M000210220

Praise for The Love of Her Kingdom

"This story will tug at your heartstrings. It's a beautiful blend of characters, magic, and emotional connection and will keep you wanting more."

~ *Gabriella Slade, author of* The Dragon Artifacts *Series*

"The Love of Her Kingdom is pure storytelling magic, eloquently woven together. I was captivated by the hearts and vulnerability of these characters. This world which Zoe has introduced to the world is on I hope to visit again."

~ *Mae Wagner, author and Collective Podcast host*

The Love of Her Kingdom

by Zoe Anastasia

with poetry by Millie Florence

Zoe Anastasia

Rosewind Publishing

First Edition, 2019

978-1-7337314-1-6 (paperback)
978-1-7337314-2-3 (hardback)
978-1-7337314-0-9 (ebook)

RoseWind Publishing
zoeanastasiastories.com

Printed in the United States of America

For all the people
who are lights in this dark world.

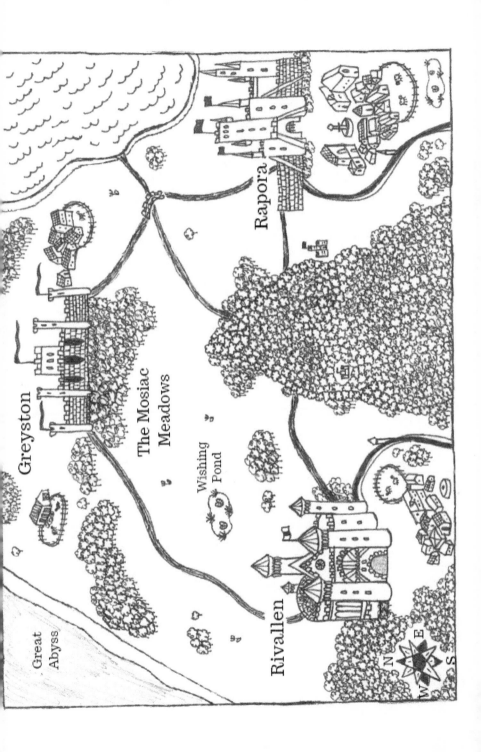

Quiet meadow,
Quiet plain,
Quiet sky,
Quiet pain.
How many footsteps would it take
To bring me to where bodies break?
Far too many to cross alone,
Far too many close to home.
In blood and spite a battle rages,
Yet I have only ink on pure white pages.
In this state of safety I find my scar
As present serenity mocks chaos afar.
So I wait with the sky,
Wait with the wind,
Wait for a sister,
Wait for a friend.

From Afar ~ by Arely

Chapter 1
Shane

I lifted my silver blade, letting the sun reflect off its newly polished edge. The skull on the hilt glittered with diamonds and sapphires and its black eyes stared endlessly into the sky.

Not a single scratch. Perfect.

I slid the sword into its sheath and looked up. The sunset cast a tangerine glow across the courtyard and castle walls, while shadows crept along the stone. It would be dark within the hour.

My horse grunted and stamped his hoof against the grass, ready to go out the gate for a walk. I turned to the chestnut steed, who nudged my shoulder expectantly.

As my bodyguards mounted their own horses, I grabbed the saddle's girth strap and finished tightening it around him.

"Okay, Triballi, we're going," I told him, placing my foot in the stirrup and hoisting myself onto his back.

I picked up the reins and urged him to move at a trot. But as we moved through the courtyard, with my bodyguards at my sides, I heard a man call my name.

"King Shane! Your Majesty!"

A couple yards to my left, a plump old man scurried down the stairs of the castle and over to me.

"What is it, Tad?" I asked, pulling my robe tighter as a chill swept through the enclosed yard.

He fiddled with his thumbs as he spoke. "We received news from Fort Oak, sir. Octavia and her army are attacking as we speak!"

"They are?" I asked, frowning. "Then I must go." I turned from the man, raising my reins again.

"What will you do, my lord?" Tad asked, shifting from one foot to the other. "Are you going to use your magic?"

"I'm afraid my magic won't help at this point," I said. "I'm too far away from the fort."

Tad frowned, creating wrinkles on his forehead. "The battle isn't going well. Perhaps you should stay here-"

"I'm going."

I didn't give him a chance to speak before I took off. Passing through the small gate, I entered a larger field enclosed with thick walls, where farmers lived in clusters of houses and tended to the crops.

Guard towers dotted the area, monitoring everything that happened inside and out, keeping my castle safe and secure. Next to the towers stood thirty-foot tall statues of knights carrying regal swords, hands clamped around them like staffs.

I passed through the last gate on the outermost wall, nodding to the guards stationed there. They bowed.

As I entered the meadow, a gush of cool air whipped around me. In the dark, I could barely make out my army in the far distance. I came to a stop and watched.

My eyes adjusted, the mass of knights becoming clearer as it marched toward the castle.

Tad had warned me only a few minutes ago. *"I'm afraid the battle isn't going well..."*

Had the army successfully held back Octavia's forces? Or had she taken over the fort? I doubted it could have been the latter.

A burst of cobalt spiraled into the air, far in the distance, and an orb of wispy magic shown throughout the night like a new moon. It was Octavia's royal magic – the symbol showing she had captured the fort and claimed it.

My jaw twitched as I yanked on the reins, turning my horse to face Rapora castle.

"Are we returning already?" one of the guards asked.

"There's no point in going to them, is there?"

I steered Triballi back through the gates, past the guards, and into the courtyard. Darkness swamped the corners of the castle walls and towers.

When I reached the steps where Tad and I had spoken, he was gone and a couple servants awaited our return.

"Servant!" I said to one of the men. "Take my horse to his stable and make sure he's taken care of."

He bowed and took the lead rope after I dismounted. I climbed the cobblestone stairs and entered the wide halls of the palace, lined with navy rugs and lanterns.

When General Warren returned, he would have to pay for his losses.

An hour later, the army general and several lords walked into my throne room as the light disappeared out the long, slender windows of my castle. The moon slowly rose into the sky.

I sat in my place on the throne, surrounded with dark blue banners and guards posted at every entry and corner. No one moved except General Warren.

"King Shane," he said, kneeling in front of me. The other three lords behind him copied his movement. "I bring you news of the battle."

I studied him. His dirty armor had dents and scrapes, as if he had been dragged through the grass. A thin line of blood ran down his cheek.

"Tell me," I ordered.

The general stood. "Octavia has captured the east lookout tower, Fort Oak. I led the army to the fort as soon as I could, but

by the time we reached it, she had invaded. The queen's army killed half the men and took the rest as prisoner. We were forced to leave."

I glared down at him, disgusted. "How many knights were there?"

"Three hundred, sir," he answered. "And I took half the army with me when the guards spotted her coming."

"Yet she still took the fort. We have the larger army, so we shouldn't have lost anything." I gritted my teeth. "I am disappointed in you, General Warren."

"I'm sorry, Your Royal Majesty," he said, staring at the floor. "I won't let her win next time."

I shook my head. "There won't be a 'next time.' You have lost too many battles, proving you are no longer fit to be general of my army." I pulled my sword out and ran my fingers across the smooth surface, waiting for his reaction.

He gaped at the blade, trying to form words. "I...uh... Your Majesty, I understand if you want to get a new general, but I ask for mercy."

"I told you no." I leaned forward. "And actually, because you lost the *key* fort to protecting my palace, it would be more fitting if I executed you."

Warren's eyes grew wide, his expression rigid. He fell to the floor, bowing as low as he could. "No, please, my King-"

One of the lords stepped forward. "Your Majesty, General Warren fought bravely in the battle tonight and it was not an easy fight. Please, spare his life."

I stood up and swiveled my sword to face the lord. "Stay out of this unless you want to be executed as well."

He shut his mouth.

"Where is Tad?" I asked, looking around. The man stood near a golden archway, looking pale.

"Yes, sire?"

"Inform the army that I will be looking for a new general tomorrow. Only the best leaders may try out for the position."

He nodded and left the room.

I turned back to Warren. "Guards," I said, "take this man to the dungeon. He will be executed at dawn. As for you three," I said, pointing to the lords, "you are excused from the room."

The guards grabbed Warren. He clenched his fists, as if preparing to strike, but the guards outnumbered him and dragged him from the throne room. The lords nervously followed after.

I waited until they had disappeared before walking to the west windows. In the woods, specks of light glowed in my lookout tower. But my army wasn't protecting it. Instead, Octavia was using it to keep an eye on my castle. She held the advantage.

I strode through the dark tunnels of the castle, which flickered with candles. A growing knot of worry filled my chest.

I climbed several flights of stairs before reaching the large, mahogany door that led to my bedroom. My guards took their places outside as I entered.

My room was gigantic. It was more space than I needed, honestly, because I was the only one using it. After my mother and father died, I didn't have any family left. I was the only heir to the throne.

A chandelier, topped with candles, cast a dim haze on everything around it. There were two different sides to the room: the king's side and the queen's side.

The queen's side hadn't been touched since my mother's death. I had draped a black cloth over the top, shrouding it in shadows, not to be seen.

Beside the balcony on my side, there was a writing desk and half a dozen bookshelves. In the far corner, I had a dresser with all my highest-quality armor and clothing. Layers of blankets covered a massive bed, which sat closest to the door.

A small fire crackled in the hearth next to me, though the embers were dying out and the room grew slowly colder. I sat down at my desk, running my hand through my inky black hair, and let out a sigh.

A pile of papers was scattered before me, shadows flickering across it from the candlelight. Tad must have left it for me to read through.

I picked it up, and written on the top was "Rapora Illness Death Count." Inside were the names of hundreds of villagers that had died from disease in the last four months.

I shook my head, dumping the papers into the fire, where they curled and fell to ashes.

I was not a medic. I couldn't heal people from the village who were suffering from the diseases that had been haunting the surrounding kingdoms. Why did they send the papers to me?

I crouched next to the fire and rekindled it, tending to the flame until it grew into a bush of swirling amber wisps.

At this time of night, I doubted anyone would knock on my door. No one dared bother me after I settled in for the night, unless it was a dire emergency.

Turning back to the bed, I laid my sword against the wall, where I could reach it in the middle of the night. "Maybe we'll have better luck with the next general," I muttered, running my fingertips along the hilt's bright jewels. "We'll find a great one tomorrow."

I listened to the silence. Most of the castle was fast asleep by now. I wished I had someone to talk to, even if it was Tad. But there wasn't anyone around.

After unfastening the buckles on my sturdy boots, I changed out of my armor and climbed into bed. A book of battle tactics lay on my nightstand, so I picked it up and began to read, until the candles extinguished and the darkness encased me.

Oh, I would find a new general, yes. And I would get my fort back from Octavia, no matter who I had to kill to do so.

Chapter 2
Arely

I held firm to the leather-bound book in my hands, turning the pages with care. My notes sat beside me, and I glanced back and forth, remembering what I had discovered in the infirmary.

Each page had tons of information about illnesses and plagues. It was gross, but too important to ignore.

It had been a problem in the kingdoms for years, as royal magic couldn't heal the sick. No one knew why, but I had learned to use garden plants to create medicine and help heal people. I enjoyed the task, especially when I could spend time with the younger children.

In the corner of the page, I caught sight of an old drawing of a blue vine. The plant was one of the rarest in the land. It had saved my life, many years ago.

I gently shut the book. As a bookmark, I had pressed a lilac and used my magic to protect it. I slid it inside, moving my gaze to the border of the woods.

Rising from my desk, I moved toward the balcony door. The wind whipped the curls in my hair as I opened it.

I sat down on the rim of my balcony, dangling my legs over the edge and watching the sun set in the distance.

Octavia had told me she'd return from the battle by now, but I didn't see our army anywhere.

It sent a shiver of fear through me every time my twin left for battle. I'd wait for hours, in rain or shine, searching the field for her ring of guards. As the only one left in our family, I needed to know she was safe.

Behind me, the click of the door interrupted my thoughts. I glanced back to see one of my guards, Nico. He stepped over and wrapped a soft blanket around my shoulders. "You look cold," he said, leaning against the stone balustrade.

I buried myself in the warm blanket and smiled. "Thanks, Nico. I appreciate it."

"It'll be fall soon," he murmured. "It gets cooler every day."

I didn't reply, but kept my eyes on the meadow. Across the field was a forest, one spreading for miles and miles. Beyond that, Rapora Castle hovered menacingly over the woods, like a foreboding mountain in an epic poem. A dragon could inhabit the dark palace, waiting for its moment to pounce on anyone who came near it.

I sat up straighter as I spotted movement near the edge of the woods. Shapes started pouring out of the trees, small specks which materialized into a large army of soldiers. The men appeared to move painfully slow at such a distance.

"Oh, I hope Tavia's all right," I said, biting my lip.

Nico squeezed my hand. "She's fine. If she needed your help, she would have sent a signal into the sky." He squinted at me, and then added, "Her magic would have dispersed into the air and created a storm if she had been killed."

"I know," I said, sighing. But it didn't help to comfort me.

My bodyguard turned back to the meadow. A moment later, he pointed to a couple knights on horses that I had missed. The men were entering the gates of the castle. "I bet one of them is an injured lord," he said. "They came back early."

"I want to help him," I said, turning away from the meadow. I entered my room, threw the blanket on my bed, and grabbed my worn notebook.

Slipping it into my dress's pocket, I hurried out of the room, where the rest of my guards waited, and ran down the winding steps of the palace to where the castle gates were located. It took several minutes, but I finally slid to a stop near the entrance.

A few seconds later, three knights on horseback rode through the tunnel and into the clearing. One of them, whom I recognized as a marquis, was pale and wore a large cloth tied around his chest, where a circle of blood seeped through. He gasped for breath.

"Queen Arely!" one of the knights called. "Can you give us help, please? We came here because my lord's wound is deep and we thought only your magic would heal it."

"Of course." I turned to the nearest servant, who was a maid. "Where are the medics? Tell them I need them to come to the infirmary. The army will be here soon and we will need everyone's help."

The maid nodded and rushed off as the three men came to a stop. Two of them dismounted their horses.

The injured knight's face twisted in pain, and he struggled to stay upright on his horse.

"I can take you to one of the guest rooms," I offered.

"Guest rooms?" one of the knights echoed, bewildered. "But there's an infirmary..."

"This will be more comfortable. Don't worry about it." I motioned for Nico to come over, and he and the two knights helped the man off his horse.

Down the hallway – not far from the gates – there were a couple guest rooms. I walked the dimly lit tunnel, and found one empty.

Holding the door open, I waited for the knights to come in. The injured man limped toward the bed and laid on the blankets, heaving a sigh as his head rested against the pillow.

I waved the other knights away and sat down beside him, studying his wound. It appeared to be a slash from a sword, too deep for my magic to heal. Blood trickled from the bandage all over the bed.

He wouldn't survive, but I could soothe him at least.

I held my hand over his wound and let my pink-colored magic seep into his skin, numbing a bit of the pain.

The marquis lifted his hand to touch mine. "Your Majesty... save it, please. For someone else who needs it."

I squeezed his trembling hand. Quietly, he watched as I pulled the blanket around him, covering the wound.

I paused to look at his expression. His blue eyes were full of pain, but he didn't say a word. I couldn't imagine what he had gone through in the battle. And not only this one, but all the battles before.

I didn't even know him.

"Thank you," I said, softly. "Thank you for fighting for the kingdom. And for defending my people."

His eyes brightened for a moment. "You are a good queen, Arely. I am proud to fight for you and your sister." He coughed, and his whole body shook. Slowly, his eyes closed and his breathing came to a stop.

I held on to his hand until he took his final breath, and then everything in the room was silent. I stayed there a moment longer, then stood and turned to Nico.

"There will be others who need my magic," I whispered. "We should go back to the gates."

He nodded and followed me through the door, passing a medic as she took over. We reached the gates as the rest of the army entered. At the front, Tavia rode on her brown warhorse.

Her brown hair had been pinned in a tight bun, and her lips were pressed thin. She didn't appear to be injured, though, and her pristine armor confirmed it.

I ran to her. "Tavia! You're all right!"

My sister dismounted her horse and wrapped her arms around me. "Yes, of course I'm all right, Arely. And – more importantly – we seized Fort Oak and secured it." She beamed at me.

"So everything went as planned?" I asked.

Her smile faltered. "For the most part."

A servant took her horse's bridle. "I'll wash your horse and put her in the stable," he said.

"Thank you," Tavia replied. Her dark brown eyes met mine. "Well, I think this calls for a celebration. Anyway, I'm starving. We should roast a hog."

I shook my head. "I need to take care of the wounded first. If you tell the servants to start a bonfire in the square, the villagers can join in. I'll meet you as soon as I can."

My sister turned and waved to the nearest servant. While she told him of her plans, I headed over to the medics gathering in the entrance of the infirmary.

Many knights had large wounds. I helped the people I could, but my limited magic prevented me from helping every soldier. There were old men and young men, even boys younger than me. I was able to heal at least seven people before my magic began to fade, signaling my limit for the day.

I leaned against a castle wall, exhausted, and my stomach growled.

"Queen Arely," I heard an older man say. I glanced over to see Sir Harding, who was the commander over all my bodyguards.

"You should take a break," he said, gently. "After you eat, you can go back to caring for the wounded."

I nodded, and hesitantly followed him through the door.

When we walked into the square a few minutes later, a massive fire burned in the center. The crackling of the flames gave me the warm, fuzzy feeling I got every time we had a celebration in the village.

A hog turned on a spit, and people gathered 'round, watching the cooks chop and spice the meat. Platters of food sat on a table, waiting for anyone who wanted it.

Around the square were dozens of narrow homes, with bright quilts and clothing hanging from the balconies to dry. Several flags billowed in the wind, showing off Rivallen's royal crest.

I found Tavia sitting on a stone ledge, eating the meat off a skewer. As I walked toward her, she met my gaze and waved for me to sit beside her. She held up another skewer. "Here. I saved one for you."

I managed a smile and took it. "Thanks." I bit into a juicy pepper, savoring every piece.

Children played in the streets, chasing each other and splashing in the water from the fountain. Adults mingled as they enjoyed the fresh, warm food and the moon glittering in the sky. I almost felt like a normal villager, and there was something special about it I couldn't explain. It's what I loved most about being in the town.

As we ate, I kept glancing at Tavia. Her forehead was scrunched together, lost in thought.

"What is wrong?" I asked her.

She glanced up. "Nothing's wrong."

"You're upset," I pressed on. "I can tell."

Tavia huffed. "I'm just tired, Arely."

I didn't say anything else, but it was clear she was lying. What could she want to hide from me?

After a couple minutes, she spoke. "By the way, I invited King Quay to come visit our kingdom for a feast. I believe I can convince him to join us in the war."

"Really?" I said. "When is he coming?"

She laid down her skewer. "He is coming next week. We'll have to prepare several days in advance."

"Quay actually agreed to come?" I asked incredulously. It didn't seem like the King of Greyston wanted anything to do with the war.

Tavia nodded. "It's a feast, which you know he loves. That's the only thing he would agree to."

"It would be great if he joined us," I said, but with a slight edge of doubt in my voice.

My twin nudged me. "If there is anyone who can convince Quay to help our kingdom, it's you. You have a special way of charming people."

I grinned at her and saluted. "I'll do my best, Your Majesty."

She stuck her tongue out at me, teasingly.

We continued to eat our food as if everything was fine, but doubt kept nagging at me. I couldn't shake the feeling more battles were on their way. They never seemed to end and we lost more soldiers every time.

The war had gone on for nearly a decade, since I was only six years old. I wished it would end.

Tavia's lack of enthusiasm also bothered me. She herself had ordered this celebration, yet she wasn't enjoying it.

I puzzled over this, trying to guess what had happened during the battle at Fort Oak, but I wouldn't know unless she told me.

Only a couple minutes after we had finished eating, our general stepped through the crowd and made his way toward us.

"Your Majesties," he greeted.

"Hello, General Ivan," Tavia replied nonchalantly. "Did you get food?"

"Uh, yes," he said, glancing back at the roaring fire. His eyes flitted to me, and then back to my twin. "Queen Tavia, I'd like to speak with you inside the castle. About the battle."

"Right now?" she said, aghast. "It's nearly midnight!"

"It'd be best if we had the meeting immediately. I have no doubt Shane is already planning a counterattack. And we need to discuss the... situation."

A bitter feeling crept inside me. Why couldn't they speak about this situation in front of me?

Tavia slowly nodded. "All right, fine. But I better not be up all night. I need rest."

She stood up and followed the general back toward the castle. "I'll meet you back in our bedroom, Arely!" she called.

I frowned as she disappeared. It irritated me that I had been left without knowledge of the battle. It wasn't the first time this had happened, but I had a feeling the information they hid was more important than any other time.

I needed to find out.

Chapter 3
Shane

The general's execution was held at the break of dawn, just as the sun was coming in through the enclosure. The black marble pillars loomed over the gathered crowd, and everything waited.

I sat grimly upon my seat, my sword resting by my side.

The executioner walked in, slowly and deliberately, coming toward the center where Warren knelt.

Wearing dark armor and robes, he stopped to the left of the general, not making a sound. The biting wind whipped through the morning air, tousling the ends of his cloak.

"Warren," I said, wishing to end this as swiftly as possible. "You have been convicted of the loss of too many battles, lack of skill, and of failing your kingdom. What do you have to say about this?"

He looked up and met my eyes. "I did my best, but no one is perfect."

I sat back, propping my chin on my fist. "Interesting. Apparently some of us are more perfect than others."

Not a word passed among the men in the enclosure.

"Very well," I said, straightening myself. "If no one has anything left to say, we will proceed with the execution."

The executioner held out his ruby-encrusted axe, the vines of obsidian flowers carved into its handle.

Warren didn't even flinch in the presence of the man of death. But the executioner raised his axe, which glinted in the sun, and with one deft movement, swung the blade.

The general's head hit the stone with a thud, painting the ground a puddle of maroon. The executioner stood still for a moment, and then turned to walk slowly back to his place.

I stood. "Warren has been relieved of his duty. We must find another to commit to the job of general."

As people started to file out of the enclosure, a couple of them sobbing, I walked toward an exit reserved for me. The knights would be waiting in the garden, and I couldn't be late.

There was a rumor passing through the castle that a small portion of knights were thinking of deserting the army.

If they couldn't handle a simple execution, they were pathetic. As soon as I heard the news, I ordered my men to find the would-be deserters and lock them in the dungeon; let them be a lesson to all.

I headed straight for my private courtyard in the middle of the castle where only I could train, but today I'd allowed the dukes and earls to join me.

The sun rose higher into the sky as I entered the royal garden, walking along the stone path until I reached a large courtyard shaped like an octagon, with golden swords lining the walls. Seven men sat on the stone benches near the back, waiting for me.

My bodyguards took their positions at the entrance of the courtyard, standing tall and holding their long broadswords in front of them. You'd have to be a fool to mess with any of them.

I walked to the men and stopped in the middle of the grassy area. All seven rose to their feet and bowed.

"Stand up," I ordered, and they obeyed.

I studied each of the earls' and dukes' faces. Their eyes were red and it looked like they could fall asleep any minute. However, each of them had cleaned up and made sure to look professional, for they wore sturdy cloaks and shoes. One of the men pulled at his coat button while another tapped his foot. The others were still.

I cleared my throat. "If you are not confident in your abilities to be my general, you should leave now."

No one moved. I glanced down the row of men, and my eyes landed on the last. Lord Collins. His eyes met mine for a moment, and he didn't flinch. This lord was bold and strong in battle.

The corner of my mouth twitched in a smile, and I turned back to the men. "You two," I said, pointing at the fidgeting dukes. "You need to leave."

At first, they looked too surprised to move, but they exited the courtyard when I motioned for them to leave.

That left the other five.

I stepped closer to them. "You know what I am looking for," I said. "It will not be easy to be the general by any means. The last one failed. I hope the person I choose today will not do the same. So show me your best, and if you are worthy, you will become my new general and you will fight to take back our lost fort."

The men nodded. Collins, in particular, had a gleam in his eye as if he already had a plan to win at Fort Oak.

"I have looked over each of your records," I continued. "I know which ones are the best out of this group. But I am not going to choose a general from that. Instead, I need to *see* it. I want you to have a duel with me."

I grinned. It was almost hilarious how quickly the men's eyes grew wide. I was known for my sword-fighting skills, because I had trained since I was old enough to hold a sword. The most renowned sword fighters had taught me every single day, for hours, because my father didn't want me to rely solely on my magic for protection.

"Oh, is that too much?" I asked.

"No, my King," Lord Collins said, stepping forward. "It sounds like a wonderful idea."

I crossed my arms. "I didn't need you to tell me it was a wonderful idea."

He lowered his head. "Right. I'm sorry, sire."

"Who is willing to take the challenge?" I asked, looking each in the eye. "If you are, stay, if you aren't, then follow the other two out the door."

One of the knights turned and left, without a glance back. Another one hesitated and then followed after. The last three knights stood in the middle of the courtyard, holding the hilts of their swords.

"You know," I said, raising my eyebrows, "that's exactly how I thought this would happen. You received the best praise from Warren when he was general, while the other four did not."

I pulled out my sword, which gleamed brightly in the sunlight. "Get your swords. We will start the duel immediately."

The knights obeyed. Although their swords were sturdy and strong, the dull metal had dents and scrapes. Mine, however, was different. I had used my magic to give it strength and durability. If I needed to defend myself, it could repel another royal's magic.

"You'll go first," I said to the knight on the left. "And then so on."

The duke walked forward into the middle of the courtyard, and the duel started. He put up a good fight, but I trapped him with my blade in a minute and won. The second fought a little longer than the first, but he met the same fate.

Lowering my sword, I said, "You both are unfit to become general and you need more training. You may leave."

The two men exited the courtyard, looking somewhat disappointed and relieved at the same time.

I glanced at Collins, who held his sword out.

"Your Majesty, if everyone else is gone..."

"Do not assume you are any better because you are last," I told him, straightening my shoulders. "Now, are you ready to fight?"

He raised his blade steadily, watching for my next move.

I dodged to the right and slashed, but he deflected my sword with ease. He moved forward and took a strike from above. I lifted my blade and the two swords clanged together, then pushed it aside and jabbed at his stomach but he leapt away from me.

We both moved around the courtyard, swinging our swords and evading blows. After several minutes, I began to tire, but I didn't give in.

"Are you sure you want to be a general?" I asked, trying to distract him.

He swung his sword and I parried. "Oh, of course," he panted. "I believe I was born to be general."

I blocked a strike from the left and said, "So you can get Fort Oak back within the next week?"

Collins fumbled with his sword and I used this chance to pin him against the stone wall with the tip of my sword to his throat.

He gulped down breaths of air. "Ah, yes... yes, Your Majesty. If you let me catch my breath."

"Congratulations," I said, stepping back and sliding my sword into its sheath. "You are the new general of my army. I hope you take this position seriously, or you will go down the same path as Warren. Don't fail me, Collins."

"I won't," he said, putting his sword away as well. "I'll do my best."

"There's a more pressing matter than the fort right now. I must ask you to address it before the end of the day." I started pacing in the middle of the courtyard. "I'm sure you are aware of the knights who did not appreciate my order to execute Warren."

Lord Collins nodded.

"I need you to step up and lead the army, be its strong leader during this transition of power from Warren to you. It will not be easy, but I expect you to bring the army together. Otherwise I suspect you will have a difficult time capturing the lookout tower."

"Of course, Your Majesty."

I stopped and met the new general's eyes. "There will be a meeting tomorrow morning about our next move in the war. You will have to be there, not a minute late. I will give you more information later, but for now, we should go introduce the army to its new leader."

I left Collins to talk to the army after introducing him. Many of the men already knew him and his confidence was clear. Collins had great potential, but I was still wary. The weight on his shoulders was great, and if he started on the wrong foot, it could be deadly.

I walked onto a bridge connecting two turrets, the breeze lightly whistling through the arrow slits in the side. I was at least a hundred feet in the air. Here, I was not far from the force field.

Any normal person would be scared at such a height. I didn't let it bother me.

When I was thirteen, I had gained enough magic to create a force field to protect my palace. Royals could gain more magic a total of three times, which were called Blessings.

Each one had a ceremony. The first was Coming of Age, when a royal turned thirteen. For the second, a royal had to be crowned king or queen.

I hadn't gained the Third Blessing, which was to marry another royal and form an alliance with them.

But I had enough magic to protect my castle, and perhaps win the war. Collins did not have the advantage of magic, and he couldn't gain experience through ceremonies.

If he worked hard, though, we would defeat Octavia.

Chapter 4
Arely

Birds chirped in their sing-song way and the fragrance of the flower garden danced around me. The day was warm once again, as if summer wasn't ready to say goodbye quite yet and the night before had simply been a trick for the mind.

I lay on a castle wall, bending over my little poetry notebook while kicking my legs back and forth as if I were a princess again. My ink jar sat to my right and I held the quill over the parchment, contemplating what I would write next.

On the pages were dozens and dozens of poems I'd written since I was first taught to write. Swirly, cursive letters covered the notebook, along with small doodles of rare flowers in the corners.

My newest piece had the title "Peace Treaty." I had written it down, knowing I couldn't use it, but still hanging on to the hope it would one day end the war.

A bee buzzed past me and landed on my hand. I gently lifted it up and smiled at the little, yellow creature. "Hello," I whispered. "Have you been tending to the flowers?"

It buzzed around and flew off, back to the garden below me. All kinds of different flora filled the garden. I was proud to take care of it all in my free time, not without the help a several gardeners. We had created an ocean of colors, a wild rainbow.

I closed my eyes and breathed in the air, when I heard my name.

"Arely!"

My sister walked across the garden to my perch on the wall. She paused and grinned. "Oh, will you ever stop climbing on the walls?"

"No," I answered. "Do you need me?"

Tavia nodded. "I'm continuing a meeting with General Ivan. I need you to be there."

Closing my notebook, I leaned over the edge and tilted my head at my twin. "Why? You never ask me to come to meetings. How would I help?"

She hesitated and squinted her eyes at me. "Well, you'll want to hear what I'm going to say. I want you to help in the next battle."

I blinked. She wanted me to help in the battle? I'd never, ever fought in one before. I had no training. "Why?"

"Come to the meeting and I'll tell you."

"I don't like this."

"Just trust me." She turned around and started to head out of the garden, not giving me a chance to argue further.

I abandoned my notebook on the wall and jumped down to the cobblestone below. I landed on my feet and yelled, "Wait for me!"

Tavia paused and waited. I picked up the skirt of my dress and sprinted to her. She glanced down at my bare feet.

"Honestly, Arely. Don't you ever wear shoes?"

"I don't need shoes," I answered, simply, and continued past her. I walked into the castle and weaved my way down the tunnels until I had made my way to the meeting room. Tavia was right behind me.

Several guards stood by the door, preventing anyone from eavesdropping on our conversations. Inside, General Ivan and several advisors waited for us. They sat around an oak table with a pile of papers stacked in the middle, while the walls were covered with maps and battle strategies that my sister had hung on nails.

General Ivan bowed as I came in. "Welcome, Queen Arely."

We took our seats on the opposite side of the general, and I stared at all the papers, frowning. Tavia had parchment in front of her, filled with notes and ideas.

The meeting must've started hours ago, when the sun had risen. General Ivan glanced at me, his lips pressed thin, and one of the advisors rubbed his forehead.

"Thank you for coming, Arely," Tavia said, tapping the papers against the table to straighten them. "I have much to tell you. Last night, I had a difficult time sleeping, so I planned our next move in the war. I have an idea that's growing on me."

I scooted forward in the chair, digging my fingernails into the soft cushion. "What's the idea?"

My sister pulled a map toward her and pointed at the edge of the woods between Rivallen and Rapora. "Here is Fort Oak. Shane is significantly weaker without it, and I'm sure he will want to get it back as soon as possible, but we won't let him."

She paused, looking up.

"Our army is in good spirits because of the victory last night. We have more knights than ever before and they are ready to fight anything. Even though Shane's army is larger, our army can beat his."

One of the advisors interrupted. "Your Majesty, the only reason we beat his army in the last battle is because we caught the soldiers off guard. We can't beat him again easily."

Tavia frowned. "It's not true. We fought bravely and his army didn't have the morale to fight as hard as we did."

"What is your plan exactly?" I asked again.

"We will attack the castle," Tavia said. "If we can—"

I stood up so fast I hit my knee on the table and hissed in pain. "*What?* Are you crazy?"

"Listen, please," she continued, calmly, as if expecting my reaction. "I want this war to be over as much as the rest of you. It has been long and I'm sick of it. We can send the army to the castle and attack it, and if we can kill Shane or make him surrender, we will succeed."

I shook my head. "That'll never work."

Tavia narrowed her eyes. "You don't know that, Arely. It can work, and it *will* work."

General Ivan spoke up. "I have concerns about attacking the castle so soon. I believe we should attack again, but maybe we should take smaller steps. It's a large leap going from a fort to the castle."

"Yes! Exactly," I said, relaxing back into my seat.

"I *understand* that," Tavia continued, "but you're not giving me time to explain. I thought about this all night. We can raid the eastern side of the village, moving rapidly, and create a path for knights to reach the castle. If we attack at night, it will make it easier to catch the people off guard. Then we'll raid the castle and his army will become overwhelmed."

She looked over at me, her gaze firm and confident.

"Arely can go with me and we'll both use our magic to fight Shane. Our twin magic is stronger when we are together." My sister turned back to the general, missing my horrified expression.

My blood ran cold at the thought of having to fight other people in a battle. How could Tavia expect me to be of any help? I could heal people. That was my job. Not fighting.

"No no no," I said, shaking my head vigorously. "I can't do it. I'm sorry."

She met my eyes. I could tell she was giving me her "you're-worrying-too-much-again" look.

"Well, I can prepare you for the battle. I'm not going to let my sister get hurt in a fight. As long as you stay next to me, we'll be fine."

"We shouldn't even attack the castle!" I argued. "The army isn't ready."

Tavia straightened her shoulders. "If we are not ready now, we'll never be."

The general stood, his expression calm and controlled. "Octavia, I think Arely is right. We aren't ready, and I don't think it's a good idea to make her go out into battle—"

"General Ivan," Tavia said, standing up to face him. "You have our best intentions in mind, but I know what my twin is capable of. She will do great in battle if only she will decide to fight. But she refuses."

I crossed my arms. "That's not fair! I do my part by healing the knights when they come back to the castle."

Tavia held my gaze. "But Arely, if it meant ending the war, wouldn't you do it?" She paused, letting the question dig into my mind. "Please? We have to stop Shane. You know that."

"I have different ideas in mind..." I murmured. "There are other ways to end a war without killing. Can't we try to have a meeting with Shane? Perhaps we could make an agreement."

My sister sighed and sat back down. "Arely... he would never agree without our heads on platters."

I gawked at her, then shut my mouth and tried again. "Maybe if we ask—"

"No." Tavia frowned and motioned for General Ivan to sit down as well. "I think we should attack in four days."

"Are you serious?" I said, more alarmed than ever. "The knights need a break! And what about Quay? He is visiting the next two days. We can't prepare for battle while he is here."

"The knights can rest after the war is over. I'll give a speech and they'll be eager to finish the battle. As for Quay, I will tell him of my plans, and he may decide to help us."

She crossed her arms, stubbornly. "The biggest mistakes we've made in this war have all been because we didn't take action."

"That's not true—" I started to say, but Tavia cut me off.

"*Four* days," she repeated. "I want all of you to start preparing."

Feeling defeated and lost, I left the room so Tavia and the advisers could continue their planning. I leaned against the gray wall, the cold touch seeping into my skin.

I had never wanted to be a queen. At least, not Tavia's definition of a queen.

Tavia thought all rulers had to spend their days doing lessons and training to become physically strong. She woke up in the morning, ate a large breakfast, then started lessons. By noon, she was finished, so she ate lunch and left to train. It would be suppertime before she was satisfied.

But that wasn't all. After dinner, she'd head off to talk to advisors, lords, and other important leaders in the kingdom. I rarely saw her.

My schedule was very different. I didn't have a set plan for each day. But I did wake up before the sun, light a candle, and read until the fiery orb peeked through the glass windows. Then I'd head into the garden to check on my plants, right before going to my own lessons.

Once I completed those, I would do whatever I wanted, whether painting, learning how to sew, taking care of foals, or spending time with Nico. I also spent time in the infirmary, helping the medics.

The only reason I was a queen was that Papa had always wanted us to rule the kingdom together. He'd told us hundreds of times how great we would be.

It was true Tavia was a great queen. Shane fought ruthlessly, and my sister had worked hard to defend our people. Without her, the kingdom would have crumbled.

But now, after several years of the war raging, it seemed neither side could defeat the other. I wanted to try another tactic, if only I was brave enough to do it.

I glanced up at the doorway, where a creed was inscribed upon the wall of the castle. It had been Papa's first order for the artists to carve it when he had become king. He never wanted to forget, and he wanted it to be the first thing he saw in the morning, before he entered the meeting room.

I paused, just a moment, so I could reread it.

The Creed of Magic

~

In the kingdoms of the earth, all royals are born with magic. It is given to protect the people, to defend them from their enemies who wish to harm them, the wounds that seek to destroy them, and the evils that ravage the land.

It was never, and shall never, be intended for the royals' own wishes, for that is to break the magic's purpose. In doing so, a royal would devastate his own kingdom and everyone within.

To that royal, he will fall. The Creator will punish him, for greediness should not inherit the crown. But for the royal who does his duty, he will be rewarded, his people will prosper, and the kingdom will stand strong.

So it is wise then to watch out for others' needs, love those who do not deserve it, and to use magic sensibly. For the king who follows these steps, he will be remembered as a great ruler.

Chapter 5
Shane

Royal families had shrunk in size over several hundred years, ever since a massacre had led to a whole kingdom's destruction in a land called Khristyna. I had read about it in multiple books, finding it fascinating, not because of the thousands of deaths, but because of the complication of magic.

The royal family was extensive: there was the king and the queen, of course, then the king's brothers, sisters, mother and father. To add to that, the king had twelve children – or in other words, twelve heirs to the throne. Heirs had the chance to gain the Three Blessings, which gave them more magic, therefore making them dangerous.

Historians didn't know for sure how many royals lived in the castle, but the estimate was around twenty.

As all kingdoms do, Khristyna had enemies. And these enemies sought to destroy the king and his family.

Over three hundred years ago, an assassin had attended one of the royal feasts. He systematically located and murdered several of the youngest heirs to the throne in less than an hour. No one noticed the missing children because the celebration was noisy and people swarmed everywhere.

When the lightning flashed outside the windows and the thunder shook the walls, no one gave a second glance. Thunderstorms were normal at that time of year.

The assassin continued on his hunt. He had help from several other men, who had hidden themselves in the crowd of people.

Everything had to happen quickly or it wouldn't work. The assassin entered the main room at midnight, targeting the king – the most powerful.

His helpers surrounded the other royals, stabbing them with daggers or slitting their throats. Within minutes, all the royals were dead and screams of the guests echoed throughout the ballroom.

The assassin's plan was far from over. He had theorized what would happen if an entire royal family was murdered all at once.

When one royal died, his or her magic released into the air, creating a small thunderstorm, or "magic storm." The assassin had noticed that the more royals who died, the stronger the storm was.

That night, when he massacred Khristyna's royal family, a tremendous amount of magic was dispersed throughout the sky.

It created a massive cloud of crackling, violent magic, and every second, bolts of lightning struck the castle walls and ground. No one knows what it was like to be in the castle during the storm.

The towers splintered and fell, the walls caved in, and the whole palace crumbled to the ground, killing everyone inside, including, most likely, the assassins.

The storm didn't dissipate for at least a week. It continued to ravish the land, sweeping over towns and villages, and killing more people.

This became known as the Massacre of Khristyna, an event which changed the way royals lived. When kings and queens had many children, they sent them to live with trusted lords and ladies, until they needed a new leader for the throne.

Kingdoms had set laws stating how many royals could be in a castle at once.

Because I was my parent's only heir, we were all allowed to stay in the castle, completely safe from the magical storms. It was the same with Rivallen's royal family. However, the kingdom of Greyston had not followed these rules.

Quay, one of my allies, repeated the same things his parents did. "We will never get attacked!" "We don't have any enemies!"

For many years, Quay and I had been great friends. We caused mischief during kingdom feasts and celebrations. Each event ended in chaos, but no one could find the culprits.

Then we started getting into fights after he was crowned king. He wasn't the oldest heir, but his father had seen a better leader in him than his siblings.

Quay and his family had no interest in war. They preferred to stay neutral, so although we were allies, they didn't help us.

Whenever we weren't around them, my father criticized their foolish decisions. They were a family of nine people, and many of them were married, so that only added to the number. They were still under the risk of the magical storms even if they never entered a war.

My father still visited Greyston, although he was always wary of thunder and lightning. At the first sign of a storm, he would sweep my mother and me into a carriage and leave immediately.

I had seen the storms before, when my aunt and grandpa died in the epidemic. I had been young, but my mother had explained them to me as I watched out the window at the colorful lightning. It had been red, for my grandpa's magic.

I had inherited his red magic, and as I looked into the storm clouds, I knew my own storm would look like his.

It wasn't the last one I'd ever see, and definitely not the worst. The worst was yet to come.

I summoned an orb of magic when I returned to the courtyard. The red mist formed in front of me and hovered, waiting for my command. I sent it to the cloudless sky, and a few seconds later, a ripple of the force field ran through the air, dipping below the castle walls. It was in perfect condition. If any unwanted person entered the castle grounds, my magic would pulse, alerting me of the intrusion.

I touched the tip of my sword, sending another wave of magic into it. Every day I added magic to it so it wouldn't lose its magical properties.

A new glimmer sprouted along the worn sheath and the scratches along the blade faded from view.

Pacing the courtyard, I set up all my targets along the walls. When I had finished the task, I stood in the middle of the yard and turned to look at them. There were twenty-one in total, and I challenged myself to hit every one in thirty seconds without fail.

My magic hovered in my hand, like a shuriken waiting to be thrown at a bullseye. I tossed a bit into the air and it started counting the time.

I sucked in a breath and began to throw the magic at the targets. I hit three in the first couple of seconds with ease. I turned around, aiming at the targets and hurling the wisps of magic at the center, not missing once.

At twenty-nine seconds, the last target clattered to the ground and I lowered my hand. The magic timer whistled and disappeared.

This was a part of my everyday training routine. In battle, aim was vital.

I picked up my sword and started practicing each of my maneuvers and poses – like my father and teachers had taught. It only took a couple of minutes.

After that, I paused from my training, sliding the sword back into its sheath, and exited the courtyard. In the center of the garden, surrounded with flowers, was a memorial for my mother and father. It was a statue, grand in size, carved with careful detail, and resembled my parents closely.

The sculptor had begun working on it as soon as my parents were pronounced dead. It took a full year to complete, but once it was done, everyone admired it.

I came here a couple times a month. Whenever I looked up at my father's face, it reminded me of what I was fighting for. At the age of fifteen I had declared war on Rivallen for killing my parents.

Three years before that, my parents had fought in the bloodiest battle of the whole war. They both died in it. I was twelve years old, and I was also the new king.

I would have sent my whole army to go kill the king and queen of Rivallen, but they had died in the battle as well.

The whole war stopped there. No one wanted to fight anymore, no one except me. But once I showed the people how serious I was about it, they could not stop me.

The twins, who were one year younger than me, became the queens of their region. Even if they hadn't killed my parents, I had to get my revenge.

It was their mother and father who had gotten us into the whole war in the first place. If King Allister hadn't stolen the rare medicine from our castle, my aunt and grandfather wouldn't have died from the epidemic that had plagued the land. My father would never have declared war on Rivallen if it hadn't been for their deaths.

But the deed was done and my parents had been killed because of it. It was only right I wanted to avenge them.

I bent beside the statue and picked up the smooth stone I had placed there two years earlier. It was my father's favorite rock because of the blue and green colors mixed inside it, making it unusual.

Brushing my finger over its smooth surface, I turned it over in my palm. I had placed it there as a promise to win the war for him. Although I was young, I was strong and determined. My years of training had paid off and my years of mischief were over. I was a king now. A warrior.

"Three weeks," I whispered to myself. "I will win the war in three weeks and no more. If I don't, so help me, I'll hang myself."

I placed the rock back down in front of my father. I would not disappoint him.

I strode out of the garden into a castle hallway, where my bodyguards waited for me, then paused near a window where I could look down at the faraway lookout tower.

Four days, I thought. *I will attack the fort in four days time and get back what rightfully belongs to me.*

My mind drifted to everything that had happened in the last day. There was one person that could help me with my problem, though I had asked for his help before. He had declined my request every time.

I headed to my room and closed the door, wanting to talk to Quay. I hoped this conversation would be different from the past ones, where he had declared that he was "too good" for war.

I didn't *need* his help, but I preferred to end the war sooner than later. After that, I would be the strongest king and no one would dare challenge me again.

I marched onto the balcony of my room, where I usually talked to the other rulers. All I had to do was use my magic to create a swirling portal so the other person could see me.

I waited for Quay to respond to my magic. Thankfully, he only took a couple minutes and no longer.

He appeared in the mist. Trees and sky surrounded his figure, showing me that he was in Greyston's royal garden. He didn't smile when he saw me.

"Greetings," he said simply. His blond hair was trimmed short, making him look older than he actually was. His blue eyes pierced into me. "I'm assuming you called for a good reason, right?"

"You know exactly why I called you, Quay." I placed my hands on the railing and leaned forward. "I need you to consider helping me in the war."

"Oh, no. Not this again," Quay muttered, shaking his head. "I have tons of work to do with other kingdoms, so you better not waste my time—"

I folded my arms. "We have been allies for years, but you have never helped me in battle. It doesn't give me the desire to help you if *your* kingdom gets in trouble."

Quay chuckled. "That's hilarious. I don't think I'll ever get into trouble. My father and I have spent lots of time and money investing in other kingdoms, so we only have allies."

I bit my tongue to keep from glowering at him. "You don't know that," I pointed out. "You could have made an enemy without realizing it. If you ever find yourself in trouble, how do you expect me to help you?"

"I am willing to bet I won't get attacked, but thank you ever so much for caring about what happens to my kingdom." Quay's eyes glinted.

"You could be kind enough to help in one single battle," I said, stiffly.

He shrugged. "I'm not that type. Blood and battles are not my thing. I'd rather read books and learn things no one else takes the time to study. I have learned much in my time and I wouldn't change a thing about it, you know."

"Learning by passive ways isn't everything," I said, frowning. "I have learned quite a bit from fighting in real battles. Besides, it's not like I don't have time to read books as well. I have learned everything a king needs to know."

"Well, kings don't need to know much," Quay mused. "That's why they have servants."

I curled my hands into fists. "Are you trying to anger me? I called on you to have a reasonable conversation. I have an offer to make, if you care to hear it."

Quay squinted his eyes, pondering my words. "All right, let's hear it."

"I will give you two hundred pounds of gold and silver if you will send a portion of your army to fight alongside mine." I straightened my shoulders, showing him I was serious about the deal. "You can use it on whatever you please."

"Two hundred pounds, you say?" Quay asked.

I nodded.

"Shane, I would help you with the war," he said, "but I need to keep my promise to my kingdom. I am not a king of war like you. I protect my kingdom with peace treaties and allies and I am not going to give up all that work for two hundred pounds of gold and silver. I'm sorry, but you don't understand."

His magic started to disappear and I shouted at him, "What *don't* I understand, Quay?"

My magic dispersed into the air, leaving nothing but open sky. I clenched my teeth.

Fine. If he did not want to help me, I would gain Fort Oak back by myself.

Chapter 6
Arely

I decided to hide my troubles of the day behind a smile, although I didn't know if it was working or not. Every minute my anticipation seemed to grow worse.

The battle would be here before long. I needed to talk about it or the fear would control me.

I walked down the barren hallway of the castle, heading to a room on the second floor. It was the middle of the night and only a few people milled throughout the castle. Mostly guards and a couple servants.

Tavia had fallen asleep, and I'd snuck out of the room and past my bodyguards. Now I was all alone.

I slowed when I reached the royal guards' section. My bodyguards switched shifts every six hours, so I had four different groups of guards. Whenever the knights weren't protecting me, they could roam the castle, train, or come to their sleeping quarters, which were here.

I paused in front of one of the doors and knocked. A moment later, Nico appeared.

"Hello, my Queen," he said, smiling. His dirty brown hair was tangled but somehow managed to look perfect.

"Ready?" I asked. "Do you have everything?"

He lifted an oil lantern and a thick, woolen blanket. "Yes. Unless there's something else you need."

"I brought a couple bars of chocolate from the kitchen," I said, grinning. "And a cloak, in case it's cold outside again."

Nico quietly shut the door behind him and locked the door with a small, silver key. "All right. Let's go."

We walked back down the hall and started ascending the stairs. Outside the window, thousands of stars glimmered in the dark sky, without a single cloud to obstruct our view. Tonight was one of the brightest nights of the year. Shooting stars could be seen flying across the large expanse of space, and we certainly weren't going to miss it.

When we reached the highest tower, Nico pushed open the balcony door and I walked out to the railing. Chilly winds whipped around me as I pulled on my cloak, glad I had thought to bring it.

I could see the Gale Mountains in the distance, plus the other two kingdoms, Rapora and Greyston. Each of them were dimly lit, with the forests to the east and the abyss to the northwest. The Mosaic Meadows separated the three kingdoms, but also connected them.

And the stars blanketed all of this.

"Whoa," I said, looking around. Although the kingdoms were small compared to ones I'd heard of in stories set far away, they never failed to reveal the land's magnificence.

I glanced back at the doorway, where a telescope stood in the corner, covered with black cloth. I lifted it and peered into the glass as Nico spread out a blanket on the ground. I looked up at the moon, so clear and bright. I didn't want to look away.

"How long do you want to stay up here?" Nico asked. "The queen needs her beauty sleep, after all."

"I don't think so," I said, lowering the telescope. I sat on the blanket, right next to Nico. "We'll stay up till we can't keep our eyes open. The meteorite shower only happens once a year. We can't sleep during it!"

Nico grinned and shook his head. "You, my friend, have a terribly excellent point."

I wrapped my blanket around my shoulders and watched the night sky. Most of the lights in Rivallen had disappeared and even the smallest stars could be seen.

I looked at Nico, who had bundled himself in another blanket. "One day we'll explore all of this land," I said. "The mountains, the meadows, the woods..."

As best friends, I had always loved to explore with Nico. We met when I was six, in the royal gardens. His family had moved in that day and he didn't know his way around the castle. I'd given him a full tour of the gardens.

As time went on, we'd gotten into tons of trouble because we kept running away into the village when we weren't supposed to, making up fantasy stories of gentle dragons and wild adventures. Of course, we didn't care.

The war kept us from going on the real adventures we wanted to go on. The land outside wasn't safe. If we left the kingdom, we could run into spies or Rapora's army. Besides, I had my own responsibilities at the castle to take care of.

"Don't worry," Nico said, reading my thoughts. "The war will end soon. I'm sure of it. As soon as it ends, we can pack our bags and go on our first real adventure."

I tried to smile. "If everything turns out the way we want it to."

"I don't think Shane will win," Nico said firmly. "He is arrogant and his people don't fully support him. Eventually that will lead to his fall."

When I didn't respond, he attempted to change the subject. "What about your garden? Are the remedies working?"

"Yes, they are. But please don't change the subject." I sighed. "Tavia proposed a new battle plan today and I wanted to talk to you about it."

Nico's face paled, as if he knew what I was about to tell him. He knew as well as I did that Tavia often made impulsive moves.

"She wants to attack Rapora Castle in four days. She wants to raid it."

His brows knit together in thought. "So she wants to end the war once and for all."

"Yes."

"That will never work."

"That's what I told her! But she wouldn't listen to me, nor to General Ivan. She's determined, Nico, and you know how she is when she's determined."

He glanced over at me. "That's not all she wants, is it?" he said, seeing my solemn expression.

"No," I answered. "She wants me to fight in the battle as well."

Nico stiffened, his eyes wide. "Wait, she's never asked you to fight in a battle. How am I supposed to protect you if—"

"We will need to face Shane, and two royals with magic is better than one. Otherwise Shane might kill Tavia."

He nodded his head slowly.

"However, I still believe we could end the war without killing any more royals," I said, hugging my knees. "No one else listens to me, though. So will you?"

"Of course," Nico said.

I stared into the night sky and started. "The other night I was thinking about how Shane has no heirs or any living relatives to take the throne. If we kill him, the kingdom will be thrown into anarchy.

"There are families and children in Rapora who want peace. They wish Shane wasn't their king so the fighting could end. But at least Shane offers them protection from attack. If we left them without a stable leadership, either the kingdom would destroy itself while trying to find a new ruler, or another kingdom would go and take it over. I don't want that."

Nico was silent.

"On the other hand," I continued, "if we tried to rule Rapora, the people would likely resent us and start rebellions. They might not like Shane, but they hate Tavia and me even more. That wouldn't work.

"The third possibility is Shane kills both of us, therefore winning the war. I believe he would take over Rivallen, and if he led this kingdom the same way he rules Rapora, my people would be doomed."

Nico wrapped his blanket around me. His expression was dark and I knew he didn't like that I had mentioned the possibility of my death.

"I *won't* let Shane kill you," he said, almost fiercely. "He'd have to kill me first."

A ghost of a smile crossed my face. "You haven't heard my plan yet," I said. "Whenever I mention it to Tavia, she says it won't work. If we could somehow manage to have a peace meeting with Shane, we might change his mind about the war. I've never met him in my whole life, for goodness sake! I mean, Tavia has, but let's be honest, she's not the best at keeping peaceful conversations with her enemies. But if *I* talked to Shane... maybe we could end this war without a knight or royal dying in the name of war again."

Nico nodded, following along.

"But every time I ask Tavia to try it, she says no. She doesn't want me anywhere near Shane, saying he'd kill me in an heartbeat. But what if she's wrong? What if I snuck out of the castle and traveled to Rapora all by myself?"

"Hold on," Nico said. "I hope you're not *actually* planning to do that."

I sighed in frustration. "You are *not* helping. No, I'm not planning on it, but what if it worked?"

"What if he killed you?"

I met Nico's eyes. He turned to look at the stars, unnaturally quiet. He'd be watching me like a hawk for the next few days.

"Look," I said, "I'm royalty, so I must put my people before myself. Papa always told me that that is why we have magic. Not to use for ourselves, but to use for others. If I am a royal for a reason, and I believe I am, then perhaps I am meant to take my ideas and use them to stop the war. If I sacrificed myself, as long as it benefited my people, don't you think it would be worth it?"

He stared down at the blanket, like he was struggling to find an answer. "I don't know. Just... promise me you won't do anything dangerous without telling me first?"

"I promise," I said.

"Arely," he said softly, "I'm always going to try to find a way around putting you in danger. That's the last thing I want to do, because it's my job as your bodyguard." He paused and glanced at me. "But, for heaven's sake, please don't be impulsive like Tavia."

I leaned against him, mostly in an attempt to hide my disappointment. "All right."

He wrapped his arm around me. "Now, I might be wrong, but I think we came up here to watch the stars, correct?"

I nodded.

"Then we better stop talking about Rapora."

I watched the sky and a few moments later, a meteor streaked across the inky blackness and disappeared as soon as it appeared. We both pointed at the same time, and then smiled.

I allowed myself to forget about the war and focus on the stars. We both talked the whole time, about nothing in particular. There were a few moments when we fell silent and watched the moon creep by.

It was nice to get a break from all the stress and worries which had plagued me for weeks.

It was early morning by the time I came back to my room. Tavia was tossing and turning in bed as if she was having nightmares. I knew she had bad dreams. Once, she had woken up yelling as if someone had died.

It had scared me so bad I nearly fell off the bed.

But that had only happened once. Usually she tossed and turned, like she was doing now.

I climbed onto the bed and lightly shook her. A moment later, she groggily opened her eyes and spotted me.

"Arely? Is that you?" she asked.

"Yes." I pulled the covers around me and laid down next to her. "Were you having another nightmare?"

My twin nodded. "The wishing pond."

I knew the pond she was talking about, and why she had dreamt of it. I hated it, but at the same time, I still loved the fond memories it had gifted us.

"Where did you go?" Tavia asked. "I woke up and you were gone."

"I went to watch the meteorite shower with Nico."

"Oh." Tavia pulled the blankets closer to her and sighed. She had no interest in the stars, so I never asked her to watch them with me.

We laid in the dark for a couple minutes before Tavia spoke again.

"Arely... I'm sorry about the battle," she said quietly. "I know you don't want to do it. And I'm sorry if I upset you during the meeting."

She reached for my hand and squeezed it.

"I forgive you," I said. "You are my twin after all. We're stuck together." I grinned, even though she couldn't see me in the dark.

Tavia continued. "It's hard trying to fight in a war. Especially when we are sixteen years old. I'm trying to keep everyone happy and win the war as soon as possible. I only hope I'm not doing it the wrong way—"

"Tavia?" I interrupted. "In the battle, when we go to fight Shane, I think we should capture him. He should get a say in what happens to his kingdom, after all."

There was a pause. "All right," Tavia murmured. "Unless someone's life is in peril if we keep him alive."

"That's better," I said, my body relaxing. Maybe this battle wouldn't be so terrible after all.

"So we're on the same page?" Tavia asked.

 47

"Yes."

"Great." She yawned. "Well, I'm going back to sleep. Quay will be here in two days, so we have to work hard tomorrow."

She turned on her side, her voice quieter.

"Goodnight, Arely."

"Goodnight Tavia," I said, sinking into the covers. I frowned. Although I'd like to say I felt much better, I didn't. Two people had dismissed my ideas in one day, saying they were irrational. I didn't know quite what to do, and this bothered me more than anything.

I could only hope that Quay would aid us in the coming battles.

Chapter 7
Shane

General Collins met me in the meeting room at our agreed time the next morning. It was foggy outside and I had decided to drink a cup of coffee to warm up and give myself energy for the day ahead.

Inside the meeting room, the servants had started a fire and it was comfortable for a meeting. Tad sat in the corner, flipping through pages of records and writing information into his notebook.

Mixing my coffee, I sat on my leather chair. A couple minutes past before the rest of the lords and battle advisers arrived.

I leaned forward as they entered. "Welcome. We have much to discuss today, so we'll get started immediately."

Everyone gathered around the table and Tad pulled a stool over to sit next to me, placing his notebook on the table to take notes.

"All right, first things first," I said, pulling my chair closer to the table and clearing my throat. "We all know the kingdom is significantly weaker without Fort Oak, so we need to get it back.

That much is clear. But the problem is how to get it back, and that's what we are here to talk about."

The men around me nodded.

I glanced over to see Tad scribbling the time and date for the meeting, including the purpose. The old man had recorded meetings for a long time, for my father and now for me. It felt good to know I had these available at any time.

"I have a date," I continued, "and I expect all of you to come up with a battle plan for taking the fort back on that day."

"What is the date, my lord?" General Collins asked.

"I want you to attack in three days," I said, "when the moon is absent from the night sky. The cover of darkness will aid in our attack, and taking the fort will be as easy as taking caramel candy away from a toddler.

"You will have to create a strong plan and execute it wisely, General," I said, making eye contact with him. "I don't want a failure on your part. It would be disappointing for you to lose your first battle as the leader, and I doubt it would help your situation with the knights, would it?"

"No, sir," he said. "I'll work hard to make sure the plan succeeds."

"Very well." I acknowledged the rest of the advisors. "We will win this fort back if it's the last thing we do. I expect the best from everyone involved. Any lack of effort will lead down a trail you don't want to go on."

Everyone nodded, without a word.

General Collins cocked his head. "Do you want us to plan the battle now, Your Majesty?"

"Yes," I answered, standing. "I will leave you all to strategize for an hour or so. When I come back, I want you to have it ready."

"Of course. We'll get to work."

I headed off to the library. Tad followed after, along with my bodyguards. I wanted to escape the chaos of the past few days, and the library was the perfect place to do so. People were always quiet, especially when I was there. I could play chess or find a new book or simply sit in a comfy chair and drink coffee, without needing to deal with the kingdom's problems.

I entered the grand library, which had hundreds of shelves full of books, on every topic you could imagine. I stuck to the history section, for the most part.

I had studied dozens of books on previous wars, reading about how they started and what kinds of mistakes the kings made, and of course, how the kingdoms finally won these wars. It had interested me from a young age, and that interest had turned into an obsession. I wanted to win my own war and so I had read and thought about that glorious moment often.

It was coming soon.

I walked over to a small table with a checkered board, waving Tad over. "I challenge you to a game of chess," I said, giving him a small grin. "If you dare to try and beat me."

He sat down across from me. "I'm assuming you want to be the black pieces?" he asked.

"Always. White stands out at nighttime, after all." I slid the drawer out and began placing the carved, wooden figurines in their special places on the board. Tad did the same. In a couple minutes, the game was set.

"All right," I said. "Go ahead."

Tad leaned over the board and moved a knight over a pawn and to the left. As soon as his fingers left the piece, I moved one of my pawns forward two spaces, clearing a spot for my bishop to move diagonally.

We played for a while before I cornered his queen and captured her, and also checkmated his king in the process. Tad sighed and sat back in his chair, defeated.

I picked up the queen from his side. I held my own queen, turning it over in my palm, and then held them side-by-side. The wooden pieces were light and dark brown.

It made me think of Octavia and Arely, and how they looked different even though they were twins. It might have been a strange thought, but my mind started ticking, and soon an idea came to me.

"Tad?" I said. "Does Arely ever go out into battle?"

He looked up, surprised. "Oh, I heard Octavia keeps her in the castle so one queen will always be safe. If she were to die, the throne wouldn't be in danger."

I frowned, staring at the figurine. "Never? Are you sure?"

"Perhaps she goes out and watches, in case she is needed, but no one has ever reported seeing the young queen."

I set the queens down on the board, thinking. "What do you think Octavia would do for Arely? How far would she go to save her?"

Tad watched me, starting to follow along. "I believe she'd do anything."

"Right. Because they are twins," I said. "And they have Tvibura Magic – twin magic – as well. So their magic is more powerful when they are together, but if I took one of them out of reach from the other..."

I pushed Tad's queen back to his side of the board, leaving my queen alone on the battlefield.

"Then I'd have control over both of them."

Tad stared down at the wooden pieces. "So you want to try to capture Arely?" he asked.

"I think that would be easier than capturing Octavia, yes." I pulled out the drawer and swept all the pieces back inside. "It's only a thought. If she never goes into battle though, I don't see how I'll capture her."

Tad nodded. "I see... but maybe you shouldn't even try."

"What do you mean?" I asked.

"If Arely doesn't fight, why should you capture her?" he said. "She hasn't done any harm to you."

"Actually, she has, in a way."

"That doesn't count," Tad argued, pushing his own pieces into the drawer and closing it. "And you know it."

"All right, but it's still war, and if I have to capture her to win it, I'll do so without hesitation."

When we came back to the meeting room, the general had a plan prepared. He began to explain it, but I only wanted to tell him of my idea to separate the twins.

I told the general and lords what I had said to Tad, mentioning the magic and possibility of Octavia surrendering to keep Arely safe.

The idea intrigued General Collins. He sat forward in his chair, listening. When I had finished, he raised his eyebrows.

"And what would you do with Arely?"

I paused. "I'm not sure."

"Wouldn't you execute her?" one of the lords said. "She's an enemy, after all."

I shook my head. "That's risky. If Arely dies, it will make Octavia more determined to win the war."

A lord stood up. "Your Majesty, what if we used Arely's magic as well? Could you do that?"

I frowned. "We don't even know if Arely will be at the battle. Besides, we'd have to force her to use magic against her own kingdom."

"But what about the tale about a royal who stole magic from his family?" he asked.

"That's a myth," I said, waving my hand dismissively. "People have tried many times before. The most important part is that she can't use hers to fight us and that will also weaken Octavia."

The room fell silent as they took in the idea. But in my mind, dozens of possibilities rolled out in front of me. I couldn't keep track of it all.

It wouldn't work unless Arely came to a battle.

If we found a chance to capture either Octavia or Arely, we'd take it. It would be the easiest way to end the war.

Chapter 8
Arely

Quay arrived at our castle as the sun painted violet streaks across the horizon. We greeted him in the Mosaic Meadow, as planned. I rode on my appaloosa named Grey Girl, whose white hair had gray splotches surrounding her neck and back.

Elated at the prospect of an ally in the war, I thought I'd burst if Quay turned us down.

Tavia had known that Quay would come, whether he was aware of our plan or not. He couldn't resist a good feast.

As he and his bodyguards walked toward us, I beamed. Quay had blond hair like mine, but it was a shade darker. He was several years older than us, and he had been king of his land longer than we had been queens.

Tavia slowed to a stop, straightening her shoulders.

"Good afternoon, King Quay," she greeted, giving him a wave. "It's wonderful you could make it."

I rode up beside her and dipped my head with respect. "We've got a great feast waiting for you. I think you'll find everything you could possibly want."

He smiled. "I appreciate it. Thank you, Queen Octavia, Queen Arely." He nodded at each of us as he said this. "Now, if you don't mind, I'd like to put my horse in the stables and stretch my legs. It's been a long journey."

Tavia nodded. "Of course." She turned her horse around and led us into the village and toward the castle.

I rode next to Quay as we passed the gates. His face wore a calm expression, though there was a bit of uncertainty to it. We rode for several minutes, entering a tunnel that connected the village to the royal stables.

"Was the trip easy enough?" I asked, casually.

"Yes, it was all right," was his reply.

"That's good to hear. Traveling can be rough sometimes."

Ahead of us, Tavia came to a halt near the stables. She dismounted her horse and servants walked over. One by one, we slipped off our horses and let the servants lead them away.

"Are you hungry?" Tavia asked Quay and his guards. "We can eat whenever you'd like."

The king glanced at the others and said, "We usually eat around this time."

"Perfect." Tavia smiled her warm smile. "I'll tell the servants."

It didn't take long to settle into the ballroom. As we entered, the smells of all kinds of food encircled us. I could almost taste the meal.

A massive dining table stretched across the length of floor, filled with mounds of turkey, bread, fruits, and vegetables. The feast would feed around two hundred people, at least.

Our guests were already seated, waiting for us to arrive and give them permission to eat. The people watched us quietly, but many smiled and waved.

Servants ran about, placing the last of the platters onto the table, and hurried to their places by the wall.

My sister ushered Quay to sit beside her, with me on her other side. Our bodyguards sat with his as if they had always been great friends.

"This is a splendid ballroom," Quay complimented, craning his neck to take it all in.

He was right. Our ballroom had stolen my heart from the time I was a little girl. The dome roof was completely made of stained glass, earning it the nickname 'Kaleidoscope Ballroom.' People claimed the shapes made pictures and stories, but no one could agree on the images they spotted. It was the equivalent to staring at the stars. The setting sun cast a glow through the glass, scattering shards of color across the floor.

"Yes," I agreed. "My mother used her magic to protect it from ever breaking. She once told me, 'Stained glass by itself isn't that beautiful. The light shining through makes it dazzling.'"

"That's poetic," Quay said, his gaze wandering.

Tavia placed a hand on my shoulder and stood up to address the people. "As you can see, our special guests have arrived. Please welcome King Quay and his guards."

The people clapped for a couple minutes, and I noticed the pleasant look on Quay's face. Finally, my sister continued, ending the applause.

"I know it's been difficult in recent months, but we have the privilege to gather for feasts and ceremonies. Everyone has arrived, so you may enjoy the meal in front of you."

She sat down and turned to me. She arched her eyebrow, which was her way to ask if I was ready for the meal ahead. It was not a simple meal, and I was starting to get nervous even though I pretended to be fine.

I put on a smile and said, "King Quay, you should try the roasted cranberries." I pushed a small bowl of the crisp, scarlet berries toward him. "They come from our best gardens in the land. A couple were destroyed in a battle, unfortunately, but the rest send a good amount of berries to the castle. They're a delicacy, in my opinion."

Quay took a small handful of the little berries and tried one. After a second, he nodded. "Those are good." He passed the bowl along to the others.

I glanced at the foods near me. There were so many choices, I always found it hard to choose what to eat. Tavia, however, didn't hesitate to make her plate. She had more important matters to think about than what she wanted to eat.

I leaned forward, lifted a turkey leg from a platter, and laid it on my plate. I created an array of bright fruits beside it and grabbed a roll last.

The whole place buzzed with chatter and joy. As time passed, the afternoon became dark, and servants walked around lighting the candles.

Tavia talked to Quay all throughout the meal, not wasting a precious moment. I wasn't always listening, but when I was, I could see how naturally she made the conversation sound, even when she was hinting at her real question.

The king wore a tranquil, at-home expression. He didn't hesitate to answer questions or ask his own. I stayed quiet. I didn't like talking during meals, but contented myself with listening to the people around me.

"How has your kingdom been faring in the last few months?" Tavia asked. "Is everything well?"

Quay ran his hand through his hair. "Well, you see, things are going great for the kingdom itself. The merchants have been doing well on their travels and the people are prospering." He paused, and I noticed the sorrow in his eyes. "However, almost six months ago, my father's illness got worse... and he passed away."

Tavia set down her fork. "Wait, really?"

"I hadn't heard!" I said, frowning.

He nodded. "I know. I wanted to keep it quiet. My father, Calloway, never liked more attention than was necessary."

"I would have thought we'd hear something," Tavia said. "I'm sorry about that, Quay."

"Were you expecting it?" I asked. "I mean, I know he had the illness for several years, but I didn't think it was getting worse."

"We had a couple weeks of notice. It had to happen," he responded. "It's probably best that it happened sooner than later. He was getting old and frail."

Although Quay looked indifferent, I could see he was not happy to be talking about the matter.

I glanced toward the servants. "I think they are bringing the desserts out."

The servants laid platters of cheesecake along the table, with several different flavors. I chose blueberry.

People began to leave the table to dance in the large open area. Tavia poked me while I was halfway through eating the cake and leaned over to whisper in my ear.

"Remember, you have to ask him if he will help us. Before the end of the night. Got it?"

I tightened my grip around my napkin. "Yes."

"I'm going to talk to Quay's bodyguards for awhile," Tavia said. "You should go dance."

She stood up and left the table. I watched her for a moment as she walked over to a couple of Quay's bodyguards, who were standing next to a window.

I finished my piece of cake and stood. If Tavia told me to dance, I'd better do it, even if I didn't know what it had to do with her plan.

As soon as I walked onto the floor, people came to talk to me. I ended up dancing with several people, which was normal for a celebration, and I was able to talk to the lords and elders. Many of them wanted to know about the latest news or discuss matters about the kingdom. Others spoke of the beautiful day we'd had.

After an hour or so, I stopped to get a drink of water.

Standing beside the wall, I drank until my cup was empty, and I took a couple moments to rest my eyes.

When I looked up, I spotted Quay walking through the crowd toward me. He slowed to a stop and offered his hand. "Want to dance?" he asked.

"Of course," I said, putting my hand in his. We stepped onto the dance floor where people swayed to the sound of the violins.

I didn't want to look nervous. This was the perfect chance to ask Quay if he could aid us in the war, but I was afraid I'd mess it all up.

Shhh, I told myself. *Don't worry. Just do it.*

I smiled. "Did you like your meal?"

"Yes, it was one of the best I've ever had. You have great cooks." His dark eyes gleamed as he smiled. "And you were right about those cranberries."

"They are just like candy, aren't they?" I paused, thinking of a way to mention the war. After a moment, I said, "So... has Shane talked to you recently?"

"Yes." Quay glanced away. "He has ambitious ideas, but they'll never work."

"What kind of ideas?"

He shook his head. "He wants to create an alliance with me, but I'm never going to do it."

My heart jumped a bit. Did that mean he would be willing to form an alliance with us? I tilted my head. "Do you think he would ever attack you? Would you fight if he did?"

We both moved closer to the middle of the floor, avoiding running into anyone else.

Quay watched me suspiciously. "You have many questions, Arely," he said.

"I'm sorry." I glanced at the ground and then to where Tavia stood, talking to guests. "I am simply curious."

I wished Tavia hadn't given me this task, but I understood why she had. *"Act like yourself,"* she had told me.

"It's just – war is hard," I said, looking Quay directly in the eyes. "We need help."

He pursed his lips, but didn't show any surprise.

 59

"I know you want to keep your kingdom at peace," I continued. "I understand that. But that's what I want too and I can't get that until we capture Shane and win the war."

I paused, holding my breath.

Quay frowned. "It's not that simple. I would help you in the war, but I promised my people to never join a war unless it was completely necessary."

"What does 'necessary' mean to you?" I asked, stopping in my place.

He eyed me carefully. "It means that I won't join a war unless my kingdom or one of my allies is attacked."

I let go of him and crossed my arms. "Are we *not* your allies?" I demanded.

Tavia rushed over to us, her brows furrowed. "What's going on here?"

Quay took a deep breath. "Please understand me. I have always considered Rivallen as my ally. However, this war started several years before I became king. My father decided to stay out of it, and so shall I."

Tavia stepped beside me. "Quay, I have an offer for you. I'd appreciate it if you would hear me out. I think you'd like it. We don't need much help in the war, I promise."

I glanced around. The guests had fallen silent and all eyes were focused on us, the three rulers.

Quay looked like he was doing his best to stay calm. "Octavia, I understand why you invited me here tonight. I know you want me to help in the war, but I can't."

As he spoke, I noticed a dark sheath dangling from his belt. It was small, the perfect size for a dagger. I frowned. For someone obsessed with the idea of peace, why would he carry a dagger at a party?

Tavia put her hands on her hips. "There is a time for peace and a time for war," she said. "I hope you understand that."

I watched her expression. She didn't flinch, even with all the pressure of the moment weighing on her.

Quay stood his ground. "If your father had worked his whole life to preserve peace, you wouldn't want to throw it out the door like that, either."

He turned and beckoned his guards to come to him.

Tavia took my hand and squeezed it, but she kept her eyes on Quay. "Don't go," she said. "There would be no honor in that, would there?"

He stopped. "If you could excuse us to our rooms, it would be appreciated. We are tired from our trip."

My sister hesitated and then nodded. "Go then. The servants will lead you."

Quay and his guards followed two servants out of the ballroom. His dagger bounced against his leg as he walked away, almost like a warning.

Perhaps it *was* a warning.

"That went horribly!" I cried as soon as Tavia and I were out of earshot from anyone else. "I thought I could do it, but I only angered him."

Tavia brushed her fingers against my arm, gently. "It's not the end of the world, Arely."

Although she tried to assure me of this, I could tell she was frustrated too.

She led me into our room and locked the door. "Look," she said. "I know it didn't go as planned, but I have other ways to convince him."

"What ways?" I asked.

Tavia collapsed onto the bed and blew her hair off her face. "I haven't worked on them yet," she admitted.

I sat down next to her. "Did you see that dagger Quay was carrying?"

"Yes. Why?"

"Well... it seemed odd that he had one." I watched her close her eyes. She was at work, thinking.

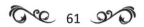

"Even Quay can have a dagger, Arely," she said tiredly. "He probably uses it for cutting ropes and stuff."

I nodded. That was true.

"Are you going to talk to him in the morning about it?" I asked hopefully. Maybe he would change his mind before he left.

Tavia shook her head. "I'll let him go back to his kingdom and when he's had time to mull it over, I can try again."

"Oh." I watched as Tavia rubbed her forehead, like she had a headache. I had completely blown it. If I had worded things differently, if I hadn't been so awkward, he would have agreed to help us.

Perhaps I wasn't any good at creating deals with other rulers. I would never be able to create a peace treaty with Shane, even if I tried.

I sank into the blankets beside my sister.

"Don't blame yourself, Arely," she said, as if reading my thoughts. "It'll all work out in the end."

Chapter 9
Shane

With the battle only hours away, I decided to head to the royal blacksmith's shop. I needed to check that my sword was in top condition, in case I had to use it.

The blacksmith's work area was on the ground level of the castle, in the west wing. My bodyguards waited outside as I walked into the room, which smelled strongly of smoke and fire. Waving my hand in front of my face, I let my eyes adjust to the surroundings.

Dozens of weapons covered the dark, ash-covered walls. Shiny halberds, razor sharp daggers, uniquely carved shurikens. Swords of different lengths and sizes lined the entrance wall, glittering with jewels and rare stones.

"Ah, King Shane!" the blacksmith's voice boomed. He stood next to a large kiln and fire silhouetted his tall, burly frame. With his calloused hands, I wouldn't put it past him to destroy a table with his fists. It was a good thing we got along.

The blacksmith grinned. "Back again, eh? You were here a week ago."

"I know," I said, shrugging. I placed my sword on his table and he glanced down at it. "Can you sharpen this again?"

"Your Majesty, it's already sharpened. It wouldn't be good to sharpen it again so soon—"

"Give me a reason to stay longer," I said, turning to study the new weapons on his wall.

He grunted, an attempt at a laugh I suppose, and then picked up my sword. "Well, if that's what you want, I guess I can polish the jewels. They are looking a little dim..."

The blacksmith went to work on the sword and I picked up a katar. Its two, sturdy blades glinted in the firelight. Designs of snakes were etched into the blade handle and onto the smooth metal.

The blacksmith had a way with art and weapons, that's for sure. I imagined if I wasn't the king, I would have wanted his job. His weapons fetched a high price for quality, after all, and he was the most renowned blacksmith in the land. It was the reason he worked in the castle for me.

I hung the katar back on the wall and spotted a new sickle. The blade was lined with small holes and the edge was jagged. "What do you call this?" I asked, picking it up carefully. It was lightweight.

The blacksmith grinned as he looked up from my sword. "Oh, that thing? I call it the flesh carver."

"The *flesh* carver?" I laughed at how deadpan he said it. "Honestly, you couldn't have chosen a creepier name."

"But it fits, doesn't it?" he asked, serious.

I glanced down at the sickle. I certainly wouldn't want to get stabbed with this blade. That would not leave you in a pretty state... if you even survived the attack.

I put it back in its place and said, "Where do you get the ideas for all these weapons?"

"From my sleep. Don't ask." The blacksmith handed my sword back, the jewels glowing like he had enchanted them. After a close examination, I placed it back in my sheath.

"Thanks," I said, throwing a handful of golden coins on the table. The blacksmith gave a crisp nod, pleased.

"Will you be back in a week?" he asked.

"Perhaps." I turned to the door and opened it. "I don't want to miss your crazy inventions. But I think you need to work on your names."

He scratched his head. "I thought it was genius."

"For an outlaw or rebel, yes. That's questionable for a king."

The blacksmith nodded, looking thoughtful, as if I meant it. "I'll have to work on that, milord."

I grinned and then left.

Somehow I felt better after the small visit, though I now smelled of smoke. I'd have to change into a new outfit.

The blacksmith was the only person who could make me laugh. At least, since Quay decided he didn't like to play pranks on people and stopped listening to my brilliant plans when I was a prince. But after that I didn't find many things amusing. Work became my top priority.

I walked up the steps to the castle until I came inside. Now that I had gotten used to the heat of the blacksmith's store, the chill of the day was a shock to my skin.

I made my way to the stables, where I mounted my horse and rode through the castle gates to the outer walls.

That morning, I had dressed with extra armor, and my bodyguards had done the same. They formed a tight circle of heavily armed men.

Thousands of soldiers covered the field, speckling it like salt and pepper. Knights rushed around the many barracks, preparing weapons, armor, and warhorses.

All the commotion made it hard to concentrate.

I waited, sitting on Triballi. General Collins must have spotted my ring of guards, because he moved closer to wait.

Once all the important lords and knights had gathered in front of me, I silenced them with a wave of my hand. "Everyone, settle down."

The crowd near me fell silent, turning its attention away from the preparation. Once it had, I began to speak.

"You all know my goal tonight: get back the lookout tower that belongs to us. All of you must do your best out there. If I catch anyone who retreats without my order, he will be severely punished. Do you understand? I want the best fighting tonight. If you want to be a coward, you shouldn't have joined the army."

A murmur ran through the crowd and most of the knights nodded their heads.

"All right. Let's get going."

I turned Triballi around and entered the vast field. The woods took a half hour to reach, and Fort Oak was only a couple hundred yards away when I came to a halt.

I motioned for my army to stop, and General Collins rode next to me.

"Are we ready to attack?" he asked.

I was about to tell him "yes" when my instincts stopped me. I glanced toward the woods and listened. In the trees, shadows started to move swiftly.

A figure on a horse stumbled to a stop right outside of the forest, surrounded by knights of high power. It could only be Octavia.

It took me a moment to recover from my shock. "Yes," I said to Collins. "Attack!"

I sent a bolt of blood red magic into the sky, marking the beginning of the battle. A second later, Octavia had disappeared from the front of the woods. A wave of knights poured from the trees instead, running to meet Rapora's army.

My bodyguards surrounded me as my knights rushed past, and I fell into the back lines.

A large chorus of metal striking metal rang out as the two armies met, along with shouts and whinnies. The soldiers collided together, creating a mass of vicious blows.

I stayed near my guards, all of whom wore defiant, stoic expressions as they monitored the area.

As the battle raged, I tried to find the queen throughout the field, but I couldn't see her anywhere. It was very possible she had stayed inside the cover of the trees.

I swiveled my head to look up as a bolt of pink lightning lit up the sky, only a couple hundred yards to the south. It struck the land like a giant snake attacking its prey.

Arely is here, I realized.

And it all made sense.

Octavia had planned to attack the castle. She had certainly brought the whole army with her, and not only that, but she had brought Arely so they could both fight me.

That's why Octavia had disappeared when the battle started. She was going to find her twin. But she wasn't going to find her, because I would get to her first.

"Where are my assassins?" I asked, turning my horse around. I didn't have to wait for one of my guards to answer, because I spotted the three knights standing several hundred yards behind me.

I kicked Triballi and he took off. He closed the gap in a couple moments, skidding to a stop near the assassins, who wore the grandest armor in the kingdom. It was crafted so that no arrow or sword, unless enchanted with magic, could penetrate the knights. Each of them had trained for years and were stronger than ten of Octavia's soldiers combined.

"I need you three," I said, out of breath. "You saw Arely's magic and where it came from, right?"

The leader nodded and spoke in a deep voice. "Of course, Your Royal Majesty. Do you want us to go after her?"

"Yes, but do not harm her. I want you to bring her back to the castle."

"Of course, my lord."

The leader motioned to go and all three of my assassins took off for the woods, where the magic had long ago fizzled out.

As I watched their steeds dash toward the battle, I had no doubt in my mind that they would capture Arely. After all, they were my best assassins, and no one had ever escaped their grasp.

Chapter 10
Arely

When it came time to leave the castle, Tavia and I mounted our horses, Patrios and Grey Girl. Sir Harding had organized all six of my bodyguards, giving each of them their orders. Nico rode beside me. He gave me a small smile, but I could tell he was nervous. I tried to ignore that.

"Okay," Tavia said to us. "Let's get going."

She reached out and squeezed my hand, then turned back to the field and nudged Patrios. Her horse started walking and she waved for me to follow.

I waited a few moments to calm myself before signaling for Grey Girl to start walking.

There was no way my guards would let me get into trouble, especially Nico. I was safe. I wouldn't get hurt.

I squeezed my legs against Grey Girl's side and she took off into a trot obediently. My guards kept close, although as we started to move faster, they spread out. I focused my eyes on the soldiers ahead and tugged my reins when I needed to change direction.

We avoided the main road that travelers and merchants used to cross from Rivallen, through the woods, and to Rapora. Instead, we traveled in the lower patches of the meadow.

Tavia had been certain about our victory tonight. She believed that our army was better, and with our magic, together we would overthrow Shane and his army.

For the sake of the people, I hoped she wasn't being overly confident again.

We reached the woods and started moving through the trees. It was so dark, Nico had to light a lantern and lead the way so we could see. Tavia had gone farther up ahead to talk to the general. She had told me she'd come right back.

As I was lost in thought, Nico rode closer to me. I looked over at him as he opened his mouth to speak. "Are you ready for this?" he asked quietly.

"I think so... but I'll be glad when it's all over," I said. "Hopefully it'll turn out the way I want, without much bloodshed."

"Well, I hope so too, but—"

Nico stopped.

"What?" I started to say, but then I saw where he was looking. I turned to look ahead and spotted another army far in the distance, beyond the trees. The dark mass of soldiers moved through the night like a shadow coming to crush us.

It was Shane's army. But how had he known we were coming? Had spies found out our plan and told him? Or was he coming to attack Fort Oak?

I jerked back on the reins too hard and Grey Girl grunted. She skidded to a stop, rearing her head up and shaking her gray hair in my face.

I patted her neck and whispered in her ear, "It's okay. I'm sorry, Girlie."

I glanced around frantically for Tavia, but I couldn't see her anymore. Both she and the general had disappeared in the thicket of branches.

A moment later, a large, blood red explosion burst in the air, visible through a gap in the trees. I had heard of this symbol before. It was Shane's signal for battle.

Sir Harding moved his horse to block mine.

"We should go," he said, using his 'that's-an-order' voice. "Octavia's plan for a surprise attack won't work now."

I frowned, remembering all the times I'd worried about Tavia while she was in battle. And now we were in the midst of a dangerous situation. This was exactly what had happened the night my parents had died. They'd left for a battle and unexpectedly ran into King Dagwood on the other side of the woods.

Suddenly I didn't want to leave.

"I'm not going." I squared my shoulders and took a deep breath. "Tavia will need my help."

Nico's eyes widened. "You most certainly aren't going to help in battle. What about the force field around the castle? Your magic will run out faster—"

Sir Harding cut him off. "Arely, there are knights everywhere. One of them might recognize you."

I backed my horse a few steps, eyeing the two armies. They were coming into contact. But the guard was right. Knights on black steeds were circling the battle to survey the fighting.

Nico glared at the knights, as if daring them to come near us. "Arely! It's time to go. The last thing we need is for a queen to get killed, and Tavia would rather know you are out of harm's way than let you help."

I didn't want to give in, but he was right. It was frustrating how little I knew about battle anyway. Perhaps I should have listened when Tavia tried to convince me to train for battle, but it was too late.

I pulled on the reins and Grey Girl turned around. She nickered quietly.

Behind me, the sound of hooves pounding against the ground filled the air. I didn't need anyone to tell me that a knight had seen us.

Fear took a hold of me and a rush of adrenaline swept through my body. I kicked my horse and she took off into a canter. Nico followed right behind me, but I didn't hear the other guards. I kept my eyes on the clearing ahead, too afraid to look behind. My hands turned white from how tightly I was holding onto the reins.

My hair flew behind me, whipping around as I raced through the trees, dodging branches and clusters of tall oaks. I dared to sneak a look back. The other guards had stayed to fight the knight, giving Nico and me more time to escape.

But I could see more knights running toward them. My bodyguards were the best-trained soldiers in the kingdom, but they were outnumbered.

Tavia had strictly told me not to use my power unless my life was in danger, but I couldn't leave them to fight alone. I pulled back on the reins and Grey Girl reared up.

Nico circled toward me. "What are you doing? We have to get out of here!"

I turned toward the knights riding the black steeds. My magic sparked, crackling like little bolts of lightning. I summoned enough energy and let it loose.

A zigzag of lightning struck the men, knocking several of them to the ground. The horses took off in all directions, scared to death of the magic. Most of the knights didn't get up, but the ones that did couldn't catch up to their steeds.

Nico grabbed my wrist. "Don't use any more magic! Go!"

I turned around and ordered Grey Girl to continue on. By now she was as panicked as I was, and she took off faster than I expected. My palms were sweaty. I couldn't cling to the reins much longer.

Nico kept looking back, as if he expected more knights to appear. That's when I realized my mistake. I had used my magic, sending a pink blast through the sky, therefore alerting everyone in the meadow that I was here.

I forced myself to keep going. All I had to do was hold on tightly to Grey Girl and she would carry me to safety.

Nico pulled the bow off his back and nocked two magic arrows at once. I whipped my head around to see three knights on our tails, and my eyes grew wide. They wore thick layers of armor, plus helmets that completely covered their faces. We were up against blocks of steel.

The steeds must've been twice the size of Grey Girl. We'd never get away by running. We would have to outsmart them.

I pulled myself closer to my horse and urged her to run faster while I tried to figure out what to do.

Nico shot an arrow at the guards, but I didn't watch to see if it met its target. The sound of the hooves grew louder.

When I glanced back, I saw that one of them had slowed down. He had an arrow sticking out of his armor, around his chest.

But that didn't help us. The other two were only yards away. My heart pounded and I wished I could be in the safety of the castle.

Nico pulled out more arrows but he fumbled while nocking them.

My horse stumbled on an uneven patch of ground and a second later collapsed. I shrieked as I was thrown into the air and hit the ground hard. A metallic taste filled my mouth and my nose ached.

Nico's horse pounded toward me. I covered my head, terrified he was about to trample my body. I felt the *swoosh* as the horse's hooves barely missed my head.

But I hadn't avoided the knights. I tried to stand up and run to Grey Girl so they wouldn't run over me, but before I could escape, one of the knights yanked me off the ground. I screamed, fighting against his grip, but he was too strong.

I sent another blast of magic at him, but it ricocheted against his armor and hit me in the face. The bright light dazed me and for a moment, I couldn't move. The knight clipped something around my wrist and suddenly I couldn't use my magic.

That something was a magic cuff, I realized, my blood running cold. Shane must've enchanted it and as long as this cuff was on my wrist, I wouldn't have my greatest defense.

I started to wriggle and kick against the knight again. "Nico!" I screamed, trying to see where my bodyguard had gone, but he was nowhere to be seen. Had he gotten injured or fallen off his horse?

"Stop, you foolish girl!" the knight growled. "If you keep struggling, I'll have to knock you out."

I stopped fighting against the guard and he forced me to sit in the front of the saddle. He chained the other side of the cuffs to the horn and grabbed the reins.

"Stay still," he commanded. "If you fall, you'll be dragged and I don't think Shane wants you to come to the castle in five different pieces."

I listened and held on to the saddle for dear life. The forest soared past us in a blur. The other knight followed close behind us.

I was too terrified to make a sound. No one from my army was around, at least where we were. The knight had purposely traced around the battle, avoiding the active parts of the woods.

If only Tavia would appear and fight the knights. But she could be in danger herself. I had no idea.

In the distance, an explosion rang through the air and shook the ground. The horse stumbled and the knight grabbed a hold of me so I wouldn't fall. My body shook and I could feel cold sweat gathering on my forehead.

Tavia had created that explosion with her magic. She was close, and yet so far.

As we neared the castle, the seriousness of my situation finally started to settle on me. After the knights took me to the castle, I would meet Shane for the first time in my life. And he would be the one person in control of whether I lived or died.

I'd heard the saying "Be careful what you wish for" a hundred times, at least. But I'd never regretted a wish until the knights rode through the gates of Rapora Castle, leaving behind the raging battle and entering a relatively peaceful enclosure with several servants hurrying about.

I did not want to be here. I did not want to meet Shane.

I had long since stopped shaking, but I didn't know if that meant I had calmed down or if my body had gone numb in shock.

The knights walked into a small stable and the two horses halted. The man who had grabbed me dismounted his steed and unchained my cuff from the saddle. "Get down," he ordered.

I slid over the edge and stumbled when my feet hit the ground. My knees buckled and I fell forward onto the dirty, hay-covered floor. The room smelled of horse manure, and while that usually didn't bother me, I didn't want to fall into it. I grimaced as I struggled back to my feet.

The man pulled me along the tunnel. It was dark in the castle, even with the candles lining the hallway. The knights walked closely beside me and held my arms, making sure I couldn't escape.

They took me deeper into the palace, until I heard water dripping from the ceiling and had to breathe through my mouth to avoid smelling the foul stench of the dungeon cells.

My stomach churned as a jail guard walked up to us and spotted me.

"Oooh... what have we here? Do I have the honor of meeting the royal princess Arely?" he asked, mock bowing.

"Queen, actually," I corrected. "And yes. It is me."

He turned to the knights, ignoring my comment. "You know there are jail cells made specifically for nobles and royals right? We wouldn't want the poor flower to have to stay down here with the real scoundrels, would we?"

"Well, we're already down here," the knight said, irritated. "Might as well. King Shane never gave any orders for where to put her."

The jail guard nodded. "All right. I'll lead you to a cell, then."

As he walked, his keys clanked against his side and I felt sick to my stomach. They were going to lock me up, afraid, without my twin, and not knowing what to expect next.

I wanted to break free and run right then, but what was the point? They would catch up to me eventually. There was no escaping Rapora now.

The guard stopped and unlocked a door. The knights forced me into the small, pitch-black room. They brought in a lantern, and the flame illuminated a row of chains on the wall. Another prisoner sat in the corner.

I gasped and fought against the knights' grip as they pulled me toward the wall. "Stop!" I said, panic filling me. "Please don't chain me up. Isn't the cell door enough to keep me from escaping?"

"Sorry, sweetheart," the knight said, unapologetically. "The times are rough. We have to make sure this queen doesn't escape or His Majesty would have our heads."

I squirmed as they tried to hold me still and put the cuffs around my wrists. The harder I tugged, the harder they squeezed my wrists, until it hurt too much that I had to give in.

The jail guard watched as they chained me to the damp, moldy wall. He clucked his tongue disapprovingly. "You know, I wouldn't want King Shane to find out you're putting her down here. His father ordered for all royals to be placed in the other cells."

"His Majesty wouldn't *care*," the knight hissed. "That only applies to the royals in his family, and he doesn't have any family. Besides, it's only for the night. King Shane will see her in the morning, if not sooner."

The knights let go of me and left the cell, without looking back. The jail guard's keys jingled as he locked the door, plunging the cell into darkness.

Tears threatened to fill my eyes, but I beat them back, biting my tongue instead to avoid making a sound. I didn't want people to think I was weak.

A ragged, old voice spoke through the dark. "You're the queen? As in, Arely or Octavia?" The voice came from my right, only a couple feet away.

I hesitated before answering.

"I'm Arely."

The man chuckled. "Ah. The one who started this whole war."

"What?" I cried, exasperated. "I never! Why would you say such a thing?"

"Oh, never mind," he said, quietly. "...You're really Arely?"

A hand brushed against my arm and I jerked back in alarm. The prisoner chuckled. "I feel terrible for you, young one."

"W-why?" I asked.

"Once Shane comes for you, you won't last long. Believe me, he *hates* you."

There's a whisper in the darkness
When kindness finds a land,
A song in the wilderness
Makes wild things understand,
A smile in the aftermath
Of battles fought and lost.
A warmth in the words
That melt the coldest frost.
Wounds cannot be healed by force
Nor a broken mind by demand,
But yet the heart finds a refuge
In the palm of a gentle hand.

Whisper in the Darkness ~ by Arely

Chapter 11
Shane

Octavia's forces withdrew at a rapid rate soon after I sent my assassins after Arely. I had no way to know if they had succeeded in capturing her, but by the way my army pushed Octavia's through the woods, I could tell that the queen and her general were distracted, and it was very possible they were searching for Arely.

The Rivallen knights didn't know what to do without command, so they fled into the forest. I sent my troops to surround Fort Oak, and in a matter of minutes, they raided the building.

Octavia never appeared in the meadow again.

A grin crept onto my face. She had meant to attack my palace and win the war, no doubt. If the knights had succeeded in capturing Arely, then Octavia lost two invaluable pieces to the war, and when she found out her sister was missing, she'd play right into my hand.

As soon as the army invaded the fort, General Collins rode his horse to me. "Your Majesty," he said.

"Is everything in proper order?" I asked.

"We captured Fort Oak and secured it. None of Octavia's men are left inside." He turned to look at the woods. "And it would appear they have retreated."

"So it would."

I glanced across the edge of the trees. Hundreds of dead knights and horses speckled the grassy meadow, where the two armies had met.

"General Collins, send knights to look for any survivors on our side," I ordered. "I am going to the castle to check on... my assassins. I believe you will take care of everything from here?"

"Yes, my King."

I nodded and we parted ways. I rode toward the castle with my bodyguards. There was only one question burning on my mind now.

Upon reaching the castle, I sought out my three best knights. I didn't have the patience to wait for a servant to fetch them, so I found them within a few minutes.

Two of the knights were sitting inside the barracks, taking off all the layers of thick armor they wore. One was missing, however.

"What happened to the third one of you?" I asked, not knowing his name.

"Your Majesty," they said, bowing as I sat down on a stool next to the door. "He was injured while we chased Arely. Her bodyguard shot him, so the medics are tending to his wound."

"What about Arely?" I asked, holding my breath.

The knight's lip curled. "She's in the dungeon, sire. Safely locked up, without her magic. I do say, she was upset."

"I'd be worried if she wasn't."

The assassin leader tilted his head. "Do you want to see her now? I'd be more than willing to get her for you."

I glanced out the doorway to the night sky. It was quite late for me to speak to Arely, but I wanted to do it tonight. There was something I had to do first, though.

"No," I said. "Bring her to my throne room in an hour."

He nodded.

I heard a familiar whirling sound behind me and turned to see blue magic swirling through the air. Octavia wanted to talk to me, and considering the events of the last couple hours, she wanted to talk *immediately.*

I left the barracks and headed to my room, while ignoring the flashing blue magic. I disregarded it all the way up the stairs even as it grew increasingly brighter. I finally used my magic to answer it once I entered my bedroom on the second highest floor. I cast a spark of magic at hers, and after a moment, she appeared through the mist.

I grinned at her.

She glowered at me, as I suspected she would.

"Where is she?" Octavia demanded. "Tell me now."

"I'm sorry, but I haven't the slightest idea who you are referring to." I started fixing the buttons on my cape that had come undone, ignoring the furious look she threw me.

"If you didn't know, you wouldn't look so smug."

"Oh, I suppose you are talking about your sister. Shouldn't she be safe in Rivallen, getting ready to sleep in her nice, comfy bed?"

By the look on her face, I could tell I had struck a nerve.

"What did you do to her?" she yelled. "What did you do to Arely?"

I waited a moment, trying to figure out the best way to answer that question. "Well, my knights locked her up in the dungeon. I haven't done anything."

"You must have a plan somewhere in that twisted mind of yours," Octavia said, still glaring at me with all of her venom.

I chuckled. "Of course. I have an offer to make her."

"An offer?" she asked. "It'd better be fair. She hasn't done anything to you, Shane."

"I assure you she'll be taken care of," I said, bored. "If she takes my deal, I'll give her everything she could need."

"And if she doesn't?"

"She'll regret it."

Octavia stared at me, and for a split second I saw fear in her eyes, but she quickly covered it.

She drew in a deep breath. "Listen to me, Shane. If you do anything – anything at all – to hurt her, I will kill you."

I laughed. "I'm sorry, but didn't you already plan on killing me?"

"I do not like to be mocked, especially by a fool like you," she snarled. "Make one wrong move, and you are done for – even if you do treat her well."

"I have a solution to your problem."

"And that is?"

"Surrender and I'll send her back to Rivallen."

Octavia fell silent, unyielding. "You can try that tactic, but I'm afraid you have made yourself predictable." She withdrew her magic and disappeared without another word.

Only a half hour later, I entered my throne room and sat down in my silver chair. I expected Arely would be here any minute, if she wanted to catch me while I was in a good mood. I could get impatient.

The servants offered me food, but I declined. "Where are my assassins?" I asked.

"They are coming," Tad said, standing a few yards away. He looked more nervous than normal, which was saying something for the old man.

I looked down at the entrance as the two knights marched into the room. One of them carried a girl over his shoulder. She looked so small, at first I wasn't sure if it was Arely, but she had curly, blonde hair and wore the queen's prominent pink dress, so it was her. My sworn enemy.

I leaned forward in my chair. I had never seen Arely in person before. I had seen Octavia plenty of times, but never Arely. Of course, I had spoken to her using magic, but it wasn't the same as seeing her in my own castle.

Her dress was torn and dirty. It looked like she had fallen off her horse.

The guards walked up to my throne, and the one carrying Arely dropped her on the floor as if she was only a sack of flour, not a queen.

I stood up and threw him a disgusted look. "Don't drop her on the floor like that," I snapped.

He took a step back in surprise, and lowered his head. "I'm sorry, milord. Forgive me."

"Why is she unconscious?"

The knights shuffled their feet. "Um, she was quite uncooperative when we tried to take her out of her jail cell, sir. It turns out she's stronger and louder than we suspected. We had to knock her out."

I knelt down beside Arely, to look at her more closely. She had dried blood on her nose and her lip was cut. She had a fair amount of dirt in her hair as well.

I noticed the magic cuff on her wrist and pried it off, dropping the metal into my cloak pocket. Then I summoned a bit of magic and touched her head, placing a new spell on her. She wouldn't be able to use her magic anymore, not here in my castle, and she wouldn't be able to get rid of the spell by breaking a simple cuff.

I stood, pleased, and walked back to my throne. "Wake her up," I ordered. "She's no good knocked out, is she?"

A servant came with a bucket of water and poured it on Arely's head, causing her to cough. After a moment, she sat up shakily and looked around.

She froze.

"Queen Arely," I said.

She whipped around and I could see the fear in her eyes.

I smiled. "Welcome to Rapora."

The second the words left my lips, she frowned, as if she thought I was mocking her in front of everyone, but wasn't sure. No one made a sound.

She didn't move a muscle, as if she had turned into a statuette and couldn't do so even if she wanted.

I looked around at the people gathered in the room. They had all fallen silent, waiting for what I was about to do next. I could feel the tension growing, and it only seemed to unnerve Arely even more. I'm sure she didn't want to be here for a moment longer.

I glanced back down as she wiped her face. I realized she had tears running down her cheeks, but she didn't make a sound. A twinge of sympathy ran through me, but I quickly beat it down. I was forgetting whom I was dealing with.

This was the girl that should have died years ago, but my grandpa and aunt had died instead, so she had survived.

Arely noticed my gaze and looked away, still rubbing her eyes.

"I have a deal for you," I said, stepping forward.

She shrank away and narrowed her eyes, distrustfully, as if calculating each of my moves. I wasn't sure how she'd react to my proposal.

"What's your deal?" Arely asked, speaking for the first time.

I hesitated before kneeling down beside her. I whispered my offer into her ear, quietly, so no one else could hear.

Chapter 12
Arely

I wanted to run as soon as Shane knelt beside me. But I couldn't bring myself to move, even if my life depended on it. I could feel the cold marble beneath me and my head ached from where the knight had hit me with the blunt side of his sword.

I honestly hadn't expected it to hurt so much.

Water dripped down my head, forming a puddle on the floor as I shivered. My curly hair was plastered to my skin.

At that moment, I could imagine Tavia thinking I was weak, but never saying anything about it. She was the one who would race into battle without a second thought. If she was fighting for her people, she would do anything and everything and face whatever challenge to win the war.

If she had been in my place now, the last thing she would have done is start crying. But I wasn't Tavia.

I wiped the last of my tears away and turned to meet Shane's gaze. I didn't want to think about what he was going to do. Execute me? That seemed exactly what a king like Shane would do. Or worse, torture me into giving him information about Tavia and her war plans. I wouldn't be able to take it.

I waited painfully for Shane to speak.

When he did, he spoke calmly. "There are several options for what I can do with you. Of course, no choice is black and white. That's where war is tricky. You would know."

When I didn't say anything, he whispered, "If you were Octavia, I'd execute you right now, but you're not Octavia."

I hesitated. "If you're not going to execute me, what are you going to do?" I asked.

At first, he didn't say anything. "...I don't plan on killing you," he said, "but I cannot let you go. There is something you can give me, and if you'll do that, I will let you stay safely in the castle until the war has ended. It's simple."

"And... what is that, exactly?"

"The Third Blessing."

I stared at him, and even in my fuzzy state of mind, the pieces fell into place perfectly. I knew what he wanted.

He was asking for us to get married. He wanted to gain the last of his magic he hadn't achieved yet. Every royal had to gain the three Blessings if they wanted to have the maximum amount of magic.

It was another one of those complicated rules that had applied to magic for centuries. It was believed that the magic worked that way so royals would marry into other kingdoms and stable alliances would remain throughout the region.

If Shane gained the Third Blessing, he would be more powerful than my sister, and with me safely locked up in his castle, I wouldn't be able to aid her in the war. He would win.

I blinked, coming back to my senses. Shane waited expectantly, and now I understood why he had whispered to me instead of letting everyone hear. The Blessings were secret.

"You want to marry me so you'll gain more magic?" I asked.

He nodded. "Then I can finally put an end to this war. I think that's a deal we can both agree on."

"Not if it means you'll kill my sister."

Shane waved his hand, brushing away my comment. "I have the right to kill her if she tries to kill me. Look, if you don't take my offer, I'll have to execute you. You're too dangerous to keep alive."

"Say I *do* take your offer," I said. "After the ceremony, what are you going to do? Kill me anyway? Throw me into the deepest, darkest dungeon to silence me? Or *torture* me? How can I be assured you won't do those things after I help you get the Third Blessing?"

He narrowed his eyes at me. "I will keep my word for a fellow royal. I won't do any of those things if you take the offer. If you think I'm some lowly liar, you're wrong."

"Well, in that case, I'm sorry," I said simply, "but I need time to think about your offer."

Shane sat back. "I'd think you would have figured it out by now."

I ignored his remark and glanced out the window. It was true, I didn't have much of a choice. If I ever wanted to see Tavia again, I'd have to do it. Would she be upset with me? Would she rather I sacrifice myself before ever letting Shane gain the maximum amount of magic? What if I never saw Tavia again *because* I took the offer? Because he overpowered her with his magic and killed her?

If only I could talk to her. I'd die to save my kingdom, if I knew it was the best thing to do. But I wasn't sure anymore. Perhaps if I found a way to escape... then *I'd* have the maximum amount of magic, too.

Shane frowned, drumming his fingers. "Are you always this indecisive?"

I pursed my lips. "You know how furious Tavia is going to be, right?" I said, challenging him.

Amusement flickered across his face. "She's already furious, but then again, when isn't she furious? Your sister has anger issues."

"That's debatable."

"Have you made up your mind?"

"All right," I said, straightening myself. "I'll do it."

Shane stood up and offered me his hand. I hesitantly took it and he helped me to my feet. I winced as pain shot through my forehead, reminding me of my headache from the knights knocking me out.

I almost wished I hadn't given them a hard time. Almost.

Shane waved one of the servants over. A wiry girl scampered toward him, waiting for his command.

"Go get one of the royal maids," he said, "and tell her to come immediately."

She nodded and ran off.

I glanced at Shane. He watched the servant go, a mysterious look passing over his face. Then he looked around again.

A short man – shorter than me – walked over to us, frowning as if something troubled him. He glanced at me, like he wanted to speak, but thought better of it and turned to the king.

"Tad," Shane said. "Go to the meeting room and I'll be there soon."

He obeyed and walked briskly out of the throne room.

A few moments later, a maid arrived and bowed low. She had silver-gray hair pulled back with a purple ribbon. A smile flickered across her face as she glanced at me, but she looked back at Shane, as Tad had done. "Your Majesty. Did you call for me?"

He nodded. "Take Arely and clean her up. I want four guards to accompany you up the stairs as well."

"Yes, sir." The maid motioned me to follow. I did so willingly and tried to ignore the guards that marched beside us.

She led me through the tunnels of the castle, and everywhere we turned, people stared at me in shock. I think a couple of them laughed at me behind my back. I must've looked like I had worked in a pigpen for a week.

The maid paused in front of a large door and faced me, her smile meeting her soft blue eyes. She had many wrinkles on her face, showing her age and wisdom.

"I suppose I should introduce myself," she said. "I'm Lori. I've been working in this castle as a maid for several decades. Don't worry, I'll get you cleaned up in no time."

I normally would have smiled back, but under these circumstances, I couldn't manage the slightest one. She seemed to understand however, because she unlocked the door to let me in the room.

The guards took their posts outside.

I walked into the large bedroom. There was a huge bed with plush, white pillows and a thick blanket tucked in perfectly. The ceiling was high above my head, and a chandelier hung from the center of it. In the corner, there was a great big tub with a dressing screen.

It was a room fit for royalty.

I hurried toward the grand windows that looked out on the meadow and forests. In the distance, I could see my own castle glimmering with thousands of lights. The sight made my heart twist in despair.

Not wanting to look away, I pressed my fingers against the glass, while behind me I could hear Lori start filling the tub with water. An amber glow reflected off the glass as she lit a flame in the fireplace, nudging the embers and kindling.

"I'm sorry, Queen Arely, but the water will be cold at first," she apologized. "It'll warm up soon though."

I walked over to her, brushing her apology away. "I'll be fine," I said. All I wanted was to wash off and change into a comfortable gown. If the water was cold, it was the least of my worries.

Lori poured a spoonful of soap into the water and bubbles began to form. I slipped off my dress, plus the armor Tavia had insisted I wear, then dipped my toes into the water. It was definitely cold, but not unbearable.

I sat down in the wooden tub and shivered slightly. After taking the brush off the small table next to the tub, I started scrubbing the dirt off my arms.

Lori rummaged around in a small cabinet and pulled out a jar of ointment. "You can put this on your cuts after you finish bathing," she said, placing it next to me.

"Thank you," I said as she bent down to work on the fireplace. She got the small flame to roar up into a blazing fire, illumining the dark room.

With all the mud covering my dress and skin, it felt good to clean off. I dunked my head under the water and began to shake the dirt out of my hair. When I lifted my head, the bubbles had grown and surrounded me completely.

I smiled. Tavia had always called me a goofball for loving bubbles so much, but they never failed to raise my spirits. I picked up a pile of bubbles and rubbed them across my face, clearing away the blood. My lip was swollen and it hurt to touch. I needed to put the medicine on it before I went to bed.

Eventually the water started to warm up. The heat of the flames wafted toward me, sweeping over my skin. It calmed my nerves enough that I wasn't shaking anymore.

Lori set a towel and a gown next to the tub. "Should I fetch you anything, my dear?" she asked. "A drink or treat before bed?"

"No thank you, I'm not hungry. But I'll take a glass of tea, please."

She nodded and left the room, leaving me all alone. I watched her leave, wondering if I could befriend the maid. I'd need a friend, after all, since it appeared I'd be here for a while.

I finished wringing out my hair, stood, and picked up the towel. It was warm from sitting next to the hearth.

I dried myself and tied the cloth over my dripping wet hair. The salmon-pink nightgown Lori had left for me was smooth and cool. I pulled it on, happy to have fresh clothes.

On the nightstand, a comb waited for me. I brushed my hair until it was tangle free. When Lori came in with the glass of chamomile tea, I had finished combing out the last of the water.

"Here you go," the maid said, setting the glass on my nightstand. "If you need anything else, you can tell the knights outside to get me, and I'll take care of whatever you need."

"Thanks. I'm good for now."

I smiled at her, but deep down inside, I knew that she wasn't able to get me what I really wanted.

As soon as Lori left my room, I raced to the window to see my own castle. Hopefully Nico had escaped and told Tavia everything that had happened. I didn't want to think he had tried to save me and died in the process. But either way, I didn't know.

I curled up on the ledge. There was a pillow and blanket sitting beside me and I pulled them close to my body.

I wasn't made for battle, even if I stayed to the side and didn't fight. What *was* I good at? None of my talents were helpful in this situation, unless Shane wanted another medic to work in the infirmary or a gardener to grow rare and delicate flowers for him.

Which was foolish.

I couldn't fall asleep. It was hopeless to even try. I sat by the window, looking over at the specks of light, wishing I could be next to Tavia, like I'd been a couple nights before.

Shane would have the wedding tomorrow and the servants would likely work all night. He hadn't confirmed it, but it made sense. The sooner he gained the Third Blessing, the sooner he could win the war. I was helping him beat my own kingdom, my own people.

I thought of an adorable girl I had once met in the village. She had given me a small stone as good luck in the war. After she had offered me the little gift, I'd taken it and given her a hug. She had run to her parents, smiling and jumping.

I didn't want to disappoint her or any of the villagers.

Maybe it would've been better if Shane executed me.

All I wanted was to talk to Tavia. But I was on my own here and had to make the right decision by myself.

I pulled my knees close to my chest, knowing I needed to stay alive so I could fight for my people, even from the enemy's own territory. I'd need a plan.

Maybe I didn't have a plan now, but I was clever, in my own unique, Arely kind-of-way. That was what Papa had always told me.

I would prove he was right.

I must've fallen asleep on the windowsill, because that's where Lori found me the next morning. She shook me gently, trying to get me awake.

I groaned quietly. I had barely slept, and I was sore from curling up on the hard wood. Today would not be enjoyable.

"Queen Arely," Lori whispered. "You should get up. You need to prepare for the wedding."

I yawned and stretched. My back was tense, and I wished my own maid was here so she could give me a massage.

As soon as the thought entered my mind, I felt guilty. Lori had done a fine job and it wasn't her fault I was stuck in Rapora.

Lori grabbed a tray off my bed. "I brought you breakfast."

I scanned the plate. There was milk, buttered toast, and freshly cooked eggs. My stomach growled, but I didn't have an appetite.

"Thank you," I said, sitting down on the bed. Hesitantly, I nibbled at the food while Lori folded my blanket. We were both silent.

I thought about helping Shane get the Third Blessing. Who would have thought I'd have the maximum amount of magic by tonight? That was the last thing I had imagined happening when I had been captured the night before.

Lori took the tray when I was finished, although I'd only eaten a couple bites before giving up.

"I let you sleep in," she said, heading toward the door. "The wedding begins in six hours. Best we start preparing now."

Chapter 13
Shane

If I had told you I wasn't the least bit nervous, I would be lying.

Not everyone understood what I was doing. After all, the Blessings were kept secret from most of the people in the kingdom. It made everything simpler.

I didn't have to do much to prepare for the wedding. I dressed in my finest outfit, which I almost always wore to feasts: grayish black armor, with woolen shoulders connected by leather straps and a silver ring. I placed my crown on my head, making sure it wasn't crooked.

The day had flown by because I'd been running around the castle trying to get everything in order for tonight. Now it was time to gain the Third Blessing.

I turned and walked out the door, meeting my bodyguards. I nodded for them to follow me, and continued down the hallway. The ceremony would start in only a few minutes. The tunnels were mostly deserted and people had gone into the throne room to wait for us.

I found my way to the entrance, where two more guards waited, along with Tad.

"Arely is coming, my lord," he said. "You should go down the aisle."

I hesitantly walked through the door and started down the carpet. My royal guards were right behind me.

My entrance was met with the blasts of trumpets, which nearly deafened me, and the guests standing and bowing. I noticed the few rows of villagers who sat in the back of the room, because they gasped and kept pointing at me. It was the beginning of the ceremony, with another half hour to go.

I already hated it.

I don't know *why* the Third Blessing had to be "get married." Why couldn't it have been "turn eighteen?" It wouldn't be too long before my next birthday. But I knew one thing: I had to get it to win the war. That's what mattered.

The navy blue drapes had been washed and hung up again, and I could tell they were brighter because of it. Along the aisle, the chairs had been decorated with dark flowers that matched the drapes and aisle carpet.

I stopped at the end, next to the priest. The guards took positions behind him.

General Collins came after me, then his chosen knights, and lastly the most prominent lords and ladies. I stopped paying attention to them, and instead watched Tad organize everyone in the very back. He waved to signal when the people could walk down the aisle, and then he would go right before Arely.

Tad sent one more knight and lady, and then waited for his turn. He walked in that silly, nervous way he always did, and stopped a few feet away from me.

I kept my eyes on the entrance, waiting, and suddenly wishing I could be anywhere *but* here. I had no idea why I'd ever thought this was a good idea. But by now, it was too late to change plans.

If I could survive this first part of the wedding, I'd be okay. That thought didn't ease any of my fear though.

Finally, Arely appeared at the end of the aisle, dressed in light pink and holding a white bouquet of flowers.

After living in a grand palace as the son of the King and only Prince, I learned how to ignore people. After all, my father had insisted that I spend half my time at incredibly boring meetings that had nothing to do with me.

So that's what I did the entire ceremony. I barely listened to a word the priest said and I tried my best to ignore Arely as well.

Out of the corner of my eye, I could see at least a couple hundred people. Old, young, weak, strong. Knights, ladies, lords, servants. You name it. It seemed like everyone was here.

That thought did little to comfort me.

I studied my kingdom's flag, which hung only a few yards from me. There was a golden hawk marked in the middle of the navy-colored flag, along with three triangles surrounding it.

I glanced back at the priest when he spoke my name. He held up a small pillow with two rings in the middle. I recognized them as the magical rings that would grant us the Third Blessing, as soon as we said the necessary vows.

"These rings have been passed on through countless generations of Rapora's kings and queens," he said, "making them an important part of the royal family. Shane, you may put the queen's ring on Arely and repeat after me."

I picked up the ring, trying to hide a grimace. It had a heart-shaped sapphire in the center, polished until it twinkled.

My cheeks grew warm. Clearly, I hadn't thought this whole plan through. Perhaps I was a bit impulsive, like Octavia, but not quite on her level.

I took Arely's hand and slid the silver ring onto her finger.

The priest droned on, and I repeated his lines impatiently, wanting it to be over.

"To you, Queen Arely of Rivallen, I promise to love and support you, in good times and in bad, in sickness and in health. I will love you and honor you all the days of my life. Take this ring as a sign of my solemn vow."

After I finished, I bit down on my tongue a little too hard and could taste blood in my mouth. I noticed Tad eyeing me carefully, and I glared back at him.

"Arely," the priest continued, "you may put the king's ring on Shane and repeat after me."

She took the second ring from the pillow, which had matching colors, but thankfully no heart-shaped jewel. Instead, it had a bunch of tiny sapphires embedded throughout the middle of the ring.

She put it on my finger and repeated the same vow as I had.

The priest lowered his voice so that only Arely and I could hear. "With these vows and rings, you each gain the Third Blessing. Your magic is at the highest power it can be. Use it wisely."

Out of the corner of my eye, Arely nodded.

The priest looked at the gathered crowd and raised his voice. "I am honored to present to you all, as husband and wife, King Shane and Queen Arely of Rapora. Shane, you may kiss your bride."

This was the part I had been dreading the most. I felt like a traitor to kiss my enemy, but I did it anyway. Then I grabbed her hand and we headed down the aisle. I cringed as the crowd cheered.

I could tell Arely was just as eager to get out of here.

As soon as we left the throne room, I dropped Arely's hand and walked toward the ballroom. She followed.

My magic became stronger as the seconds ticked by and a wave of confidence filled me. I had gained all three Blessings.

I was glad that the first part of the ceremony was over. It had been a nightmare from start to finish, and it had taken all my strength not to clobber the priest on the head with the words he had spoken. Maybe he had to say those things because they were of royal tradition. I still didn't appreciate it though.

But the hardest part was over. I could relax a little more and stop worrying.

Hundreds of candles lit the ballroom. The cooks were placing the final platters on the long table. There were so many different foods that it would be close to impossible to count them all.

By now, night had fallen, and the ballroom was nice and dark. It reminded me of the parties my parents had thrown years ago, when everyone had stayed up all night, dancing and talking, while eating dozens of desserts. The cooks had constantly brought out new plates full of pastries.

I looked down to the end of the room and spotted the table in the center, where everyone who had been in the wedding procession would sit.

Arely followed me as I walked toward it. She was quiet.

The other knights and ladies came in, walking right after us. I walked around the long table, which had silver plates, knives, and forks. There were folded, blue napkins with crystal-clear glasses.

I found my chair and sat down, and a second later, Arely sat next to me.

She didn't look at me, but instead watched the steady flow of people entering the ballroom. I got the feeling she was doing her best to pretend I didn't exist.

That was fine with me. Everything was easier that way.

I made myself comfortable in my chair. It would be awhile before all the people came in and sat in their places.

A servant walked toward us, holding two pitchers. "Would you like spiced cider, Your Majesty?" he asked, talking to Arely more than me. "There will be more drinks on the way, as well."

I nodded, nonchalantly, and Arely said, "I'll take cider, please."

The servant smiled and filled her cup with the steaming cider.

The cider was my favorite drink for a large feast. As the last of the guests seated themselves, he filled my cup to the brim. I nodded my thanks.

Tad stood in front of the crowd and got everyone's attention by clapping loudly. It took a few moments, but eventually the people settled down.

"Ladies and gentlemen," he said. "Thank you all for coming tonight. I hope you enjoy this meal the cooks have been working on all day. I must ask you, however, to wait until the King and Queen, as well as the special guests, have been served. Thank you."

Servants came up to Arely and me first and asked each of us what we wanted to eat. Arely squinted at them in confusion, like she wasn't accustomed to this way of feasting.

I told my servant to fetch me grilled salmon with fresh lemon to pour on top, along with the royal salad. He left right away.

"And for you?" the second servant prodded Arely.

"Uh, that sounds good. I'll have what he said."

I glanced over at her, amused. I didn't know if she was too nervous to know what to get or if she actually wanted salmon and a salad. My guess was the first.

"Do you not do it this way in your kingdom?" I asked casually.

She shook her head. "We always get our food alongside the guests."

"Why do you do that?"

Arely scrunched her eyebrows together. "I don't know. I mean, we've always done it that way. Tradition, I suppose."

"Hmm." I thought about that for a second. My parents would never be caught dead getting their own food next to the villagers from the streets. It would be considered a royal crime to do so.

A shame to the family.

Chapter 14
Arely

As midnight drew nearer, we sliced into the wedding bread, which was twisted into a braid and sprinkled with sugar. Later, we danced to a couple songs, but not for long, because Shane decided to sit back down. I agreed.

I silently took a warm roll and spread butter across it. I still had a little bit of spiced cider left from a second refill.

Splitting the bread into several pieces, I slowly ate them. The bread was sweet and I could taste cinnamon hidden inside, reminding me of the bread Mama always cooked for Tavia's and my birthday. I liked it much more than the wedding bread.

After I finished eating, I pushed the plate to the edge of the table so that the servants could take it. The ballroom had started to clear and I guessed half the people had decided to head home before it became too late.

I lifted my cider to my lips, about to take a drink, when I heard Shane suck in a breath and the glass cup shattered in my hands, raining down my lap.

I shrieked and nearly fell out of my seat. A burning sensation crawled across my skin, where the glass had cut through my dress. I leapt out of my chair, gasping from the pain. *What* had been in that glass? I knelt on the floor, trying to ease the burning sting.

A puddle of cider stained the chair's velvet cushioning and smoke rose up from the liquid. I whimpered.

Shane scrunched his forehead together, staring at the mess of glass and smoke. He had several cuts on his hand that dripped blood, and it took me a moment to realize he had tried to knock the glass away from me, but it had shattered instead.

He glanced at me. "Someone poured poison in your drink," he said. His gaze cut through the crowd of people, as if searching for anything out of place.

"How... could you tell?" I asked, panting.

"There were thin vapors rising from your drink." He pursed his lips. "You didn't see them?"

I shook my head and looked down at my dress. The pain had subsided, so I tried to stand up, but as soon as I did, more pain shot through my legs. If that's what a little poison did to my skin, I would've been dead if I had drank it.

I staggered to another chair and sat down shakily.

A moment after I had done this, Lori scurried over to me. "What happened?" she asked. "Are you all right, Queen Arely?"

"I'm burned."

She studied the small burns that speckled my legs, and clucked her tongue. "Ouch. You are. Let me take you into another room and I'll put ointment on them."

The little man, who I had seen several times, walked over to Shane. The king turned to him and said, in a steely voice, "Tell everyone to leave. The wedding is over."

He nodded, and Lori tugged on my sleeve. "We'd better hurry with those burns."

When we reached a deserted room, Lori found a medicine kit and gently rubbed an ointment on my burns. It immediately lessened the pain and felt cool on my parched skin. She wrapped the burns with soft fabric.

"There. It should heal in the next few days," she said, patting the fabric to make sure it was secure.

"Thank you, Lori," I said.

She smiled up at me. "You are very welcome, Queen Arely."

"Please," I said, "just call me Arely."

"Oh!" Lori said, raising her eyebrows. "All right... May I ask why?"

I shuffled my feet. "In Rivallen, none of my royal guards or maids call me 'Queen'. I don't think it feels right when they do, and I prefer they simply call me by my name only."

Lori rested her chin on her hand. "I like that."

I turned as footsteps echoed outside in the hallway. Shane walked into the room, looking flustered. "How bad are the burns?" he asked.

Lori stood and told him the burns weren't serious and I would be fine.

"Okay." He looked over at me. "I assume you're tired."

I nodded. After not getting much sleep last night, I could fall asleep sitting on the bench.

I slid off the seat and gave Lori a hug. "Goodnight," I said quietly.

"Goodnight Arely." She smiled at me as I turned to follow Shane out the door.

My legs felt much better already and it didn't hurt to walk as we went up the stairs and wound our ways through many hallways.

All the guards nodded at Shane as we passed.

"You were lucky you only got burned," he said, not looking back at me.

I bit my lip, knowing he was right. I should have thanked him for saving me, but I couldn't find the proper words in time.

He stopped at an oak door, with several royal guards protecting the entrance. Shane pushed it open and I stepped into a room almost identical to the one I had slept in the night before, although this one had a balcony outside. It also had several bookshelves packed with books, which I hadn't expected. Apparently Shane liked to read.

He turned to me, his expression cross. "Listen, Arely. I have a few rules you have to follow while you're in my castle. Clearly, you are not safe here. There are people who want to kill you and I'm sure you'd like to live, so I'd suggest you obey the rules. They will keep you safe."

"What are your rules?" I asked. I glanced down at my ruined dress. The layers were singed and torn. Shane had kept his side of the promise so far. He could have watched me drink the poison and not do a thing when I collapsed. I was at his mercy, anyway.

But instead he had saved my life...

Shane walked over to the fireplace and dropped a new log inside. "First of all," he said, "you cannot leave the castle. The only exception is tomorrow, when we will take a carriage ride around the village once, for tradition's sake. Any other time you need fresh air, you may go to the royal garden.

"The second rule is that you can't use your magic, but I already placed a spell on you so you couldn't. I am certain you understand." He poked at the logs, making sure they were in place. "And the last rule is that you cannot talk to Octavia, for whatever reason."

I frowned. I knew he would say that, but I wished he hadn't. I wanted to talk to Tavia right now.

"Can I talk to her once?" I asked, hopefully.

"*No*," he said, sounding impatient. "I just told you that." A couple seconds later, Shane lit a spark and a fire spread across the wood in the fireplace.

He walked back to the bed and sat down on the edge. He drew his sword, took a cloth, and started cleaning the blade, taking time to polish it and make it shine. "Will you follow those three rules? I'm giving you permission to roam the castle as you please."

I nodded hesitantly. "Yes, I will."

"Good."

Shane nodded toward the back of the room, where a black cloth covered a large piece of furniture. "You can use the bed in the back," he said. "Just take the cloth off."

He didn't speak again, so I walked to the bed and tugged on the fabric. A shower of dust flew into the air as it fell to the ground.

I waved my hand in front of my face, trying not to inhale any of the gray fuzz.

How long had this blanket been here? If no one had touched it since Queen Kora died, that meant the top had gathered five years of dust.

Across the room, Shane sat down on the sofa and pulled out a book, apparently not noticing the mess I'd made.

I sighed, then looked around, wanting to change into my nightgown. Lori – or I assumed Lori – had left it hanging on the dressing screen.

After changing, I sat on my bed, undid my elaborate hairdo, and began to brush. Soon, I was lost in thought.

My Papa had told me many stories when I was little. A few of them he had told me dozens and dozens of times. I never forgot them.

As a small child, a couple of them hadn't made any sense to me, but I had loved the expressions my father used to tell the story of the characters. He used different voices for each of the people, and Tavia and I would laugh at many of them. They were so strange and comical.

But in the end, each one had a little lesson hidden inside it, and Papa would challenge us to see if we could figure it out. Most of the time we did, but a few times we were stumped.

I remembered one of the stories he had told us. Many years ago, a young farm boy had worked on his father's farm with his brothers. It was grueling work at times, but they all worked as hard as they could.

The boy did little gestures of appreciation for his father every day, and his father loved him greatly.

His brothers noticed this and it annoyed them. Each of them had their fair share of work to do, anyway. So one day they decided to send the boy off to the army, without their father's knowledge.

The boy continued to work hard even though he didn't want to. He started as a squire and later became a knight. Not long after, he found himself working for the king as a royal knight.

The king was childless and had never named an heir, so he decided to hand the throne to the boy, who had grown into a strong man. He was stronger than most kings of the land and his power was unmatched.

As soon as he became king, he sought out his family. When the guards found them, they brought the brothers to his castle.

His brothers were afraid, but he held a feast for them and roasted the fattest cow in the kingdom. He told them he was glad to be together again, and they needn't be afraid because he had forgiven them.

After Papa finished this story, he would always ask, "Why do you think he forgave his brothers when they disowned him?"

I'd always moan and say, "I don't know! I'd be angry with Tavia if she ever did anything like that to me. But I know she wouldn't, because we're twins."

Tavia would grin mischievously and then say, "If I were him, I'd have punched my brothers in the face!"

Papa would cover his face with his hands and sigh as I burst out laughing. And it always ended this way. I had to wonder why he even tried.

I had spent long nights trying to figure it out though, but I could never quite understand it. How could he forgive his brothers and become friends with them again?

It didn't make sense, but as I slipped into sleep that night, I decided it was time to learn.

In the morning, as Shane had said, we planned to go on a carriage ride in the village. Lori led me, carefully, into a dressing room lined with dozens of dresses. I had a slight limp from the burns the night before, but it wasn't terrible.

She helped me put on a bright red gown, with white laces in the back that tied into a big bow, and afterward twisted my hair into a bun, leaving a couple strands to dangle around my ears.

When she was finished, I stood in front of a mirror, studying myself. I looked over my shoulder to where Lori stood. "I don't think Shane is thrilled to go on this carriage ride," I said. "If he doesn't want to do it, why does he bother?"

She tidied a wrinkle in my skirt. "His Majesty thinks a couple of the royal traditions are ridiculous, but he believes keeping the traditions alive is one of the most important parts of being king. His parents were, after all, big on traditions, and it was unheard of for them to skip one."

"Well, I'm excited to go out into the village. I think the people are interesting."

Lori smiled at me. "Really? Why is that?"

"I always wondered what it was like to live in the village. I had a strange obsession with the idea. I'm used to living in a castle and I can't imagine what it's like to live in the town. Though, I've learned much about it in the last couple of years."

Lori placed a brush down on a table and stared out the window. "I can't tell you either, because I lived on a farm and took care of horses. After that, I moved into the castle and started working as a maid."

"Ooh," I said, grinning. "You worked with horses? That sounds like it was nice."

"It was. But it was also hard. I went out in the fields and caught wild mustangs with my best friend, Trevan. I don't know how he and I did it, but the money was great and we needed it."

Lori picked up a necklace and clipped it around my neck. I gawked at her. "I fell off my horse and she's the mellowest creature I've ever met! I can't imagine trying to *tame* a horse."

"It came with a fair share of injuries," she said, the smile disappearing from her face. "For sure."

A knock on the door ended our conversation. A knight came inside and told me it was time for the carriage ride. I nodded and followed him out the door, waving to Lori as I left.

It was time to see Rapora Village.

Chapter 15
Shane

The waiting carriage had a broken spoke on one of the wooden wheels, chipped paint that crumbled with a touch, and dirt covering the windows.

I frowned, turning to the nearest servant. "You didn't get the royal carriage? Why will we be riding in this pathetic excuse for a carriage?"

He looked uncomfortable. "Well, the royal one hasn't exactly been, um, repaired from the last 'incident'."

"Fine," I said, although I wasn't sure what incident he was talking about. At this point, what did it matter? I wasn't going to enjoy the ride either way.

At least two dozen knights stood behind and in front of the carriage, ready to defend it in case of an attack. The village could be a dangerous place for me and I didn't want to deal with any rebels.

The servants opened the door and Arely and I climbed into the cabin. It had red velvet cushions as well as curtains to open or close as we pleased.

Two guards already sat inside, waiting for us. They sat on one side, forcing me to sit next to Arely.

I settled down, scowling, and gazed out the window.

No one said a word as the coachman and horses drove us through the gate and into the streets of Rapora.

The plan was to stop at the Royal Inn, which wasn't actually an inn, but a place where we had stored precious royal artifacts for centuries. It was in the cleanest part of the village, the place where the wealthiest merchants and lords lived.

People could only enter the Inn with special permission from the castle, which kept it fancy and free of poor people.

As the carriage bumped down the street, I saw that many people had already come into the roads to watch the carriage travel by. I rarely entered the village, so people usually wanted to get a look at me, but this time, all the attention was directed toward Arely.

These villagers had never seen her before, and *everyone* was coming out of their homes to watch us pass by.

I tried to ignore that as best as I could.

It wasn't a long ride, but it was long enough to start making me motion sick. The coachman didn't take us through the dirty parts of the village. However, I still saw beggars and homeless people sitting on the streets.

Arely didn't say a word the whole time, and neither did I. I noticed she had brought a fur coat and bundled herself inside it. It was chilly, all right, but I didn't think it was *that* cold.

I was surprised by how mellow she was, unlike her twin. She didn't seem to have much to say, and I wondered if Octavia always did the talking instead. Or maybe she hated it here and didn't want to talk, which was probably the case.

Either way, I didn't care. I had plenty to do without her talking to me. If she wanted to be silent, good.

I stared up at the sky most of the ride, trying to ward off my growing headache. I didn't feel like looking at the villagers, plus I was bored. This was certainly one of my least favorite traditions of the royal family.

I did not belong in the village.

After a while, Arely let the curtains fall over the windows, blocking her from the view of the people outside, then scooted away from it.

I grinned at her. "Tired of everyone staring?" I asked.

She shrugged, as if it didn't matter, but she looked uncomfortable.

Most of the people didn't like her, even if they had come out to see her. I could only imagine the looks they had given her.

A couple minutes later, the carriage crawled to a stop. The coachman leaned back to look at me. "Here we are, Your Majesty."

Servants walked up to the carriage and opened the door for us. Arely was closer, so I let her go first, then I stepped down.

People were gathered all around us, whispering as we left the carriage. Everyone stared at Arely, inspecting her every move.

I paused a moment before walking forward. The servants rushed to the door of the tall, brick mansion, opening it wide.

When I reached the door, I glanced to check that Arely was behind me, but she wasn't.

I spotted her next to the villagers. She had stopped in her tracks and bent down to pick up something on the ground – a ragged, old doll. A little girl, around three or four years old, stood a few steps away.

I frowned and started to speak when a woman cast a worried glance at me and swooped the little girl into her arms. "We're leaving," she huffed, turning away and disappearing into the crowd as quick as lightning.

"Wait!" Arely said, bewildered. "What about—"

"Arely!" I hurried over to her and grabbed her wrist, pulling her toward the building. We stepped through the entryway and I slammed the door behind me.

I whirled on her. "What were you thinking?"

She froze in surprise. "What?" she panted. "What do you mean? I picked up a doll!"

"Exactly!" I said, exasperated. "Why did you do that?"

"I was giving it back to the little girl. Is there something wrong with that?" she asked, her cheeks turning bright red like her dress.

I gritted my teeth. "We don't interact with villagers. We're *royalty*, not peasants. You shouldn't have even touched the doll."

The room fell silent for a moment. I was painfully aware of all the servants and guards standing by the door and down the hallways.

Arely held the doll behind her back and sucked in a breath. "Well, I don't see what is so wrong about interacting with the villagers," she said. "They are normal people, after all."

"They are *poor* people," I argued. "They do not have royal blood, or magic, or a castle with riches. Some of them live on the streets and beg for food, or even worse, live in barns with their pigs. I certainly don't want to be around people like that."

She pursed her lips.

"They have no choice but to do that. It doesn't mean they aren't wonderful people, because many of them are, once you get to know them."

I frowned, crossing my arms. "I highly doubt that."

"If you spent any time in the village, you would know that I'm right," she said, a new fierceness in her voice. "In Rivallen, the royal family has always spent nights celebrating with the people and talking to them."

I glared at her, but she didn't back down. "It's not of my kingdom's custom to spend time in the village," I said, choosing my words carefully. "My kingdom is not your kingdom and you better learn to follow my rules, because you'll probably be here for awhile."

She opened her mouth to speak, but I turned to the servants before she had the chance.

"Prepare the second carriage," I ordered. "I don't want to stay here. I've seen this stuff a hundred times."

When we arrived back at the castle, I marched up to my room.

I didn't like the fact that so many people had seen Arely pick up the doll. People spread news faster than a fire burned down a forest.

I didn't want it to ruin my reputation or how my people saw the royal family. We were the highest ranking, the ones who didn't associate with the lower class citizens.

I couldn't understand why she had done it. Why bother with picking up a doll when the little girl could pick it up herself? After all, she was the one who had dropped it, not Arely.

I remembered the look on the woman's face when Arely had tried to hand the doll to her. Shock, fear. She understood the way the kingdom worked, and she was afraid her daughter would get in trouble for bothering a royal, so she had taken off.

Now, instead of the girl having a doll, she had no doll and the whole point of Arely bending down to get it was ruined.

I frowned, sitting down in my chair.

Arely was different. More different than I had guessed two days ago. I couldn't fathom why she had done it, but I had seen the look on her face as she picked up the doll. She had looked thoughtful and when she had tried to hand it to the girl, she had smiled.

And I had noticed.

A knock sounded on my door. I was hesitant to answer, but thankfully when I opened the door, it wasn't Arely. It was Tad.

"Hello," I said, in as pleasant a voice as I could muster. "Do you need something?"

"My lord, I have news about Octavia," he said.

"Then come in," I said, waving him over to my coffee table. He sat down in one of the chairs and I took the other. "Is it urgent?"

Tad picked up a jar from my table, which was filled with chocolate-covered coffee beans. He chewed on one before saying, "Well, one of our spies came back this morning and told us information concerning King Quay."

I leaned forward. "Wait, is he working with Octavia?"

"No, no. The spy said Quay went to Rivallen for a feast, but it ended with the three rulers getting into an argument. People left the feast quickly after that."

I pursed my lips. That didn't mean much. Quay had always been clever and he could fool the smartest people.

It could have all been staged so that any possible spies would think no alliance had been formed. But on the flip-side, it might have been real. The only way I would know was if I talked to Quay himself. His attitude could give me hints.

Before I could change my mind, I summoned a bit of magic and cast it into the air. I glanced at Tad and said, "I'm going to call Quay. You can stay and listen, but don't make yourself known."

He nodded and a second later, Quay appeared in front of me with a scowl on his face. That wasn't a great way to start a conversation...

"Ah, Quay. Nice day, isn't it?" I greeted him.

He shook his head. "Shane, whatever weather you are having in Rapora is nothing like the weather here. It's been storming for two days straight."

"I have a new deal for you," I said, sitting straighter. This was true, of course, but I hadn't had a good reason to call him until now, when he had visited Octavia's kingdom.

"Clearly," I continued, "since two hundred pounds of gold and silver aren't enough for you, I'll have to offer more. Mind you, I won't give you whatever you like, so don't test me to see how much you can get."

"You sound like your father," Quay hissed.

I decided to ignore his comment. "If you help me win the war, I will give you five hundred pounds of gold and silver, along with a dozen of the best jewels in my kingdom. Maybe I can throw in a couple of the greatest trained horses in the land, as well." I folded my arms and looked him squarely in the eyes.

Quay chuckled. "Oh Shane. Won't you grow up?"

I frowned at him, trying to read his expression. "And what on earth does that mean?" I snapped.

"Here's the thing about your little deals. You might make them seem grand, but I know you have much more wealth than that. It's honestly like you don't even want my help... or you don't respect me enough to offer more." Quay sat back in his chair, looking at me expectantly.

"I shouldn't have to give you anything!" I countered. "Our kingdoms have been allies for years and yet you won't help me win the war."

Quay shook his head slowly. "No Shane, we *haven't* been allies. Once your father died, your kingdom stopped helping my kingdom. And whose fault is that? I believe it would be the king's fault. Also known as *you*."

He continued. "I learned that it would be better to stop aiding you in any battles or wars until you learned to respect me and my kingdom. It seems that hasn't happened yet. You can go on fighting this war alone, for all I care. I quite enjoy being neutral in the fight."

I glared at him. Why did my words not bother him?

"Octavia has been talking to you, hasn't she?" I accused, knowing the answer well.

Quay nodded. "I can tell you this: she makes much better deals than you do."

"You haven't made any deals with her, have you?" I demanded. I could feel fear building inside me, but I pushed it down.

"No," Quay said, his eyes like ice. "I told her the same thing I'm telling you. I don't want to be in this war, so keep me out of it."

I gripped my sword's handle. "What would it take to get you to do one thing for me in the war?" I asked. "One *little* thing?"

He ignored my question. "What about Arely?" he asked. "You made her marry you so that you could have more magic. And what do you plan to do with that power? Destroy her kingdom. All you do is use people to your own advantage, whether or not they like what you are doing."

I bit my lip, trying to contain myself. He had no idea. How could he judge my actions?

Quay paused, tapping his fingers against the handle of the chair. "That's your weakness, Shane. It's why you have no allies. No one likes you, not even your own people."

He waved his hand and his magic disappeared along with him. I stared into the void of my magic, not sure what to think or feel.

I tried to process his words. Was he right? Many people in my kingdom hated me, though I did my best to ignore it. There were still people who liked me. He didn't know what he was talking about.

One thing was for sure though: Quay wanted nothing to do with me.

I remembered that Tad was still in the room and turned my glower toward him. "Get out of my room," I ordered, stiffly. He didn't hesitate before placing my jar back on the table and pulling open the oak door.

I sat back down and opened a book, though I didn't read the words. Quay's words filled my head like a horrible headache. A headache that I didn't want to deal with.

Closing my eyes, I tried to slow my breathing. Although Quay didn't want to help me in the war, I had the Third Blessing.

If I continued with my plan alone, I could attack Octavia's second lookout fort in the woods and spread my control closer to Rivallen's borders.

Chapter 16
Arely

I clutched the doll in my hands with a death grip, not wanting to accidentally drop it or let someone snatch it.

The castle walls surrounded the royal garden. Outdoor hallways lined the circular enclosure, weaving high into the sky, and the sun shone through the center, bringing the area to life.

I could see knights and maids hurrying up and down the stairs, though they didn't appear to notice the garden. Perhaps they had grown used to the beauty of it. I, on the other hand, was sure I could lie in the grass and watch the birds flit through the trees forever.

The leaves and flower petals glittered in the brilliant light. A fountain gushed water into a large, pentagon-shaped basin. Paths, created from millions of tiny, colorful stones, wound their way around the plants and shrubs.

Royal knights, who had stayed close to me throughout the morning, stopped and stood next to the entrance. I assumed Shane had assigned them to guard me, though I didn't see the need for it.

Hundreds of knights protected the castle, and there was hardly a moment I was alone.

I wandered the labyrinth for a while, until finally settling upon a bench and opening my hand to reveal the little doll I had picked up.

It was smashed, and I assumed the girl who had owned the doll had loved it well, carrying it with her everywhere. The flattened features of the doll indicated she had hugged it tightly, as if her life depended on it.

Brown strings hung from its head, braided together for hair. The doll wore a yellow dress – or what I guessed had once been yellow, for now it was smudged with dirt and grime.

The doll had small, black buttons for eyes and a smile that had been stitched on. In the end, whether it was perfect or not, the doll had been made for the little girl and she had loved it. It wasn't right for me to have it. I wished to return it to her, but I had no idea how I would find her.

I spent the rest of the day in the garden, pondering this question. No answers came to my mind that didn't include breaking one of the three rules Shane had given me.

There was no way I could help my kingdom either. My mind felt numb, blocking any ideas.

Giving in to the fact that I couldn't come up with ideas, I resorted to writing a poem on a piece of parchment that Lori had given me. It wasn't my greatest work, but it was better than nothing.

At last, when the sun started to set in the sky and the garden was bathed in darkness, I headed inside. It wouldn't be long before I could get my badly needed rest. I hadn't slept well the last two nights.

Perhaps after I slept for a couple hours, I would be able to answer the questions that burned in my mind.

I climbed into bed early that night and drifted off to sleep minutes later. The night was quiet and my imagination took advantage of the peace, slipping into a dream as soon as I closed my eyes...

The air was humid. Fireflies blinked on and off, on and off. Papa and Mama sat beside each other next to the Wishing Pond. Tavia giggled and splashed me with the water.

"Ah! Don't get me wet!" I laughed, splashing her back.

She ignored me and scooped up more water, ready to spray me again.

That ended in a large water fight. Tavia jumped into the pond and started splashing me as hard as she could. I was laughing at how soaked she was, while trying to shield myself from the water.

"Okay girls, that's enough," Mama said, laughing.

I ran to Papa and jumped on his lap. He wrapped his arms around me and I closed my eyes. Tavia came over and sat with Mama, who didn't mind getting wet. She hugged Tavia like Papa was hugging me.

"You two are crazy," she said.

I knew Papa was smiling. "They're going to be great leaders one day though. Both of you will rule the kingdom together."

"When will we do that, Papa?" Tavia asked.

"One day when your mother and I pass the throne to you. One day when you are old enough to take care of the kingdom yourself," he answered.

"But you're a good king, Papa," I said, looking up at him.

He grinned. "You think so? Well, I'm glad to hear that."

"I want to be a good ruler too," Tavia said.

"I'm sure you will both be amazing. The people already love you. You know how to be fair to the villagers and have spent time learning with them. We may be a part of the royal family, but we're not that different from the people in the town. That's an important thing to remember."

I laughed as Papa cuddled me. I wanted to stay right there listening to what he had to say.

"What's that?" asked Mama, her voice rising.

I looked up, confused. *That's not what's supposed to happen,* I thought. But how did I know what was supposed to happen?

Mama was looking to the west, where the Great Abyss carved its way through the Mosaic Meadows. No one ever went near it.

A rumble broke through the land.

Papa stood, picking me up. He looked scared. "Papa?" I asked. "What's going on?" I looked over at Mama. She was carrying Tavia.

My sister met my eyes. She looked just as scared as I felt.

Another rumble shook the ground. "Get to the horses!" he yelled to Mama. They both started running, and I clung to Papa, terrified.

This isn't what happened.

I looked back at the Great Abyss. A dark, shimmering monster rose out of it, like a massive cloud of smoke during a fire. It had blood red eyes that pierced through me like daggers, and it was coming straight for us.

"Papa!" I screamed. He looked behind him for a split second and saw the great beast. I had rarely seen Papa get scared of anything, but I knew he was terrified when the color drained from his face.

"Run faster!" he yelled.

Part of me wanted to cry, but I was too terrified to shed a single tear. I stared at the black monster as it zoomed toward us. *We're never gonna make it,* I thought.

I gripped Papa so tightly, I wouldn't be surprised if I had completely cut off the circulation in his arm. He was holding on tightly to me, too.

Papa tried to run faster, but everything seemed to slow down. I could see him panting and sweating, but we barely moved across the ground. Mama had slowed down too.

The monster was catching up to us. The horses weren't far away. If we could only get to them, maybe we could make it.

My family disappeared. I fell to the ground, hitting my head. I was alone. Where had everyone gone?

I looked around and screamed. The beast was right in front of me, opening its jaws to devour me whole. I covered my eyes.

"Papa!"

My eyes shot open.

I was in my bed again. Moonlight shone through the window, casting a serene glow throughout the room and the books that lined the wall.

I understood now.

It had been a nightmare, not reality. That had never happened. I could remember that night clearly. Papa and Mama had told us stories until it was quite late. I had fallen asleep against Tavia's shoulder, and Papa picked me up and put me on his horse, while Tavia rode with Mama. The night had been peaceful. But it was the last time I had seen my parents.

The next day Tavia and I played with the children from the village. We didn't know when Mama and Papa had left for the battle.

That night, a few of the royal maids had come and found us playing. They all had been crying. That's when they told us what had happened. Both our parents had been killed, and not only that, but the king and queen of Rapora as well.

The war was over, but neither side had won. And it cost more than I had ever feared.

I breathed deeply, trying to calm myself. Tears stung my eyes, but I wiped them away quickly. This was when I needed Tavia most. She had always been there for me and I had always been there for her. If we hadn't had each other, those next few years would have been torture.

I closed my eyes and focused on my breathing for a couple minutes. By the end, I already knew what I wanted to do. What I *had* to do. The next night I would sneak out of the castle into the village.

Later that morning, Lori brushed my hair, tied it into a long braid dangling over my shoulder, and helped me into a bright yellow sundress. As she wrapped a ribbon around the tip of my braid, I rested my elbow on the windowsill and let my gaze wander to the village below. Tonight, I would explore those narrow alleys and houses. Tonight, before I changed my mind.

Just once. No more.

I sighed and Lori paused in her work. "You've been awfully quiet," she said.

"I miss home," I admitted as I watched the city. I could make out tiny specks moving around the streets and squares. "I know it hasn't even been three days yet, but it feels like it's been months."

Lori's voice was soft. "I see. That's a tough one."

I chewed on my lip and then blurted, "It's hard because I've never *not* been with Tavia. We were always together when we were young, and after our parents died, we stayed close to each other and ruled the kingdom. And now I haven't seen her in days. It doesn't feel right."

"When was the last time you saw her?" Lori asked.

"Right before the battle. We entered the woods, and she said she was going to talk to the general. I didn't see her after that, because Shane appeared and the battle began."

Lori nodded. "It's easy to miss home, but at the same time, it's when you leave home that you learn new things."

I pondered her words for a moment, and then said, "I'm worried about Shane. I know I'm going to mess something up and make him furious. And I don't know what he would do. He's already upset with me now."

She released my braid, letting it rest against my back. "I understand. But you shouldn't worry about that."

"Why?" I asked her.

She gazed out the window at the clouds, then back to me. "Well, I'm afraid I can't explain it."

I propped my chin on my palm. "He has executed servants for messing up little, unimportant things," I pointed out. "And he executed General Warren."

Lori winced. "Yes, but that was different. It's just... I think it's good for him to be around you."

I tilted my head at her, surprised. "What do you mean?"

"Shane has always hid his problems from other people. So did his father. But when his father and mother died, people tried to help him get through it. Of course, he wanted them to leave him alone to deal with it himself. Everyone in the kingdom was talking about how he was going to become king soon. Many people had heard about his reaction to the servants trying to help him, about what he had said to them, which I won't repeat."

Lori continued. "They called him a spoiled brat behind his back. They thought he would be a terrible ruler. Shane knew, of course. No one wanted to be around him, so as he got older, he became more and more independent. He pushed people away and masked his feelings with anger. It's hard to tell what he's thinking most of the time."

I nodded slowly. "But what does that have to do with me?"

"Well, you were born into a royal family, like Shane. You know what it's like to lose your parents at a young age and have to take on the role of being leader. I can guess, but I'll never know what it's like to go through that. But you know."

I looked out at the clouds lazily drifting across the sky. Lori was right. I hadn't thought about it like that before. It had been awful the first year, even with Tavia. I couldn't imagine what it would have been like without her.

"He'll never admit it," Lori said, "but he needs you, Arely, because you are the only one who understands. And I have reason to believe he is lonely."

Throughout the rest of the day, her words echoed in my mind. Did I understand? I had never pushed people away until they thought I was a brat and talked badly about me behind my back.

But had I done something similar? I wasn't perfect myself and I had my fair share of moments creating trouble and pain for the people around me.

Lori was right. Even though it seemed absurd to think Shane and I were more alike than I had imagined, the more I thought about her words, the more I could see the truth of the matter.

And I had to do something about it.

Chapter 17
Shane

I didn't wait for night to advance my army.

Perhaps I ran the risk of alarming Octavia and her advisors, but I had to attack swiftly and take control of her second fort in the woods. If I did, Fort Oak would be more secure than before.

The army gathered around the gates. When we left, the sun peeked over the forest, where we were headed. A couple hours passed, and we reached Fort Oak and entered the dense trees.

I rode along a small trail with my guards surrounding me, anticipating the moment when I would test the limits of my new power.

We didn't stop to eat. I packed a small lunch for while we rode, which consisted of two apples, a chunk of bread, and dried meat.

By the time we came into proximity of Octavia's fort, we slowed and didn't speak.

It was on the opposite side of the woods, closer to Rivallen than it was to Rapora.

I'd only attempted to conquer it once, two years prior. I lost hundreds of men. After that, I'd decided to wait until I had a clear advantage and was sure to win the battle.

Now, I was sure.

With the Third Blessing, I had better control over the outcomes of a battle.

The tall trees provided shade as my army charged forward. They climbed the walls as Rivallen knights began shooting arrows from the slits in the building. Men rushed from the doors, wielding swords and shields.

I stayed back, hidden by a cluster of tall bushes and trees.

Although the fort didn't have reinforcements from Rivallen, they put up a strong fight. It took several hours before my knights broke inside the building.

Within the next hour, the army had successfully driven out Rivallen's knights.

I doubted they had expected us to come. With that surprise, we had won.

I rode into the glade and dismounted my horse, ignoring the sounds inside the stone building as the knights cleared it out. With my bodyguards watching, I lifted my hand and let magic pour from it.

It expanded into the air, stretching across the expanse of the fort. It covered the entire glade, forming a new force field. I lowered my hand when it was complete.

"Perfect," I said. "That was easier than I thought."

One of my advisors turned around, studying my work.

"So your plan is for this force field to protect Fort Oak?"

"Yes," I answered. "If Octavia's army comes here, unaware of it, then I will know they are attacking. It will help my army reach Fort Oak if she advances farther."

I circled the fort, making sure I had used my magic correctly and it covered the entire area. The sky turned purple as twilight descended over the woods.

I turned to my guards. "We need to head back. It'll be midnight once we reach the castle."

They agreed and we followed a different path to the palace. General Collins would take care of the army and give orders.

If Tavia saw me then, I'm sure she would have been alarmed. The battle barely crossed my mind. Rapora's army had won without my intervention and her men had been ill-prepared.

I settled down as I rode Triballi, aware that my day had passed in a blur.

As we walked, a pounding pain began to spread through my forehead. I didn't know what I had done to get a headache, but that's what it felt like.

It was a mere headache, though, nothing I couldn't handle.

I didn't take a break for water or food, but perhaps I should have. Traveling was exhausting, even in the cool of the autumn air.

All the while, my headache grew steadily worse until I had to bury my head in my palms, overwhelmed by the pain. I needed to stop.

Whatever had caused the headache would soon go away and the headache would fade. The next day, I'd feel better. I didn't regret placing the force field around the fort, however.

When we finally reached the castle, I found my way to the stairs, forcing myself to climb. After only a couple minutes of walking, a man carrying a stack of books nearly collided into me.

He looked up and squeaked. "Your Majesty! I'm so sorry, I didn't mean to almost run into you."

I casually leaned against the wall and rubbed my forehead, trying not to show my discomfort.

"Hello, Tad. Have you heard anything from Octavia recently?" I asked.

He frowned. "No, actually... she's been rather quiet over the last few days. It's disturbing, if you ask me. She's never this quiet."

Tad appeared to be struggling to hold the books, and I was ready to collapse on my bed, so I decided to let him move on.

"All right. Tell me if anything significant happens."

"Of course, Your Majesty," he said as I stepped up the last of the stairs.

I wound my way to my room, where the guards greeted me, and I pushed open the heavy, oak door. A maid was washing and folding the blankets on my bed.

She spotted me and immediately ducked into a bow. "Your Majesty, is it all right if I stay and finish making your bed?"

I nodded, tiredly, and sank into my reading chair. "Yes, yes. Be quick."

I picked up a book from the coffee table and flipped to my current page while the maid dried the blankets and put new sheets on the bed.

I don't know if I dozed off or lost myself to the rhythm of turning pages, but when I looked up from my book again, the maid was gone and the candlelight had dimmed dramatically.

A moment later, Arely opened the bedroom door and padded in. She must have been completely lost in thought, because she jumped a foot when I spoke.

"What have you been up to today?" I asked, trying to sound casual.

She shifted on her feet and I realized she wasn't wearing any shoes. She had walked around the castle with bare feet, which wasn't royal behavior at all.

A smile tried to creep its way onto my face, but I squashed it with a frown. "Don't you wear heels?" I asked, cagily. "It's not queenly to walk around without them."

Arely glanced down at her toes, as if the fact she wasn't wearing shoes hadn't occurred to her. "But it's much more comfortable like this," she said. "Heels are a pain."

"I wouldn't know."

She bit her lip, and a tiny hope flickered through me that she was trying to hide a smile. That she had understood it was a joke.

"Right. Well I'd hope not."

I sat up a little straighter and deposited the book onto my table. "But really, what were you doing today?"

Arely glanced up at the chandelier, and counted on her fingers. "I visited my maid, Lori. I went to the garden. And... I ate food?" She looked down at her hand. "So not much."

After a moment she glanced over at me, her eyes squinted. "Are you not upset with me anymore? Because of yesterday?"

I crossed my arms, remembering the doll and the girl and the crowd of villagers.

"I don't know about that," I said. "It was a dumb move on your part."

"Oh." She sank onto her bed. "All right, then."

Arely turned away and started brushing through her hair, but I decided to ignore her. I picked up my book again and continued to read, even late into the night.

Of all the nights I might have had a dream about my parents, I wouldn't have guessed it would be that night. But I did.

"Shane, darling," my mother said, walking into my bedroom. "Are you ready for the masquerade?"

She wore a voluminous red dress adorned with hundreds upon hundreds of rubies. Her hair was done up in a large, brown bun, with a silver crown encircling it. The mask of a raven hid her face in shadow.

"Yes, Mother," I said, standing to face her. I straightened my own raven mask before she could rebuke me.

"Good, good. Your father is waiting for us."

The queen ushered me to follow after her. We left the room and carefully stepped down several flights of stairs. Her dress swooshed back and forth. It took up more than half the staircase and the servants passing by us had to press against the wall to fit through.

I was dressed in all black, as I suspected my father would be as well. My mother refused to dress in anything less eye-catching, like a bright dress that was five times her size.

A grin crept onto my face.

"Shane!" my mother said. "Remember: no shenanigans." She reached the bottom of the stairs and turned around. "Of course, I wouldn't expect my precious son to cause any problems."

She smiled and pushed a curl of rebellious hair out from under my mask.

"I assume Prince Quay will be here soon," she continued. "After we enter the ballroom, you may go find him if you wish."

"Thank you, Mother."

She grabbed my hand and pulled me toward my father, who was standing at the entrance of the ballroom.

"Sweetheart!" my mother called. "We are ready."

He turned and looked down at me, and even through the mask, I could tell he was studying me carefully. I stood taller, putting my weight on my toes.

"Father," I greeted.

"Shane, you must remember the rules. Stick close to other royals, avoid the lower class guests, and don't let anyone treat you as less than royalty."

"Yes, Father," I said, resisting the temptation to roll my eyes. Did he think I would let someone treat me less than I deserved? "I always obey the rules."

"Very good."

He turned back to the doorway and my mother joined his side. "We are ready," he said to the servant next to the door.

The servant nodded and lifted a trumpet to his lips. I covered my ears as he blew it to get everyone's attention.

"Presenting His Royal Majesty, King Dagwood of Rapora, and his wife, Queen Kora!"

The crowd applauded as my parents walked down the steps onto the large marble floor. I stepped up to the doorway, waiting patiently for my turn. I wanted to wait until the people's excitement for the king died down and they would give me their full attention.

"All right," I said to the servant. "My turn."

He nodded and blew the horn again. "Presenting His Royal Highness, Prince Shane of Rapora!"

I stepped into the ballroom, making a show of marching down the steps. I grinned as the crowd clapped once again – for me.

I reached the floor, and took a bow, before heading into the crowd to find Quay.

It wasn't hard to find him. He was surrounded by his family after all: his father, Calloway, his mother, Osanna, and all six of his siblings.

He walked over to me as I approached. He wore a fox mask, which hid a couple tufts of blond bangs, and gave me a wary look.

"Welcome to our masquerade, Quay," I greeted, grinning.

"Are you planning more trouble, Shane?" he asked.

I raised an eyebrow at him. "That's hardly the proper way to greet a prince. I'd imagine you know that because you're a prince, too."

"You don't have to remind me," he said, his voice even. "Thank you for inviting my family to your kingdom's masquerade. Now, are you planning a prank or what?"

"Think music," I said quietly, letting my gaze drift to the band in the corner. They were setting up their instruments, getting ready for the dances.

"This should be interesting," Quay muttered, but his lips quirked into a smile.

"Always interesting."

My father climbed onto a platform and the servant blew the trumpet again. "His Royal Majesty wishes to make an announcement!"

The room instantly went silent. No one wanted to make the mistake of interrupting the king. That almost always led to an execution.

"It is time for the dances to begin," he said, his booming voice carrying all the way to the back of the ballroom. "We will start with..."

I blocked out his speech as I summoned my magic. Quay watched me carefully. I sent a signal to the rodents I had placed spells on.

After a painful minute of waiting, the four mice ran across the floor toward me. I stepped back, not wanting them to touch me. Quay feigned a gag.

"What were you thinking putting a spell on those things?" he whispered through the corner of his mouth.

"They were easy to find," I answered simply.

As my father continued to ramble on about the dances, I sent the mice skittering toward the band, which had placed the instruments back on the floor to hear the king speak.

The corners of my mouth twitched as the mice lodged themselves inside the instruments: the tuba, the trumpet, the drums...

I looked back up at my father as he finished his speech. The guests all clapped and continued to clap until he stepped off the platform. He joined my mother on the ballroom floor and took her hands.

Other couples entered the dance floor with them, ready to dance when the music started. I, on the other hand, sat down in a chair, barely able to smother my mischievous smile.

Quay was shaking his head. He was much better at hiding his emotions. Then again, he was four years older than me.

My father signaled for the band to start playing.

A loud, high-pitched honk rang through the room. I covered my mouth with my arm before I could laugh out loud. Everyone around me looked at the band, wearing expressions of surprise, amusement, and horror.

The last one was my mother, her eyes as wide as if someone had struck her in the face with a pot.

I was glad no one could see my eyes well through the raven mask, or they might have known it was my fault.

"Sorry, sorry!" the band member called out. "I must have hit the wrong note. Let's try again."

This time, all the band members lifted their instruments and started to play. The cacophony that came next was neither beautiful nor elegant. It was a horrific clashing of squeaky notes and beats, along with the screams of ladies.

People started running around like the castle was on fire. Duchesses covered their ears, lords attempted to calm everyone, and several knights tried to stop the band from playing any more music.

However, the band members had discovered the mice and were trying to rid their musical instruments of the creatures by blowing or pounding as hard as they could.

I wasn't hiding my reaction anymore. I leaned back in my chair, snickering. Quay had sat down on the edge of the table, a giant grin on his face as he laughed along with me.

It was the best prank I had ever pulled off.

Finally, after several minutes of complete chaos, the band members blew the mice out of the instruments and a clang reverberated through the room as they dropped the instruments.

There was a moment of silence.

Then my mother stormed up to the band. "What on earth was that? That was the most atrocious music I've ever heard in my life! Get out of my castle right now!"

The band members didn't hesitate before fleeing the room.

I glanced over at Quay, who still wore a smile. "One out of ten?" I whispered into his ear.

"Ten," he said.

I grinned. "I thought that's what you would say."

It didn't take long for my mother to get everything back into order. Another band arrived to entertain us. The dances began. People went back to milling around and chatting.

My laughter faded away and the smile slipped from my face. Quay nudged me. "Did you see that group of barons over there? We should go over to meet them."

"Why?" I asked. "They are only barons."

"Because, we should get to know all the guests. My siblings are talking to them right now."

"I am not going toward those people," I said, stubbornly.

"Why not, Shane?" he asked, squinting at me.

"They are among the lowest class here," I replied. "I do not mingle with them, like my father won't either."

Quay wrinkled his forehead. "That's a terrible reason to avoid them."

Though he was a foot and a half taller than me, I didn't budge. I looked right up into his eyes, frowning. "It's our royal ways. I will barely look at them, much less talk to them."

"Fine." Quay stormed off toward where his siblings gathered, talking to the barons.

He could be so impossible when it came to lower class guests. His parents clearly did not go by the same standards mine did.

My frown deepened and I turned around, snapping my fingers to summon the rodents who had blocked the instruments. When they appeared, I released the spells on them.

"There you go. You're free. Go and enjoy the rest of your pathetic lives."

Each of them scurried off into the shadows of the room, disappearing under tables or crags or tunnels.

Now that the prank was over, the rest of the night would be boring. I certainly was not about to let anyone pull me out onto the dance floor, no way. I hated dancing.

I sat near the dessert table and ordered the servants to make a large plate of sweets for me. They did just that.

I grinned, thinking of what my mother would say if she spotted me eating so much sugar. Across the room, I could see the court joker doing tricks and poking fun at people.

No one ever suspected I was a prankster prince. No one ever punished me for my pranks. No one ever knew of my sense of humor.

I suppose that's part of the reason no one ever understood me except for Quay.

Chapter 18
Arely

When the moon rose in the sky and the time fell past midnight, I was ready.

I knew of the danger I'd put myself in, with the possibility of assassins finding my location. It reminded me of the burns on my leg. Though they were healing, they were a sign of the people who wanted to kill me.

I sat up and looked at the dress I had left out for the next day. Inside, the ragged doll was safely wrapped up, hidden from anyone who would want to toss it. In other words, Shane.

Although it was risky business, it'd be worth it to see the doll returned to its rightful owner.

I slid my feet from under the covers and stepped into my slippers, then pulled the doll from my dress.

I knew where I had to go. The village had always been my favorite place to go during the day to hang out with the people, but when I got older, it had been my favorite place to go at night when I snuck out of the castle to explore.

Nico had always insisted on going with me, to guard me from danger. We loved to explore and we knew every corner of the castle. But whenever we went into the village there were new people to meet, woods to explore, berries to pick, and walls to climb.

Every once in a while, the guards would catch us, but they only told us to get back to the castle, saying it was too risky in the town at night for a royal. As the princess, I didn't get in to much trouble.

I quietly changed into my dress in a matter of minutes and checked myself in the mirror. If I was careful, no one would catch me sneaking out, especially since I'd been preparing since dawn.

I glanced at Shane in his bed. He was fast asleep and I didn't think he'd wake up any time soon.

If I left through the door, the guards would catch me. If I slipped out from the balcony, I actually had a chance to pull this off.

I stepped out on the balcony and closed the door with a quiet *click!*

Hundreds of feet below me lay the castle garden, with the statue in the middle illuminated by the moon's glistening glow. Besides the whistling of wind, everything seemed eerily quiet. Towers reached into the night sky all around me, and although I could not see as well as I could in the day, I made out many crevices in the walls of the castle.

I would climb down that wall and onto the windowsill a couple yards below me. It was the only way to insure the guards at the door wouldn't catch me leaving.

Was what I was about to do stupid? Probably.

Would I regret it? Probably not.

Besides, I had already scouted out the small room during my free time. The window was unlatched and ready for me.

I swung my leg over the railing and pulled myself to the other side. It was quite difficult in a dress, but I had done this dozens of times before.

Nico and I had always climbed the castle walls whenever we wanted to escape lessons or boring meetings. It had always been easier for him because he wore pants and a shirt, neither of which were as fancy as my dresses. He could scratch and scrape them and no one would give him a second glance. I did not have those advantages with my attire.

Another thing that made it harder was the fact that I didn't have Nico to help me, or my magic, for that matter. If I slipped and fell... well, that would be the end of Queen Arely.

I held on tightly to the railing and lowered my right foot down to an inch-thick ledge protruding from the stone. After I steadied myself, I lowered my other foot.

Slowly descending the wall, I chose good footholds and held on tightly with my arms. The wind was freezing and I had to clench my teeth to bear it.

By the time I reached the windowsill, I had probably been climbing for fifteen minutes. I lightly pushed on the glass until it came loose and opened into a small closet.

I breathed a sigh of relief as I stepped into the room and quietly latched the window shut behind me. My heart was racing, but I had made it.

As I exited the closet, I looked around for any guards standing in the hall. There were none. I continued down the hallway until I came upon four guards standing and chatting amongst themselves.

All of the guards jumped into position as soon as they saw me. One of them said, "Queen Arely. What are you doing out at such a time?"

"I can't sleep," I said. That was the truth. "I'm going to the library. If King Shane asks, you'll know where I am."

I walked down the hallway without glancing back, expecting one of the guards to follow me. But I had already planned for that.

Winding my way through the castle, I found the path to the library and entered the massive room. The sound of the guard's footsteps wasn't far behind.

On the far side of the room, there was a circular reading area where I sat, and pulled out a random book. It was a book with mysteries in the Gale Mountains, and I probably read a quarter of the book before I was confident the guard had left.

I stood, glancing around, and abandoned the book on the sofa. I found a cloak that I had stuffed behind one of the pillows and carried it.

I needed something to wear that would disguise me as a traveler or merchant. It would be freezing outside, as well, so I needed something warm. This would be perfect.

I was finally ready to sneak into the village.

The gates that led into the castle were large. People constantly came in and out, and even during the night, a few merchants would come to and fro.

Going out would be the easy part. Finding my way back in would be trickier.

As I neared the gateway, I pulled the cloak on and covered my hair. When I reached the doors, I paused. There were guards everywhere, all carrying sharp, royal claymores. If they noticed me, I didn't want to know what would happen.

I waited in the shadows until a man leading a horse walked toward the gates, and then walked into the open, following the merchant.

No one took a second glance at me.

I smiled as I reached the edge of the city. People sat on their doorsteps, breathing in the cool night air and talking to their neighbors. A few young children ran around the streets even though it was so early in the morning. Adults milled around, doing their own thing.

I decided to take a walk around the village, stretching and warming myself up.

At one point, a dog barked loudly at me, but a woman scolded him. I turned down another street.

Even though it wasn't anything like Rivallen, I enjoyed being among the villagers and away from the castle.

I sat on the edge of a fountain and pulled down my hood, letting the wind brush my hair.

Two children were playing a board game on the side of the road. I watched them out of the corner of my eye. Both of them had dirt-covered clothes, with holes and tears in the fabric.

One was a little girl and the other was a boy. They seemed to love the game they were playing, because they kept giggling.

I knew when they noticed me. The two children fell silent, then started whispering and pointing at me. I pretended not to notice, but instead watched the moon slowly sink toward the rooftops.

After a few minutes, the young boy tentatively walked over and tapped my shoulder. "You're Queen Arely," he said shyly, his light brown bangs covering most of his eyes. He must have been around seven years old.

I looked down at him and smiled. "Yes, I am. And who are you?"

"My name's Ashton, Your Majesty."

I giggled. He had the sweetest little voice. "I like that name," I said. "What about your friend?"

"My friend?" he echoed, looking back at the girl who hadn't moved from her place. "That's Scarlett."

I stood up and walked to her, with Ashton following. At first, this seemed to scare her and she scooted closer to the wall.

"Hey," I said, kneeling a few feet away from her and the board game. "I'm Queen Arely. I guess you already know that though."

Scarlett had red hair and freckles on her cheeks, and she appeared to be a couple years older than Ashton, but I doubted they were siblings. They looked nothing alike.

When she didn't reply, Ashton sat beside me, his shyness gone. "Are you supposed to be out here?" he asked, curiously.

I blinked. "Uh, I mean, technically no, but I think we can keep that a secret between the three of us, right?" I asked, looking at each of them. I know that got them interested. Who didn't want to know a secret that only the queen knew?

"Okay," Ashton said, perking up. "I can keep a secret. I'm great at that."

Scarlett tilted her head at me. "Did you sneak out?"

"Yes." I pointed at my cloak. "I wore this while walking out the gate. The guards didn't notice me."

"Whoa!" Ashton exclaimed. "That's amazing!"

I laughed. "You think so?"

"Nobody knows you're here but us?" Scarlett asked, a tiny spark of excitement in her eyes.

"Yes," I said, leaning in. "Can you both keep my secret? It's *really* important."

Scarlett nodded her head this time. "All right. I'll do it."

Ashton jumped in. "Will we be like spies or rebels?"

"If you want to be." I grinned at the awed look on his face.

Scarlett studied me. "Why did you leave if you could get in trouble? Did you come to do an important thing?" she asked.

"Well, actually I did." I pulled out the crumpled doll from my pocket and showed it to the two children. "I want to return this doll to its owner."

Their eyes lit up.

"That's the doll you picked up yesterday morning!" Ashton said.

I studied him. "You heard about that?"

Scarlett rolled her eyes, but not in an unfriendly way. "Oh, *everybody's* heard. They all think you're crazy."

"Crazy?" I echoed, frowning. "Why?"

"Anyway—" Ashton interrupted, "you want to find the doll's owner? I mean, I don't know who it was, so... I have no idea how to do that." He pursed his lips as if he didn't like that fact.

I turned to Scarlett. "Do you know the little girl? She looked like she was three years old and she had dark brown hair."

Scarlett shook her head.

I thought a second, then tucked the doll back into my cloak and pulled out a little coin purse. Inside, there was enough money for a family to live on for a month. I took out two shiny coins and

held them. "Here's a deal," I told them. "If you can figure out who that girl was in the next week and tell me, I'll give you all the silver and gold in this pouch."

I showed them the inside of the purse and they gasped. It had to be more money than they had ever seen before.

"But, first I'll give you each a coin, as a promise that you'll get the rest if you complete the mission."

"The mission?" Ashton said, his eyes lighting up. "So it's important?"

"Yes," I said. "Extremely important."

"We can do it!" he said, and Scarlett nodded, smiling at me. "We can find her in *half* a week, I bet."

"Great. But remember, you can't tell anyone I asked you to do this for me. It's top secret, after all."

Ashton saluted, making me giggle again. "Yes, milady!" he said, then glanced at his board game before he could accidentally step on it. "Hey! Would you like to play our game? We made it ourselves! Pretty please?"

I smiled. "All right. Teach me how to play it."

I loved playing the board game with the two children. They were hilarious and endearing, and reminded me of the little boys and girls in Rivallen, especially of the girl who had given me a lucky rock and told me to win the war.

But as the moon dipped lower into the sky, I knew I needed to head back before anyone could realize I was missing.

"I have to go," I told them.

"No!" Ashton said, grabbing my arm. "Please don't go. I like you."

I smiled, but kept my voice serious. "I like you too, but I need to get back to the castle. I'm sure you both have places you need to be as well."

"Can you come back tomorrow?" Scarlett asked.

"Yes!" Ashton said, tugging on my arm. "Please, please, please?"

"Not tomorrow," I said, laughing. "But I'll come in two nights. How's that sound?"

"And you'll meet us right here?" Scarlett asked.

"Right here," I assured her.

Ashton hugged me tightly. "Thanks Arely. You're the best queen *ever*."

I ruffled his hair. "I'll see you soon." I gave each of them a hug and then pulled the hood back over my head. More guards would start pacing the village, and I definitely did not want them to catch me.

As I was walking down the street, a woman stopped me. Her face was gaunt and she towered over me. I nearly jumped out of my skin.

"Queen Arely," she said, staring at me in disbelief. "What are you doing out here?"

"I'm taking a walk."

"You are playing with children!" she said. "I'm sorry, but I must ask, what do you think you are doing?"

"I love children," I said, defending myself. "And I needed to get out of the castle."

"You are still young." The woman shook her head. "I know King Shane won't be happy when he finds out about this. And I hope he doesn't blame us for your foolish mistake."

I bristled. "You can leave me to make my own decisions, thank you."

I turned and left the woman behind. The stars were starting to disappear in the sky. I needed to find a way into the castle quick.

Several blocks from the entrance, there was a flower garden. It appeared to belong to a wealthy family, because the flowers were crisp and bright, without the presence of weeds.

I sat down on the rocks surrounding it, and, trying to be as nonchalant as possible, I took a handful of dirt and rubbed it into my hair. I let it smudge my skin and sprinkle across my dress, as if I had fallen.

There were many merchants entering the castle. Surely I could sneak in with one of them, if I pretended I was in a group.

A group of merchants led donkeys, which carried large bags packed with supplies for the castle. I stepped in with the rest of them.

The guards interrogated each of the groups of merchants. They had to verify they had permission to sell goods in the castle.

I stuck close to the group as they talked to one of the knights. After a few minutes, they let us through. The darkness was on my side.

But as I past the guard, he stopped me and said, "Are you with this group?"

Thinking better of lying to him, I said, "No, sir. I'm a tailor."

He narrowed his eyes at me. "You look like a peasant. Where did you come from?"

"I am not a peasant, sir. I work for Lady Teal. I simply took a nasty tumble on my trip."

He sighed, rolling his eyes. "Do you have the token?"

I blinked. "What token?"

"The token that shows you have permission to sell here. *Everyone* must show it."

My heart started to pick up speed. "N-no, sir. This is my first time selling here."

The knight glared at me. "Well, why didn't you say that first?" He waved me to the side of the entrance and another guard took his place.

The darkness was still on my side.

He told me to take off the cloak and then searched all the pockets. When he pulled out the doll and coin purse, he frowned.

"Didn't you bring anything to sell?"

I paused. "No, sir. I thought I'd see what other people were selling before I sold anything."

He handed me my cloak, considering my words. "That's wise."

After that, the guard sent me with another servant to go through the process of gaining this 'token.'

I told him a fake name and fake information, and by the end, he had filled out a list of requirements for selling in the castle. The servant barely paid any attention to me, but instead complained under his breath that he had the worst shift.

"All right, you may have your token," he said, handing me a silver coin, with the same symbol that was on Rapora's flag: an eagle with three triangles in the background.

"Thank you," I said, pocketing it. This token would get me in and out of the castle with relative ease.

After he let me go, I hurried toward the stairs. The sky was lightening. I ripped off the cloak and stumbled on my way up.

I had a plan for what to do when I reached the room. There would be a new group of guards at the door, and if I told them I had gone to the garden, they would believe me.

I looked at my dirty dress. Unfortunately, they would also believe I was clumsy and had actually fallen into the dirt. But the most important part was that I was safely inside the castle.

Chapter 19
Shane

I woke up coughing.

It was the kind of cough that makes your chest hurt and makes your sore throat ten times worse. I groaned.

In the last couple of weeks, the fever had been going around and many servants had stayed in their quarters after falling prey to the sickness. I should have expected it to get to me eventually.

Now the headache from the day before made sense.

I was sick.

I had to get up and work though. A king couldn't take a break when he got sick, especially in the middle of a war. I had several people who wanted to meet with me today, plus a list of things to complete before nightfall.

I cursed under my breath. Why did I have to get sick now, of all times?

I tried to sit up, but as soon as I did, I fell into another fit of coughing. My throat was raw and I needed water.

"Are you all right?"

I glanced in the direction of Arely's voice. She was sitting on the sofa, leaning over the edge to face me. "You don't sound well."

"I'm fine," I said. "Just a cough."

I started to sit up again, but she stood and walked to my bed. "No, you don't look well either," she persisted, resting a hand on my shoulder and gently pushing me back onto the pillow. "You should stay in bed." Her voice was firm, as if she had gained a new confidence in her words. "I'll take your temperature and see if you have a fever."

"I am not staying in bed all day," I argued, but I didn't try to get up again. Why on earth did she think I would *ever* let her take care of me?

I watched Arely silently as she walked over to my desk.

"Do you have a thermoscope in here?" she asked. I remembered the item she spoke of, which a royal had created in the last decade. Although I'd barely used it, I knew it was one of the only medical items made with magic.

"Yes," I said, pointing to the drawer to the farthest left. "It's in a box full of bandages."

She rummaged through the drawers and pulled out the metal box, along with the thick glass thermoscope, and then walked over to me. She placed the red stick in my palm. "Let's see what your temperature is."

"Okay, but I'm only staying in bed if my temperature is above 107 degrees."

Arely stared at me. "You'd be dead if your temperature was that high."

"Exactly."

I hesitated before putting the thermoscope in my mouth. After I did, I closed my eyes, wondering how bad the fever could be. I felt nauseous.

Arely sat back down on the sofa and waited a few minutes before taking the thermoscope from me.

She turned the vile toward her. "102.6 degrees," she read, and glanced at me. "You should definitely stay in bed, Shane."

I shook my head. I didn't understand why she was telling me what to do. I'd dealt with this situation before. "I've *always* worked when I had a fever," I told her. "I'll be fine."

Arely frowned. "If you rest, you'll get better more quickly." She paused and ran her fingers across the blanket, smoothing a wrinkle. "And I will take care of you until you get better."

"I have my own medics," I pointed out, puzzled.

She ignored my comment. "I can tell your adviser that you don't feel well. What's his name again? Oh, Tad."

"No, wait, don't tell him that." I sat up and instantly felt dizzy. "Tell him I'm going to spend the next few days strategizing for the war."

She paused and raised her eyebrows. "Why not tell him?"

"I'd prefer people didn't know that I am sick."

Arely frowned and I thought she would argue with me, but instead she sighed and nodded. "Okay, I'll tell him that, *if* you promise to stay in bed."

I studied her. What was her motive? Did she want to keep me from working until Octavia could attack me? Or did she want to try to keep me sick by giving faulty medicine?

But she looked at me, and her eyes didn't give any hint of a threat.

I released a breath of air and sank back into the blankets. "Fine. I promise."

Arely stood and walked to the door. She didn't bother to change into something other than her nightgown, which I found odd.

"Can you get me a glass of water first?" I asked as Arely opened the door.

"Sure," she said, and then stepped into the hallway.

I pulled the covers closer to me, while watching the door close behind her. My only thought was, *That was strange.*

Worry crept inside me. No matter how I felt, I couldn't take my mind off all the things I needed to do. If I fell behind, I was afraid I'd never be able to catch up again.

That wasn't something I wanted to happen.

Tavia was working on a new plan as I lay in bed, my fever above a hundred. The papers on my desk would pile up, and when I recovered, they would overwhelm me.

A dozen people would want to have meetings with me and the force field would be weakened, increasing the chance of a surprise attack. I'd be behind in all my studies.

I rubbed my forehead, the ache growing stronger. People had said I was addicted to work, but I was sure that was a good thing. They'd said the same thing about my father, after all.

A while later, Arely came back to my room with a cup of water, like she had promised. She placed it on my nightstand.

"I mixed honey and thieves into it to help your sore throat. Do you mind?"

I hesitated, thinking of the person who had tried to poison Arely. "You didn't put anything..."

I stopped speaking when I saw her expression. She narrowed her eyes at me, and said, "Would I poison you after you saved my life? I didn't add anything else to this water."

I shifted under the blankets and shrugged. "It'd make me feel better if you tasted it first."

"Fine." She lifted the drink to her lips and drank a little bit. She grimaced. "It's not pleasant to drink, but it will help you."

Arely handed me the glass, not appearing pleased with my request.

I drank the warm water. It felt good on my throat and after a few moments, I swallowed the last of it.

I laid still as Arely walked to the windows and pushed them out a crack. A cool breeze filled the room.

"Don't open the windows," I said. It already felt chilly in the room.

"You're burning up," she replied quietly, heading back over to me. "You need the cool air. It'll help, believe me."

I buried myself deeper into the blankets, knowing she was right. I decided to switch the conversation.

"Why don't you send for medics?"

Silence followed. I had a feeling I was offending Arely more and more with my words. Though I didn't care if I did or not.

Her voice carried over from somewhere near the fireplace. "I thought you didn't want people to know you are sick."

"Yes, but…" My voice trailed off. "I need a medic."

"Well," Arely said, coming over to face me. "You're in luck, because I am a medic."

I let out a surprised laugh. She had clearly lost her marbles. "You're a *queen*, not a medic."

"Who says I can't be both?"

I squinted at her, trying to read her expression. "You're not kidding."

She tilted her head. "I have no reason to lie. I study herbs and epidemics and try to find a way to use my magic to cure people from illness. It's important."

I fell silent. Arely returned to the fire and a second later, I heard the clink of a pail and a splash of water. I lifted my head to see her pouring water on a dying fire.

"Why are you putting out the fire? You already opened the windows!" I said, exasperated.

She glanced at me grimly. "If you hadn't noticed, it's exceptionally warm today. There is no need for a fire."

I opened my mouth to argue, but a pounding headache started to fill my head again. I turned on my side and closed my eyes. All I wanted was sleep.

Arely's voice was softer when she spoke again. "I'll get you whatever you need, whenever you need it," she said. "Try to sleep."

Only a couple moments after she had said this, I was out, and the rest of the day, I went in and out of sleep. I ate a couple crackers and drank the medicine Arely gave me, but for the most part I didn't do anything at all.

No servants could pester me, no knights could ask me endless questions, no merchants could try to sell me their goods. I didn't have to worry about the war or Octavia or getting revenge for my parents. None of that mattered.

And I had to admit, it was pretty great.

Chapter 20
Arely

After I gave Shane his water and left him to rest, I skipped down the steps, knowing exactly where I had to go to find Tad. My heart raced as I thought of what had happened. Had I actually offered to take care of Shane?

What was I thinking?

How could I help Shane, my enemy, when his parents had killed mine and he planned to destroy my kingdom? I couldn't.

Stop thinking like that, Arely, I told myself sternly. *Remember what Lori said. This is the chance you've been wishing for.*

I stepped onto the third floor, where the library was located. Shane had told me Tad always spent his early morning reading a book.

Letting my thoughts drift back to Shane, I headed down the hallway. I knew plenty about helping someone with a fever. The medics in my castle had allowed me to care for patients before, and I memorized what they had taught me. I also remembered when I had been sick myself.

I came to a stop and glanced out the window at my reflection. My blonde hair fell around my shoulders in curly wisps, but that wouldn't do.

I gathered it all in my hands, began a braid from the top, and continued down until my hair rested in a side braid. That way, it would stay out of my way.

I raised my chin, looking directly at my reflection in the glass. *You can do this – for your kingdom, if nothing else.*

I would find Tad and tell him exactly what Shane had told me to. In a couple minutes, I reached the grand library, which turned out to be larger than the library we had in Rivallen. The shelves towered around me, with several balconies wrapping around the walls.

As I walked inside, I slowed for a moment to take it all in. There were so many books and I wished to look around, but I had a task at hand.

Tad was sitting at a table with his nose in a book. He looked so engrossed in it, I almost didn't want to bother him.

I walked to the table and said, "Hello, Tad!"

The old man jumped so high, it was as if I had tried to scare him. He settled down quickly, however, and laid his book on the desk. "Oh, Queen Arely! Is there something you need from me?"

"I have a message for you," I said, sitting across the table from him. I repeated everything Shane had said, avoiding the fact he was ill.

Tad nodded his head slowly. "All right. I suppose he needs time by himself. It's been crazy in this castle lately. Perhaps he needs time to rest and recuperate?"

I shrugged my shoulders. "Maybe. I think he mostly needs space to think."

"Yes, of course." Tad smiled at me kindly. "Thank you for telling me this, Arely."

I left the library soon after my talk with Tad, but not before I grabbed several books containing legends and myths about illnesses. I'd read them in my down time.

I had to get back to the bedroom, to stay with Shane.

I walked down the hallway, trying to keep my pace. I didn't get lost as easily anymore, now that I had wandered the halls of the castle for a couple days.

While I navigated through the tunnels, I came upon a knight walking toward me. At first, I didn't give him a second glance, until he paused a few paces in front of me.

"Queen Arely."

The words came in a hushed voice, as if the knight didn't want to be heard.

Confused, I stumbled to a stop, glancing at the knight. None of the knights had ever bothered me since I had arrived at the castle. Why had this one stopped me?

"Follow me," he said, motioning to the end of the hallway. I hesitated, wary of what he wanted, but I supposed it would be best to listen.

The knight continued walking until he showed me into a small room down one of the deserted hallways and closed the door behind him.

He stopped and pulled up the armor that covered his face. At first, I had to blink, but I recognized his dirty blond hair and tired eyes.

"Nico!" I cried, throwing my arms around him. "How on earth did you get here?"

He took the helmet and set it on a small stand. "Well, I could tell you the whole story, but that would take a while, and we don't have much time. Long story short, your sister spent many sleepless nights trying to find a way to get you out of here."

He smiled at me with that goofy grin I loved.

"Wait," I said. "You mean we could leave right now?"

Nico nodded. "We'll need to leave soon. I have horses waiting outside the castle. You can disguise yourself as a villager and cover your head. We'll run for it. The alarm for the force field will go off, but if we can get to the horses in time, we can race back to Rivallen and be there by morning. I brought the fastest horses in the kingdom."

I stopped, trying to take it all in. I could go home to Tavia right now. We could be together and I could stay in my own castle, in safety.

But another thought flickered through my mind. "What about Shane? He'll be furious once he knows I'm gone."

Nico shook his head. "Tavia will deal with that. Believe me, she worked everything out. It's not like her last plan. But we need to leave now, Arely, before they find the guard I knocked out." He took my hands in his. "Come with me."

I looked into his eyes, and knew he would get me out safe and sound. He'd take me back to Rivallen, to my sister. She would be thrilled to see me. She was my twin, after all.

But it couldn't happen that way and if I went with Nico, terrible things would follow. I had to avoid that. I felt it in my gut.

"Nico..." I said, my voice faltering. I took a breath. "I'm sorry, but I can't go-"

He gripped my arm, as if fearing I would leave. "Wait, why? Arely, everything is ready! I promise. I won't fail you like I did last time."

"It's not about that. It's about Shane. If I leave here, it'll upset him. He spared my life because I helped him gain the Third Blessing and promised to stay in Rapora."

"I don't understand!" Nico said, waving his hands. "We're in a war and he's our enemy. If you break that promise, why does it matter?"

"Look, I can't explain. I have a plan and if I leave the castle, it'll never work. I... I believe that Shane isn't as bad as we thought."

He shook his head. "He's awful."

"But if he were as awful as we thought, wouldn't he have tortured me and let Tavia watch? She'd surrender the whole kingdom in a day. But he hasn't done anything of the sort. In fact, I think he can make fine company when he's in a good mood."

Nico rubbed his forehead. "Arely, do you know how distressed Tavia will be when I tell her you wouldn't come? She's been working hard on this rescue mission..."

I hugged him. "Tell her I'm sorry. I wouldn't do this if I thought I didn't have to. But it *is* war, like you said, and sometimes we have to make sacrifices."

He was silent for a moment.

"Arely, if you won't go with me, then I'll have to force you to go," he said, clutching my arm. "I have to protect you."

"No, Nico. You don't understand!" I cried. "You must let me stay here."

"Not when Shane could decide to kill you any day," he said, his grip tightening as I tried to pull away.

My heart pounded. He was stronger than me, but I needed to find a way to escape.

"I'll scream," I blurted.

He stared at me, his expression contorted in confusion and frustration. "No, you won't."

"And then he'll kill you," I continued, my voice shaking. "Please, I'm warning you."

Nico paused, and for a second I hoped he would listen. But in one swift movement, he clamped his hand over my mouth and dragged me into the hall.

For a moment I couldn't breathe. I struggled against his grip, terrified, as he pulled me down the hallway. I tried to scream, but his hand muffled any attempt.

Tears stung my eyes. I remembered I had worn my garden boots, which were sturdy and hard.

I kicked at his feet, aiming for his ankle. Nico stumbled down the stairs, dropping his hand, and gasped in pain as he landed awkwardly on his foot.

I screamed. My throat felt like it was trying to suffocate me as my heart pounded in my chest.

He lowered himself to the ground, reaching to touch his foot. I covered my mouth, knowing I'd injured him.

I could see pain and betrayal on his face. "I came all this way, Arely."

I'm sorry, I thought, but didn't say.

Footsteps echoed in the hallway, nearing us.

When four knights rounded the corner, the first demanded, "What is going on here?"

"I-I saw him fall," I said.

The man turned to Nico. "Are you injured?"

"No," Nico lied, slowly standing up. "I'm fine. I'll get back to my post."

"Good."

I backed up. The guards didn't seem concerned.

When they left, I turned from Nico and started up the stairs, moving quickly and not looking back. I couldn't explain myself. I couldn't risk him trying to persuade me to leave again.

I didn't stop until I had reached the top steps.

I took a deep breath, sinking onto the stairs, and wiped at my tear-stained cheeks.

I had a plan and I had to stick with it. It was time to be strong and work toward my goal, even if it meant giving up what I wanted most.

Strange is the flower who dares to grow,
Beyond the safety of earth
Yet where would the world be
Were it never given birth?
Strange is the flower who dares to stretch
Out into the unknown
Yet where would the world be
Would it not depart from home?
Strange is the flower who dares to wait
Through anger's ice and snow
Who peers at the heart
that the enemy does not wish to show.
Strange is this flower true
And yet I know it well
For where would the world be
if not the blossom of forgiveness swell?

Strange Flowers ~ by Arely

Chapter 21
Shane

I didn't know why, but being sick wasn't quite so bad with Arely. I would never tell her this, but I liked her attention. She was gentle, and whenever I needed anything, she would go and get it for me – even in the middle of the night.

I didn't understand why she was being so kind to me. I had puzzled over it for hours.

Whenever I awoke, she was either sitting on the sofa or laying on her bed, reading. She always stayed in the room. Who knew how many books she was able to read while I was sick?

When I was little, my father had always worked, even when he was sick. I grew up thinking that's what kings had to do. But now I wasn't so sure. It certainly was nice to get the rest I needed. I believed Arely was right about me recovering quicker.

The next afternoon I awoke feeling nauseous. I took a small sip of my cool water, trying to make my fatigue go away.

I turned, looking toward the sofa, but it was abandoned, so I glanced at the queen's bed. The only thing was a wrinkled quilt. Arely wasn't there.

Where did she go? I wondered. Maybe she had gone to the washroom or to get a drink of water for herself.

My head hurt terribly. I took the glass of water and drank more, because it seemed to sooth my headache.

There was a little water in the glass and I soon drank it all.

I sank against the pillow, hoping the pounding in my head would stop and the nausea would go away.

As I closed my eyes, my magic pulsed as if sending me a warning. I sat up, frowning.

The warning was different than the one I received when someone unwelcome entered my castle. It took me a minute to realize what it was.

Arely had used her magic. Tried to, anyway.

I'd placed a spell on her to warn me if she ever tried to use it. She wouldn't be able to, of course, but I wanted to know if she tried.

It was the second day I'd had the fever, and I wanted to stay in bed, but I also wanted to see what Arely was up to. According to the magic, she was in the gardens and I needed to make sure she wasn't trying to escape.

I climbed out of bed slowly, to avoid irritating my headache. If I hid it well, none of the guards would even suspect I was ill.

I'd make it downstairs and back. I had worked from dawn to dusk when I was sick before, anyways.

After changing into a pair of clothes, I grabbed my sword and headed through the door.

The guards outside jumped to attention quickly, but they seemed surprised to see me.

I quickened my pace to a walk and marched down the stairway. It took a little longer than normal to reach the royal gardens, but I didn't stop until I found myself at the entrance.

Shivering, I stepped outside. The sun was shining and the fresh air tasted sweet. I almost wished I could stay here until I recovered, but that could never work.

I looked around for Arely and spotted her next to the fountain.

 157

She was slumped against the side, with her head buried in her arms. As I stepped forward, I could hear her crying.

Something inside me made me stop. She hadn't noticed me yet. I would've bet anything she had tried to talk to Octavia.

A twist of shame filled me, unexpectedly, and for a moment I wasn't sure what to do. I was the reason she was crying. I was the reason she was stuck here. I was the reason she wouldn't be going home any time soon.

For a second, I regretted putting the spell on her. But I had needed it to make sure she couldn't use her magic against me. It was a means of security, nothing else.

I watched her for a moment longer. She'd appeared to be happy the last few days, though it could've been a façade. Now she was crying next to a fountain.

She still hadn't noticed me.

I turned and left the garden, never saying a word.

An hour later, when Arely entered the room, I was lying on my bed reading. I didn't look up.

Out of the corner of my eye, I saw her pause, holding a wooden box. "How do you feel?" she asked. Her voice was tired and the fact that she had been crying was clear.

"I feel well enough to read, but that's not saying much." I looked at her. "What are you carrying?"

She walked over and opened the box, revealing a board full of wooden pieces. "A chess set... You said you wanted to play earlier, so I thought I'd bring it."

I took it, opening my mouth to say something, but I didn't know what to say. I picked up the light brown queen, turning the piece over in my hand.

"I'll get you more medicine," Arely said, sitting on the edge of the bed and rummaging through a small chest. She'd been using the herbs inside to help me recover.

"You know how to play chess?" I asked.

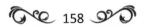

Her cheeks turned a slight shade of pink. "Not really," she said. "I'm afraid I won't be much competition."

I shrugged, dumping the pieces onto the quilt. "I'll do anything to distract myself from this fever."

Arely handed me a cup of medicine, and I had to choke it down. It was nasty, but it helped my sore throat and cough.

After I placed it aside, I set up the board. Arely sat on the opposite side of the bed, watching to see where I put my pieces on the checkered spaces.

"You get to go first," I said, nodding to her side of the chessboard.

She moved a pawn, and I did the same.

I had to suppress a smile when she tried to move the knight forward one space. "Wait," I said, "the knight moves like this." Reaching across the board, I traced the two paths she could take.

She decided to move to the left, and I took my turn, moving the bishop.

After a few rounds, I found a strategy to trap her king. She moved several pieces forward, capturing my decoys.

I moved a rook to the top row, cornering her king with her own men, and said, "Check." But as I said it, several coughs racked my chest and I doubled over.

When the pain subsided, I glanced at the board. Arely held onto the corners, but the pieces had scattered all across the bed.

"Oh, no," I groaned, "Did I knock the pieces over?"

Arely smiled. "Yes. But we both know who was going to win."

I gathered the figurines into a pile with her help. I paused before setting up the board. "Do you want to play again?" I asked hesitantly.

"Why not?" she said, setting up her small army.

With that, we entered another game.

She might not have been the best, but I could tell she was trying, and with each round, she became better. I pointed out tips that would help her strategize and improve.

We had played six games by the time my mind started to whirl. The last time I had played chess was with Tad, only a few days before. That was when I had gotten the idea to capture Arely in battle.

Now I was playing chess with her.

I decided to lie down because I was feeling dizzy and Arely thought I should sleep.

She packed up the board by herself and gave me another glass of cold water. Outside, the sun had fallen and I could see small stars when Arely blew out the candles for the night, keeping only one lit so she could read.

I knew what I needed to do. But it made me nervous and I wasn't sure if it was a good idea or not. What would she think?

I rose in my bed, enough to see her sitting on the sofa.

"Do... do you want to talk to your sister?" I asked.

Arely looked up from her book, titled *Historia of Papaver orientale*, and scrunched her eyebrows together. "What?"

I braced myself. "I mean it. Do you?"

"...Yes," she said, laying the book down, a question lingering in her eyes. *How did you know?*

"Then go ahead," I said. "The balcony is the best place to do it." I sent a spark of magic through the open doors and the mist appeared.

Arely sat frozen in place, her lips slightly parted.

"Well, don't waste your opportunity," I said.

I was surprised by how quickly she jumped up and ran to the balcony. She leaned against the railing.

I couldn't see the magic from my position, but after a couple minutes, I heard Octavia's gasp.

"Arely!" she cried. "How did you—"

"Shane's letting me talk to you," she answered. I couldn't ignore the happiness in her voice.

There was a pause, and I imagined Octavia crossing her arms and raising an eyebrow.

Arely continued when Octavia didn't answer. "I've missed you," she said.

I dug myself deeper into the blankets, averting my gaze from the balcony.

"I've missed you too," Octavia said. "Have you been all right?"

"Yes." I watched as Arely twisted her hair around her finger. "Is Grey Girl injured?"

A new voice drifted through the doors of my room.

"Her leg is broken, but it's healing nicely. I've been caring for her. You don't have to worry."

"Thank you," Arely said. "I appreciate it."

Octavia spoke again, sounding a little impatient. "Are you really all right? You look like you have been crying."

Arely shifted from one foot to the other. "Because I wanted to talk to you! I'm great, Tavia."

The wind picked up, and it swept away whatever Octavia said next. After a moment, it died back down and I could hear their words again.

"I'll see you as soon as I can," Octavia promised. "I will do everything I can to end this war."

Arely glanced back at me, and I looked away. "Okay," she said. "Don't do anything impulsive like last time."

"I do what I must."

"I love you," Arely whispered. She was so quiet, I could barely hear her.

"I love you too, little sister," Octavia said.

Her tone was so gentle, I could hardly believe it was Octavia who was talking. But it was. Obviously, she had never used that tone while talking to me, so I hadn't known she was capable of sounding nice.

After this, the magic must have faded away, because no one spoke after that. Arely stayed on the balcony, shoulders slumped, looking at the view. I didn't understand why she looked so down all of the sudden. Hadn't I given her exactly what she wanted?

I wondered what it was like to have a sibling. I had never had any brothers or sisters. And I only had distant cousins whom I'd rarely seen.

Arely and Octavia made it seem like it was great. But Quay, on the other hand, made it look awful. Granted, they were twins, and he was the middle child of seven siblings.

One had to wonder though, how differently this whole war would have happened if I'd had a sibling or two.

Chapter 22
Arely

I couldn't believe Shane had let me talk to Tavia.

I'd regretted trying to call her as soon as I had done it. It was foolish, but I had wanted to talk to her so badly, I hadn't been able to contain myself.

As soon as Nico had left the castle, a realization hit me. I was stuck here. There was no going back now. And that led to my attempt to call Tavia, which of course had failed.

But Shane wasn't upset. He'd let me talk to Tavia using his *own* magic.

It didn't make sense.

I continued to take care of Shane until nightfall. He probably wouldn't wake until the morning. He needed sleep, so he slept long and hard.

I should have gotten sleep myself, but I was too fidgety to think about sleep.

When I was sure Shane wouldn't wake, I took to the stairs. There was one thing I wanted to do before I left the castle, and that was to talk to Lori. The last few days I hadn't seen her and I wanted to tell her what had happened a couple hours prior.

I had no idea when Lori went to bed, but I hoped to catch her in time.

When I asked a guard for my maid, he helped me find her. As it turned out, she had stayed up late doing extra chores, tending to the horses in the stables.

"Lori!" I called, quiet enough to not disturb the horses.

"Ah, Arely!" she said, smiling as she turned. "I wouldn't expect to see you up at this time."

I smiled sheepishly. "Oh, I actually stay up pretty late."

Her lips curved into a grin as she fed a horse a handful of oats. "I see. Did you want to talk?"

"Yes. I... well, let me tell you what happened today," I said, leaning against one of the wooden poles jutting out of the dirt floor.

"All right," Lori said, raising her eyebrows.

I told her how Shane had let me talk to Tavia after I had broken two of his rules by trying to use my magic. She nodded silently as I finished. "Before, he said he would never allow it, but he changed his mind."

Lori gently stroked the horse's muzzle, thoughtfully. "Hmm... interesting. I hoped he would do something like that."

"You did?" I asked.

"Yes," she replied. "That's the king I see when I look at Shane. The king Rapora's people need." She paused, staring at the ceiling. "Though he is hidden behind a mask and I don't know if he will come out. He is stubborn."

"Like my sister."

Lori looked down, squinting.

"Yes. Just like your sister. Which, now that I think about it, is probably why they don't get along very well."

I raised my eyebrows. "Very well? They don't get along *at all*." My smile faded as a thought entered my mind. "And that will make it harder to end the war... How am I supposed to make them get along?"

My maid shook her head. "They are going to have to choose to get along themselves. You can't make that choice for them."

I bit my lip, uncertain.

The sound of clanking echoed through the stable, and a knight appeared around the bend. "Are you done with the task yet?" he asked, directing his voice toward Lori.

"Not yet," she admitted, then glanced at me. "I best get back to work. I'll see you later, Arely."

I left, storing her words in my mind, and headed for the kitchen. I'd remembered a recipe that the medics in my kingdom had taught me years ago, for treating fevers.

No one was in the cooking area when I entered. It was the perfect time of night.

Shelves lined the walls, filled with tiny bottles of dried leaves and flowers. I pulled out a couple wicker baskets, trying to find what I needed, and placed the items on the wooden table.

A pile of stalk-less red roses, saffron threads, and poppy, along with a couple other ingredients formed on the table. I took the ashes of a flower from a small pouch that I'd kept in Rivallen.

It was a plant I hadn't used much, but it had shown promising results. It belonged in a different climate, but with care and magic, I was able to keep it alive.

I ground the dried ingredients into a powder, then laid cheesecloth inside a basket, brushing everything inside. Taking the cloth, I dipped it in a water basin and began to strain it. Lastly, I placed it back onto the counter and formed tiny balls easy enough to swallow.

The process didn't take long. I had done it so many times, it was like second nature.

I poured a glass of boiled down wine and took a couple of the medicine pastilles. I stuffed the rest into a corner where no one would find them, and left the room.

When I reached the royal chamber, I quietly opened the door and slipped in.

Shane was asleep, curled in his blankets, shivering.

I left the items on the nightstand, planning to give it to him when he awoke in the morning.

Ashton and Scarlett both sat on the edge of the fountain, flicking water at each other as they waited for me. I took my hood off, walking into the square.

They lit up and Ashton ran to me. "Arely!" he said, his eyes dancing. "You came!"

"Of course," I said, smiling. "I promised, didn't I?"

Scarlett stood, holding her hands behind her back. "I couldn't bring my game," she said, "so we'll have to do something else."

Ashton raised his hand. "We could play tag!"

She raised her eyebrows skeptically. "I don't think Arely wants to play tag."

The little boy looked at me curiously.

"How about you show me around this part of the village?" I suggested. "Have you found any sign of the little girl who lost the doll?"

"Oh!" Scarlett exclaimed, her face falling. "I almost forgot. We looked, but we haven't found her yet. I'm sorry."

"It's fine," I said. Ashton pulled on my hand, leading me toward one of the roads.

"I'll show you the village," he said as Scarlett scrambled to catch up. "We have lots of interesting places here."

I asked him what these places were, but he put a finger to his lips. "It's a secret."

As we moved farther into the barren streets, more people were sitting or lying on the stone ground. It appeared they had no home.

My skin prickled. Even in my own kingdom, I had never gone into areas like this. But by the confident steps of Ashton, he must've been used to it.

After several minutes, he slowed next to a tiny shack tucked between two larger houses, although each one had holes in the rotten wood.

Scarlett opened the door, letting us in. Ashton let go of my hand and I blinked in the darkness.

"This is where you live?" I asked, hesitantly. I could see several blankets in the corner, along with a crate and small lantern.

"Yes," Scarlett said. "We live here, on our own. We steal what we need to avoid the orphanages. It works... I guess."

Ashton reached into his pocket and pulled out the single coin I had given him. "We'll find the girl soon, too."

"We should go back," Scarlett said, with a hint of disdain. She kicked the blanket and marched through the door.

Ashton frowned. "She hates this shack," he explained. "I don't think she wanted me to bring you here."

I fell silent as we followed after Scarlett, back into the alley. A sliver of moonlight grazed the rooftops, the moon peeking through a thin cloud.

Scarlett, who was several yards ahead, led the way to the fountain. Ashton spoke softly. "I guess that's the end of our adventure."

"I liked it," I began to say, but a shout echoed through the streets and I froze, just inside the square. I glanced around to see where it had come from, but I didn't see any soldiers.

Scarlett stood and whipped around. "We need to leave," she whispered, pulling Ashton closer to her. She looked at me. "You should go, too."

I didn't need her to explain what was going on. I pulled my hood back over my hair and stepped back.

Ashton tugged on my cloak before I could leave. "You will come again, won't you?" he asked quietly, looking hopeful.

I hesitated, looking at each of the children. They were both holding their breath, as if they wanted me to say yes.

I nodded. "Of course."

Scarlett pulled on Ashton's sleeve. "Time to go."

 167

I watched as they left the square and headed in separate directions. Several knights ran into the area, and I slipped into the shadows.

"I heard voices over here," one of the men said, mumbling under his breath.

Another one snapped at the knight who had spoken. "Well, if he was here, he's gone now!"

"We need to keep searching," the leader said.

I stepped into the street and quickly headed toward the castle before the knights in the square could stop and interrogate me.

Who had the knights been talking about? Had Ashton done something wrong and now he was in trouble?

I hoped not.

If Ashton got caught, I didn't want to think about what they might do to him.

Chapter 23
Shane

By the fourth day, I woke up feeling better than I had any of the other days. I didn't wake with a painful headache or stomachache, but instead felt simply tired and fuzzy-minded.

I had never recovered from a fever so quickly. It seemed impossible.

I glanced at the other side of the room. Arely was snoring softly, curled up in the blankets of her bed. Her hair was tangled together in a curly mess, and she looked so comfortable, I didn't want to wake her up for anything.

I shook my head in disbelief. It didn't make any sense why Arely had offered to take care of me. But I was glad she had.

I sat up, looking out the window. The sun's light seeped through the corners of the window, shining orange and yellow against the wall.

My head didn't feel nearly as warm as it had the days before.

Arely rolled over sleepily and saw me sitting up.

"Do you feel all right?" she asked, yawning.

"Yes... I feel better. Can you take my temperature?" I paused, and then added, "Please?"

A smile flickered on the corner of her lips and she nodded. "Of course." She slipped out of her bed and began her morning routine.

She gave me the thermoscope and made sure I had enough water. Then she rested her hand on my head, and finally took the thermoscope back.

"You're at 99.8 degrees. Much better than yesterday. Hopefully the fever will be completely gone in a couple days." She looked over at me. "Are you going to rest more, or are you going to work again?"

I took a drink of water. I needed to work on the war plan, see what was going on, and lead the army in the direction I wanted.

However, part of me still wanted to stay in bed and rest. I doubted Arely would mind.

I shook my head. No. I had to get back to work. I couldn't waste any more time.

"I have to work," I said, pulling back the blankets and getting out of bed. My head didn't pound when I stood and walked a few steps.

I reached the dresser and changed into my armor with the black robe, while Arely made the bed and opened the balcony doors to let fresh air in.

As soon as I was finished, I walked toward the door, but paused, looking back at Arely. She tucked in the corners of the bed and picked up my glass of water that I had left on the nightstand.

She handed it to me. "Here. You should drink lots of water. It'll help."

"Thank you." I leaned over and kissed her on the cheek.

She turned a slight shade of pink and whispered, "You're welcome."

I paused before leaving. An idea popped into my head, and before I could stop myself, I said, "Do you want to go to the garden first? We could both use fresh air after the last few days."

She smiled, dazed, and then nodded. "All right. I'll go."

I opened the door for her and we headed to the gardens. It didn't take long to reach the sunlit enclosure. The day was cooler than the past few ones.

Arely walked beside me, running her fingers along the flowers as we walked down the stone path. I breathed in the fresh air, glad to be better again.

I actually felt at peace for once.

Arely stopped next to a bush with purple flowers and plucked one from its stem. She twirled it with her fingers. "This is an interesting flower. I've never seen anything like it in my garden. I wonder what it is."

I shrugged. "Well, I don't know anything about flowers, so I can't help you there."

She giggled. "I wouldn't expect you to." She stepped gingerly along the path.

We continued on the trail, letting the sun warm our skin. I couldn't help but smile to myself.

"Have you come here often?" I asked after a moment.

Arely nodded. "It's peaceful." She tilted her head and then her smile turned into a frown.

I stopped. "What's wrong?"

She bit her lip, looking at the ground. "Do... do you ever wish that the war had never started? And we could have our parents back?"

I narrowed my eyes. "Yes."

She shuffled her feet. "I'm sorry. That was a dumb question. It's just... the war seemed to start over nothing. That refugee came to our kingdom and your father found out—"

"What refugee?" I asked, confused. "I don't remember a refugee being a part of it."

She wrinkled her forehead, glancing at me. "The criminal that your father wanted to behead. He came to Rivallen and Papa decided to give him a place in our castle in return for his work. When your father found out, he declared war on us."

I shook my head. "Arely, that's not why my father declared war on your kingdom."

By the look on her face, she had no idea what I was talking about. I realized she must not have known. After all these years, had no one told her the truth, not even Octavia?

Chapter 24
Arely

"Didn't your father tell you?" Shane asked.

I clutched at my skirt, perplexed. A trickle of worry ran through me. What did he mean? Didn't my father tell me *what*?

I shook my head, unsure what to say.

"He stole rare medicine from our kingdom when the epidemic happened," Shane said. "He stole it to heal you when you got sick. My grandfather and aunt – on my father's side of the family – caught the sickness. We didn't have the medicine anymore, so they both died. And that's why my father declared war on your kingdom."

I opened my mouth and shut it again, shocked. I had always believed the war had started because of the refugee. That's what my family had always told me.

I remembered the horrible days when I had fallen sick. Tavia wasn't allowed to sleep with me, or even be around me, for months. Mama had cried and Papa had too.

The pain had been immense, and I had thrown up many times each day. I never felt like eating, but the kind medics had sat next to me, gently coaxing me to eat until I did. My fevers had grown so bad, I'd had to stay in bed for days, not moving a muscle.

Mama sang me to sleep every night, letting me squeeze her hand as hard as I needed to, and Papa had read me stories.

Whenever Tavia was allowed to see me, she snuck me chocolate, even though I wasn't supposed to eat it.

But no matter how well my family and servants took care of me, I steadily grew worse until the medics feared the worst. The kingdom seemed to hold its breath. My parents stopped all their work to focus on me.

At the time, I was too young to fully understand how dangerous of a situation I was in.

All I knew was how much my stomach and head hurt, and how miserable it was to lie in bed all day. I wanted the sickness to pass and to be like all the other children.

Finally one night, when I felt especially awful, the medics took my parents into a corner and whispered together. My mother had walked to my bed and sat beside me, brushing the hair out of my face. My skin was on fire.

Papa stood next to her, but his mind was somewhere else. I could tell because he was staring at my pink, stuffed animal, which used to be fluffy, but I had squeezed it so hard in the past months, its fur was matted and thin.

I had looked up at Mama, who had tears in her eyes and my heart sank like a stone. She squeezed my hand and I asked her, "Mama, am I going to die?"

She began to cry, and I did too. She wrapped her arms around me and cradled me as if I were a little toddler, and I wished I was.

Papa sat next to me and took me in his arms. "Arely," he said, with a certain intensity. "Listen to me. You are not going to die. I will make sure you get better, okay? Trust me."

My mother had watched him with concern. "Allister, what are you talking about?" she whispered.

"I'm going to Rapora," he claimed, standing up. He met my mother's eyes. "I'll bring back what she needs."

He left my room quickly. Mama began to follow him, but I cried out, not wanting her to leave me, so she stayed the rest of the night.

I fell into a restless sleep and when I awoke in the morning, I couldn't open my eyes or hear much of anything. I felt drowsy and didn't want to move. My whole body ached.

I felt a hand hoist me into a half-sitting, half-laying position and I mumbled nonsense to whoever had raised me. A hand caressed my cheek and someone said my name.

"Arely, you need to take your medicine, sweetie."

I didn't budge. I had no intention of moving, for fear of pain, so I stayed in place, with my eyes closed.

I heard a younger, familiar tone beside me. "Arely, Papa brought you special medicine. Wake up!"

I opened my eyes slowly, but the light was blinding. I started to cry again.

My sister sat beside me, watching my expression fixedly. She grabbed my hand, trying to comfort me.

"Arely," my mother said again. "The medicine's going to heal you. You have to take it now though. Open your mouth, darling."

I obeyed, and although I couldn't see through my blurred vision, I felt the cold medicine as soon as it touched my tongue. I closed my mouth, swallowing all the bitter medicine from the spoon.

For three days after that, I took the same, yucky-tasting medicine, with no results at all. I hadn't gotten worse though, and that was something.

On the fifth day, I woke up feeling different. I didn't have a fever or a headache or even a sore throat.

I sat up all by myself. I almost couldn't believe it was happening. It seemed too good to be true.

My parents and sister walked into the room and I stood and ran to them. They were so surprised, we all ended up in a laughing, crying mess on the rug. I felt better than I had in forever.

The kingdom celebrated for a week afterward and I was so happy to ride through the village again and visit my friend Nico.

In all the time since then, I had never thought to wonder how, exactly, my father had gotten the special medicine. It hadn't mattered to me.

It hadn't occurred to me that it might have been the reason King Dagwood declared war on Papa six months later.

Now it felt like a blow to the stomach. How could I have not known? I knew instantly that Tavia had known all along, but she had never told me. Perhaps my parents had told her to keep it a secret, knowing full well I would take the news horribly.

They had been right.

My parents died to save me? And all those thousands of soldiers? Both of these wars, they were only fought for a sick princess?

I stumbled, suddenly feeling nauseous. Shane reached out and grabbed my hand. "Arely–" he started to say, but I broke free and ran inside the castle.

I found a bucket of water sitting in the hallway. No one else was around. I collapsed beside it and threw up.

My throat burned and tears welled in my eyes. I began to sob.

I didn't notice when Shane sat down next to me. "Arely..." he said, touching my arm.

I jerked away. I couldn't help myself. I didn't understand how all this could possibly be true. Was it all my fault?

Shane fell silent, staring at the floor as I continued to cry. My body shook with every gasp of air I took. I didn't want to believe it. My head was reeling.

I stood and tried to walk a few feet, but my feet faltered and I curved into the wall. I was a wreck.

Shane took my hand. "Let's go upstairs," he said gently. "You should lie in bed for awhile."

I nodded numbly and let him lead me through the castle and up the stairs to our bedroom. I was glad to have him with me.

Chapter 25
Shane

I knew exactly why no one had ever told Arely the real reason for the war as soon as the words left my lips. I hadn't expected her reaction, nor prepared myself for it.

I led her up the stairs, not entirely sure what to do. She clung to my hand, not letting go.

The best thing I could think of was to go to our room. Maybe she would calm herself down. I doubted I could help her much. That was something I wasn't good at.

When we reached the bedroom, I bent down next to the fireplace to try to revive the dying embers. Perhaps a little warmth would help.

Arely sank beside me, sniffling. She wiped the tears from her eyes and didn't say a word.

I placed a new log in the center and pushed kindling into the ashes of the old fire. After a couple moments, the flame caught and grew into a decent fire.

Although I didn't need to do anything else, I took a stick and pushed the kindling around. It didn't help the fire much, but I needed to stall. I didn't know what to say to Arely.

I guess I didn't need to say anything though. She leaned against me and laid her head on my shoulder. Her breathing was soft, so she had stopped crying.

The fire radiated warmth, which felt great on the cool fall morning. I felt strangely at peace sitting there with Arely.

"I guess I should have known that was the cause for the war," she said quietly. "It makes more sense than the fugitive story."

"The fugitive was part of the reason, now that you mention it," I said. "It just wasn't... the main reason."

"I see." She lifted her hand closer to the flames to warm it. "There are always multiple reasons for wars."

We didn't speak for a couple minutes, but listened to the fire crackling.

Arely sighed. "I wish the war had never started in the first place. I wish no one had to die because of it. And it seems so unfair that we both lost our parents... Nothing good came for either side."

I watched as she trailed her finger along the maroon-colored rug, spelling out a couple words. M, a, m...

Mama & Papa.

She stopped, letting her hand rest against the softness of the rug. She took a deep breath.

"I know," I said. "I wish it hadn't happened, either. But I..."

I had started it again though.

I stared into the ashes of the burnt wood shavings, realizing what this meant. A bitter feeling grew within me. I remembered the pain all those years ago, when I was all alone and everyone seemed to hate me. I had lost my parents, and my best friend didn't want to spend time with me anymore.

Nothing had made any sense then.

And I remembered the feeling that had stayed with me each night. The need for revenge, no matter what it took.

Revenge. On Arely. On Octavia. And Arely was sitting beside me, leaning against my shoulder. She was my enemy, wasn't she? But if she wasn't, then who was she?

I stood up quickly, making Arely jump. "Is something wrong?" she asked, squinting at me.

"I - I need to get back to work. I've been wasting time."

When I reached the royal stables, I found my horse Triballi sleeping. His head rested on the door of his stall, lulling to the side. I tilted my head at him.

"Triballi, wake up! We have a task to do."

His eyes slowly opened and he turned his head to the side to look at me.

"Yes, it's me. Get your head off the gate so I can open it!"

He stepped back and I unlatched the gate, letting it swing open. I took his bridle and led him out. His hooves clip-clopped along the ground and once he was in place, I tied the rope around the pole, and began to saddle him.

My bodyguards had joined me after I left my room, and they gathered their own horses from the other stalls.

Once I was done with Triballi, I pulled myself onto the saddle and steered him into the field.

"Want to know where we're going, boy?" I asked, and his ears flicked back at me. "We are going to Fort Oak to see how everything is going. After all, we don't want Octavia to take it from us."

Triballi picked up his pace and cantered toward the gates and into the meadows. My bodyguards spread out enough to give us room.

Far in the distance, the fort stood next to the forest, waiting for us. It wouldn't be too long before we reached it.

As soon as Triballi and I reached the fort, soldiers came out and led my horse to the stables. The head soldier of the fort, Lord August, took me inside and offered me a drink.

"No, not now," I said. "I came to see that everyone is prepared for new attacks. This fort has seen many battles in the past weeks, and although it is more protected than ever before, we must stay on our guard."

"Of course, sire," he said. "I will call the knights to attention, if you wish."

I nodded and Lord August marched from the main room.

I sat on the sofa next to a fire while I waited. Although this place was nice, it had seen much death, and the evidence of that was clear.

Blood stained the walls. The furniture was scarce. The walls showed signs of crumbling. It had once been grand, but now it was a humble place for the knights to stay and protect the castle and woods.

A portrait of myself sat above the fireplace mantle, with my title below. That was the only picture in the entire room.

A selection of windows was placed in strategic places, with small spaces that people couldn't climb through. Outside of the window, I could see dozens of freshly dug dirt piles. That was the graveyard. But the army only buried the most important soldiers.

All the rest of the bodies were burned. The surviving knights simply didn't have enough time to dig all the holes necessary to bury everyone. Not if they wanted to prepare for and survive the next battle.

There was a single sign in the middle for all the knights who had died and weren't buried. It read: *To the defenders of Fort Oak, who sacrificed their lives for the greater good.*

I cringed at the sight of all the new holes. The last battle had gone in my favor, but the battle before had been disastrous.

After a couple minutes, Lord August returned and a line of soldiers rushed after him. They all filed outside and I watched through the window as they created a perfect formation within a minute.

When they had done so, I stepped out of the fort and onto the trampled grass.

The knights stood stiffly at attention, facing the lord. He motioned to me.

"The King, I believe, would like to speak to all of you. Pay close attention. We have hard work to do in the coming weeks."

The lord stepped away and I took charge.

"All right," I said, clasping my hands around the hilt of my sword. "The last few weeks have been interesting. We've had our losses, but we've also had our gains. In the end, it's all in the past and what matters is the present and the future. Those are the two things we can control."

I walked along the front line, making eye contact with many of the soldiers.

"We cannot lose this fort again. And we won't, because we are going to fight harder than ever. Octavia is going to make another move soon, and we have to be prepared, especially if we lose the second fort in the woods. No exceptions."

I stopped in the middle. I had much work I needed to do with the knights and with the fort. I would have to spend the rest of the day here, making sure the fort was as secure as possible.

The men were ready, I could tell. They were ready to work.

"We have the upper hand now. We will win this war. Once and for all."

Chapter 26
Arely

I certainly wasn't in a state to leave the castle, not after learning my family had kept a secret from me for years, one that I had every right to know.

After Shane had left, I'd laid on my bed, trying to wrap my mind around the truth. It only resulted in more tears.

But I was sick of staring at the gray walls of the bedroom and sick of being alone. The sky was darkening as I pulled on my boots and cloak. Shane hadn't returned from wherever he'd gone.

A terrible feeling filled me as I left for the third night. Beside what Shane had told me, the things I'd heard from the knights in the village worried me, cluttering my mind like unwanted weeds in a garden. Were they looking for Ashton? Had they found him?

Scarlett had been insistent on getting away from the fountain and I believed she knew something was wrong. I wanted to check on the two of them, to see that they were all right.

As I neared the meeting place, I saw each of them sitting by the wall, playing their game again. The night was quiet, like any other.

The wind whistled softly and dim lights shone in the homes around us.

A smile spread across my lips and I started to head over to them. The soft leather of my boots was silent against the stone streets. I didn't want to call out to either of them, or else I might wake the nearby families sleeping in their homes.

Before I could reach Ashton and Scarlett, however, the voices of knights stopped me.

A half-dozen men were walking in formation down the road, with the leader at the front. He waved for them to enter the square.

I slipped into the shadows of a nearby alley, for fear of being spotted. I did not want to get caught outside of the castle, especially at night. But I peeked around the corner to see what was going on.

At first, the knights didn't go over to the children, but instead looked around the square, their eyes alert. Scarlett and Ashton ignored the knights.

"Remember what I told you," the leader said, speaking to another knight. "He's been a problem before."

My breath caught in my throat. I hoped that my assumptions were wrong, but I couldn't help but believe the knights were talking about Ashton.

I wished he and Scarlett would move away from the men, but surely they would have been spotted immediately.

After a couple minutes, one of the knights saw the two of them sitting in the shadows and walked over. I held my breath, watching from a distance.

Ashton jumped up and started to run, but the knight grabbed the back of his shirt. The little boy shouted and wrestled against his grip.

"I found him!" the knight yelled to the others.

They all circled around Ashton, while Scarlett tried to stop the knights. But she was no match for the tall guards. One of them growled, "You rascals think you can get away with anything! But we saw you steal bread from the bakery, young boy. You will pay for what you took."

Ashton fought against the knight. "I needed that bread! Let go of me!"

One of the guards pushed Scarlett away. "It's the King's rules. You steal something, you pay for it. Or you can go to jail."

As the guards started to pull the boy down the street with them, I stepped into the middle of the road. My heart pounded in my chest, knowing how much trouble I would get into, but I had to help Ashton.

I pulled down my hood, revealing my curly blonde hair, and headed after the guards.

Scarlett spotted me as I marched past her, and gasped. "Wait, Arely! What are you doing?" she whispered.

I didn't reply, but paused a few feet away from the guards. "Stop!" I said, keeping my voice steady and commanding. "Let that boy go."

All of them turned to look at me. Their expressions changed from angry to stunned.

I narrowed my eyes as the top guard stepped forward, studying me. "Queen Arely. If I do remember right, all the guards are under strict orders from King Shane to not let you leave the castle. This—" he said, pointing in a circle at the village, "—is not the castle. It's Rapora Village. May I ask why you are here?"

I stood my tallest, even though the knight towered over me. "I'm sorry. Maybe you haven't heard the new orders, but King Shane allowed me to go into the village, as long as I don't leave the perimeters of the buildings."

He glared at me and spit on the ground. "And why on earth would His Majesty do that?"

"I have been here for awhile now," I said, trying my best not to flinch or show any doubt on my face. "It's not easy to be stuck in a castle all day long, even if it is massive. I asked him several times, and today he said I could go out into the village."

"How about the fact that it's nighttime? The King let his own enemy wander his village without guards? Am I supposed to believe that?" The guard took a step toward me, but I didn't budge.

"Excuse me," I said, raising my voice, even though uneasiness fluttered inside me. "It's terrible manners to lean over a queen like that." I pushed him away from me and raised an eyebrow.

His eyes widened at my sudden boldness, but then he puffed up his chest. "You didn't answer my question, missy. You may be a queen, but you're not in charge."

"I needed a breath of fresh air, to help me sleep. And about the guards? I'm allowed to walk around the castle without them. After all, in both the castle and the village, there are guards everywhere. It's not like I'm *not* being watched all the time."

"Well—" he started, but I cut him off.

"This doesn't have to do with me. It has to do with the orders the King gave to you." I frowned at him, not losing eye contact. "He is allowing me to go through the city because I asked. If you want to question his orders, you can bring me to the castle now, and tell him what happened. I'm sure he'll be thrilled about one of his guards waking him up in the middle of the night."

The guard paused and then looked up at the dark castle towers, thinking.

"Oh," I added. "How much was the bread? I'll pay for it, but you have to release the boy. Do you hear me?"

"Yes, yes," the guard said, turning to look at Ashton, whose eyes were wide with fear. "It was three copper coins."

I reached into my pocket and pulled out my coin purse. I dropped the money into the guard's palm. He signaled for the other knights to let go of Ashton.

"All right," he said to me. "I'll let you go, but if I return to the castle and hear that this is a lie, the King is going to hear about it."

With that, the guards turned and left the block, leaving me with the two children. But two stayed by the street, keeping watch of my movements.

I walked to Ashton and crouched next to him. Tears began to run down his face and I wrapped my arms around him.

"It's okay, Ashton," I said, trying to soothe him.

He shook his head vigorously. "Did you tell them the truth? Did King Shane really tell you that you could come here? Tonight?"

"No," I said quietly. "He didn't."

"Then you're going to get in trouble because of me!" Ashton wailed. "The guard is going to tell him that you came out here and King Shane's going to be mad!"

"Shh." I hugged him tighter. "I don't care what happens to me. I can deal with it. But I want *you* to be safe."

Ashton didn't say anything else, but buried his face into my cloak. Scarlett walked over and sat down.

"That was brave," she said quietly.

I smiled slightly and ruffled Ashton's hair. "Everything will turn out fine. Here, I'll give you the rest of the money I have in this pouch." I pulled out the white bag and handed it to Scarlett. "There's not much left, but I know you'll be able to use it."

"We didn't find the little girl for you, though," she said. "We don't deserve it."

I shook my head. "It's all right. I'll find a way to give the doll to the little girl myself. But I want you to have this money, okay? Take it."

Scarlett accepted the coin purse, tucking it into a pocket on her dress and patting it. "Thank you."

Ashton looked up at me. "I wish you didn't have to leave. I want to see you again."

"I know." I reached out and Scarlett joined the hug. "Listen. I'm going to go back to the castle. You don't have to worry about me. All right? I won't be coming back to the town though. I want you two to watch out for each other, and I know you already do. Things can get hard, but if you have good friends by your side, everything is much easier. Remember that."

Ashton wiped at the tears that had dried on his cheeks and sniffed.

"I want to be like you one day..." he said. "You're a good queen. One day I want to be a good leader too. Even if I don't get to be the ruler of a kingdom, I want to be a good leader in the town. And I'll help the people who don't have everything they need! Just like you."

I smiled. "I think you'll be great at that, Ashton."

Scarlett squeezed my hand. "Arely, you have to win the war. Please. I don't want Shane to win. He's not great like you are. He never comes out to the city or talks to the villagers."

Ashton chimed in, a smile appearing on his face. "And you're great at board games!"

I laughed. "I appreciate your compliments," I said, squeezing them.

"One more thing," Ashton said. "Will we ever get to see you again?"

I paused, looking up at the sky. I didn't want to say that it seemed highly improbable.

"Hopefully, one day, I'll be able to see you again. I promise I'll do my best to make sure it happens. But as for now, I can't come back."

He nodded slowly.

All three of us sat there in the middle of the road, in silence, hugging each other. No matter what happened to me, I wouldn't have changed what I had done, for that one moment under the stars, where I had become one of the children of the village again.

At last I had to leave. I said goodbye to both of them, and they said goodbye in turn. But as I stood and turned around, I saw a patrol of guards.

It was the same guards as before. They had come back.

My gaze swiveled to the leader, the one who walked in front. My blood turned to ice.

Shane.

He was here. How had he gotten here so quickly? It was still the middle of the night. But I knew the answer: he must have woken up and seen that I was gone. If he had left to find me and ran into the patrol of guards, they would've told him everything.

I pushed Ashton and Scarlett away from me. "Go!" I whispered to them. "Now, and don't come back!"

I didn't need to convince them. Their scared expressions said enough and they took off into the night.

I turned back to where the knights stood.

Shane had stopped, his face livid. I had never seen him this angry, not even when I had picked up the doll. The confidence I'd had with the guard evaporated in an instant and I shrank back.

"Arely," he said, his dark eyes flashing.

"Y-yes?" I asked.

"You should never have come here."

I gulped and nodded. "I'm sorry."

"I don't believe that."

"I really am!"

Shane waved the knights over and I stiffened.

"I have *rules*," he said. "And everyone has to follow them, including the queen." He turned away from me and to the knights. "You can take her to the dungeon."

I didn't bother to fight as they grabbed my arms, but I kept my eyes on Shane. "Can I at least explain myself?" I begged. "Please, Shane."

"No. And you will call me either King Shane or Your Majesty." He folded his arms. "I kept my promise, Arely, but you didn't keep yours, so the only person you have to blame for this is yourself."

With that, he turned and left, and the guards pulled me away.

Chapter 27
Shane

Arely had snuck out of the castle when I'd been sick. She'd taken advantage of the fact I wasn't on top of security. But the guards at the gate had also failed, and I'd have to deal with that in the next few days.

I had begun to trust her. I didn't know how to feel. Angry? Betrayed? Indifferent?

How many times she had snuck into the town? What had she been doing with those two children? The only way to find out was to ask her, but that was the last thing I wanted to do.

I decided to head to the planning room, where I doubted anyone would be at this time of the day. But as I entered, I found General Collins, Tad, and several of the spies I had sent to Rivallen. They must have come back with information for me.

"What's going on?" I asked. "Did you learn anything new?"

A spy stepped forward. "I believe, sir, that Octavia will attack any day. She's been preparing her army and strategizing for an attack. And, by what I saw and heard in Rivallen, she might try to attack Fort Oak and Fort Maple in the same night. There's a rumor she completely changed her battle tactics."

I nodded, listening as he told me every detail, even the ones that didn't seem to matter. When he was finished, I sat straighter.

"All right. If she has changed her tactics, we can't expect her to be predictable," I said, turning to the general. "Alert the army leaders and tell them to go into defense mode. I want to be ready when she attacks. I'll check the force field and prepare the catapults."

"Yes, sir." Collins rose from his chair and left the room, leaving me with Tad and the spies.

I turned to them. "The current round of spies will stay in Rivallen and report to me with any new information." I waved them out. "You are dismissed."

The spies bowed and left.

Tad turned to me as the door banged shut. "Your Majesty, I was wondering about Queen Arely. What do you plan to do with her after the war ends?"

I narrowed my eyes at him. "Well, I suppose that depends on the way she acts."

He squinted at me. "What do you mean?"

I crossed my arms, bitterly. "A couple hours ago, she snuck out of the castle, but several knights caught her and told me. Now she's in the dungeon."

Tad's eyes widened. "Really? But— Your Majesty—"

"She asked for it," I said.

And with that, I left the meeting room.

I spent all my time focusing on the battle ahead. The knights were at work cleaning armor, washing horses, repairing saddles, and sharpening weapons. The maids were clearing the halls of any obstacles that could cause knights to trip while rushing outside to battle. All the other servants carried boulders to the catapults on the outer wall. With all this work going on, the castle rang with shouts and clangs. But that was good.

Octavia. Would. Not. Win.

I walked the castle halls, meeting with leaders to see if everything was going well. It took my whole day, but I didn't mind. I had nothing else I needed to do.

While I was walking down one of the hallways, a guard stopped me.

"Your Majesty," he said. "May I have a word with you? It's about Arely."

I hesitated, but then nodded curtly. "Tell me."

The guard told me what Arely had said to him while he and three others were guarding her cell. "She wants to apologize in person, if you'll let her."

I paused. "She said that?"

The guard nodded.

"All right. Thanks for the information."

I continued on my way down the hall. I supposed the guard had expected me to say more, but I didn't care.

I had other things to think about. It wasn't simple, letting Arely out of the jail. It would be easier knowing she was in there rather than wondering where in the castle she could be. If she remained in the dungeon, I wouldn't have to worry about what she was up to while I was working.

I passed the archway to the garden. Rain pounded against the drooping flowers and plants, drenching my shoulders and clothing as I stepped underneath the dark sky and walked toward the statue of my parents. I remembered how they had prepared for battles.

My father had never shown any fear. He spent hours talking to the advisers and generals, while my mother oversaw the servants, making sure they were working hard to secure the castle and prepare the weapons.

My job had been to stay out of the way, but also watch and learn. I'd learned a ton by doing this.

I had done everything my parents had done to prepare for battle. Whenever Octavia attacked, I would be prepared.

Looking at the statue made my thoughts return to the promise I had made. *I would win the war in three weeks.*

Two weeks had passed. I had one week left.

When night came again, I laid in bed reading while the stars and moon cast pale gray stripes across the floor. All was silent. The book was about war strategies. I had been reading all the books I had about it for months, and still wasn't close to finishing all of them.

The night grew cold, so cold that I walked to the balcony door and shut it, then climbed back into my bed. But I didn't warm up much, even under the thick blankets.

Nothing felt right, sitting here alone. It was too quiet in the room.

A familiar feeling fell over me. I knew it all too well, and it was something I had tried to ignore for years, although it had never quite left me.

The feeling of loneliness.

I didn't know why Arely had left the castle. And it bothered me. How could she be so quiet and innocent, then go and break rules? I guessed I hadn't quite believed she was capable of getting past the guards.

Arely had asked for her punishment. She knew of the consequences of sneaking out. But she had done it anyway. *Why?*

I put the book down, frustrated. I couldn't read with all these thoughts floating in my head.

I stared out the window, where the land stretched for miles and miles and endless amounts of creatures roamed. A river wove through the middle of it, sending water throughout the meadows. It seemed so peaceful in the night, but a battle would soon rage there, ruining its beauty.

Not that I cared, of course. What mattered was that I won that battle.

I sighed. Two years ago, I had planned on defeating Octavia in a matter of months. Now here I was and I still hadn't won. I had learned a great deal though, about war and tactics. I had learned winning a war wasn't as easy as I'd thought.

But I had never given up. That was against my personality.

Something in the war felt off, however. It made me uneasy. Why didn't I feel confident about this upcoming battle?

I could beat Octavia. I had won the last battle, after all, and crushed her army. The soldiers had fled from Fort Maple and I had gained new territory. I was destined to win again.

But *still* that uneasy feeling remained.

I threw my pillow across the room, in anger and confusion.

A shatter broke through the air and I looked up to see what the pillow had crashed into. A million glittering shards of glass reflected the roaring crimson of the fire. A frame lay on the floor with a pale gray picture sprawled across the mess.

I jumped up and ran to the picture, picking it off the ground. My father was in the back, with one hand resting on my mother's shoulder, and his other hand resting on mine. I had been significantly shorter in this picture, because I'd been twelve. It was the last picture we'd had the artists create.

The glass had shredded the corners, but other than that, it was fine. I gently slid it behind the frame again.

My parents' smiles were bright. They looked happy. I was happy, too. That was my family, my only family. But... they weren't with me anymore.

So my only "family" left was...

I shoved the picture back onto its stand and sparked a curl of magic. With that, I whisked away all the glass from the floor and dumped it in a trash pail.

Why did Arely have to act so sweet and kind? Was she trying to make everything harder for me? I had spared her life and given her everything she needed. She didn't have to do this to me.

I blamed her for all the uneasy feelings about the war. It had been confusing ever since she had stepped foot in the castle. Like she wanted me to feel guilty about fighting her kingdom. That must've been her plan all along. If she treated me like an ally, I wouldn't want to win the battle, because I was fighting Arely's own people.

She'd treated me so well when I was sick. She had stayed with me the whole time, but it had never been about me. Everything she had done was for her own kingdom.

How had I been so foolish to think that? Not even my own people liked me. Quay had gotten that right. I'd denied it for years, but I had never been able to escape it.

So why had I thought that, for even the slightest second, one of my enemies would come into my castle and decide to be nice to me, just for the sake of being nice?

No one in his or her right mind would do that. Of course she'd had her own motives. I should have known that she'd find a way to help her kingdom, even if she was trapped here.

Arely had preyed on my weakness.

I cursed under my breath, glaring out the window.

A blue shimmer broke the air, the sign of Octavia's magic. She wanted to talk again. It was a good thing for her that I wanted to talk as well.

I got out of bed and strode to the railing of my balcony. One spark of my magic and Octavia was standing in front of me.

"Long time no see," I spat.

"Oh, aren't you in a pleasant mood," she snapped. "I heard about what you did to Arely."

"Yes." I raised my eyebrows. "After all, you are Queen Paranoid when it comes to your sister. I'd be surprised if you hadn't known."

Octavia shook her head. "That's not okay. You are asking for trouble, throwing her in prison!"

"I know I am. And I'm ready for whatever you throw at me. I crushed you in the last two battles." I smirked.

She ignored my comment. "I called to give you an offer. If you let Arely out of the dungeon, I won't attack you. But if you keep her in there, you can watch your army fall as my army destroys it. Believe me, you have no idea what's coming."

I couldn't ignore the confidence in her eyes. It wasn't her normal confidence in her own skills. It was the confidence of a secret plan I couldn't imagine, waiting to be hatched and used against me.

Octavia knew what she was letting me see. She was trying to intimidate me, and although she was good at it, I wouldn't let her succeed. She could never crush my army.

I had the upper hand.

"Excellent," I said, smiling. "I can't wait to see you try."

Chapter 28
Arely

The dungeon was colder than I remembered. The guards took me to a different area than all the regular prisoners. The air was musty but it didn't smell bad. There weren't any windows to let light in, so candles lit the halls.

They placed me in a cell that had a bed with one thin sheet and a small bucket. At least I had that. These were much nicer than the other cells.

When the door banged shut, a shiver slipped down my spine. The memory of my last night spent in the dungeon still lingered in my mind, with the chains, strange people, and *way* too many horrid smells.

This cell was better, but the memory was not welcome.

I laid on the bed, staring at the black ceiling. I stayed there for quite awhile and before long, I lost track of time. At first I hadn't contemplated what had happened. But as I lay there, I realized what a bad predicament I was in.

Who knew how long Shane would keep me here? Would it be weeks or months? What if the war ended before I got out? That would mean my whole plan had failed, and I should have left with Nico when I had the chance.

I pulled the sheet around me as the room grew colder. Although I had arrived in the morning, I was sure it was nighttime by now.

The cold stone walls pressed against my arms, adding to the distress I felt inside. I'd put myself into this situation, as Shane had said. I'd known the consequences, yet I had ignored them.

Tears began to stream down my face. I buried my head into the pathetic pillow I had, trying to muffle my sobs. No matter what I did though, the guards could hear.

I thought about the last conversation I'd had with Tavia. The confidence in her voice was clear, but I had to wonder if she'd feigned it, only to comfort me. Either way, she'd told me not to worry, implying that I could count on her to get me out of this mess.

I needed to give her time.

Tavia was stubborn and tough. When she was determined to get something, she always got it.

These thoughts didn't stop my tears though. I wondered what tonight would have been like if I hadn't left the castle. Was it worth it? To meet Scarlett and Ashton?

After a couple minutes, I took the silver ring off my finger and turned it in my palm. The blue, heart-shaped jewel glittered in the candlelight. To imagine, queens had worn this ring for decades, maybe even centuries. It still shined as if it had been crafted yesterday. It must've been enchanted with magic to keep it in perfect condition.

I lifted my fist and hurled the ring as hard as I could. It bounced against the wall and fell to the floor, clinking as it came to a stop on the opposite side of the cell.

Before any of the guards turned to see what I'd done, I turned toward the dungeon wall and curled into a ball. If any of them saw the ring, they said nothing.

I thought back to the beginning of this huge mess. Nico and I had dashed through the Mosaic Meadows, but I hadn't escaped the knights. They had taken me to the castle, and there I met Shane. He gave me the deal to spare my life if I helped him gain the Third and Final Blessing. We traveled through the village, where I had picked up the doll and upset Shane. Then from there...

Everything got muddled. There had been moments when Shane was upset with me, but also the moments when he had almost been like a friend. When he had told a joke, and I had understood.

But now we were back to being enemies. My plan, it seemed, had failed.

Something would have to happen in order for me to get another chance. Something significant.

And whatever that significant thing was, it was out of my control.

I mostly laid on the bed, drumming my fingers on the wood, trying to keep my boredom at bay, but that was about as impossible as using my own magic to entertain myself.

I attempted to start conversations with the guards, but no matter what I said, they remained silent. Every few hours, they would switch shifts, and I'd try again, but it never worked.

Counting all the times this had happened, I believed I'd been here for more than three days, but maybe it hadn't been that long. It almost felt like a month.

I flipped over on my bed and glanced at the tin of milk. I hadn't eaten much. They gave me enough food, but I didn't have an appetite to eat. However, I had drank plenty of milk and water.

I picked up the tin and drank the last of the milk, then walked to the bars. "Can I have more milk?" I asked. "Please?"

The guard closest to me hesitated and then nodded. He took the tin and left the hallway.

I sat on my bed and rubbed my arms. It still felt chilly in the dungeon, but I had gotten used to it, for the most part.

I needed a plan. I needed to do something so Shane would let me out of here.

I stood back up and walked to the guards. "I want to tell Shane something," I started. Like I imagined, the guards didn't say anything.

"Can one of you give him my message, please?"

Silence.

I continued anyway. "I want him to know that I'm sorry about sneaking into the village. I had a nightmare one night, and I wanted to leave the castle for a moment. I left three times, explored the town, and met two kids. They begged me to come back, so I did. We played games and talked, but nothing else. I know I shouldn't have left the castle though, so I'd like to apologize in person, and I'd like to have a second chance. Please, I can't stand being in here any longer."

The guards stayed in their positions, not saying a word.

I sighed and sank back onto the bed, wrapping the blanket tightly around myself, and mumbled quietly, "Just thought I'd try..."

I didn't get up when the other guard came with my milk. He set it on the floor and went back to his position.

I didn't want to think my own adventurous side had ruined the plan that could've saved my kingdom, my people. If it had, there was nothing I could do now.

As I lay in the darkness, I pretended that Shane was there, that he was listening. I plowed through so many explanations of why I had sneaked out of the castle, but each time I was unhappy with it, and started over.

Why would Shane care about the two children on the street, playing games in the middle of the night, and stealing bread to survive? He despised the villagers and I couldn't change that.

To him, the village must've been like a play, with puppets that never showed real emotion on the stitches of their fabric faces. A mask covered them, showing only the things he wanted to see.

I wished I could show him the village through different eyes, so he could experience the emotions of the people, and see how much they needed a strong leader to watch over them.

But the kingdom was a disaster, and the only ones who prospered were the residents of the castle.

Words could not explain what had drawn me to the village; it could only be experienced with the people.

But Shane never came down to the dungeon, and I remained trapped behind the bars.

Chapter 29
Shane

Rain poured across the glass windows as thunder boomed in the distance. Night had fallen once again, but Octavia's army hadn't appeared. Hopefully she wouldn't want to travel through the meadows during the storm.

I sat in bed, too restless to sleep. I tried to focus on all the things I had done to prepare the castle. But I couldn't.

The night my parents died had been just like this night. Cold. Bitter. I remembered it as if it had happened yesterday. The memory wasn't going to leave me any time soon.

Every day it haunted me, forcing me to wonder what life would have been like if my parents hadn't died.

One thing was for sure, it wouldn't have been like this life.

That night had been chaotic. And in the chaos, the general and his guards had managed to come to me and explain what had happened:

They all had solemn faces, as if they had seen terrible things but didn't want to scare me.

"Prince Shane," said the general. He bowed low, and I could tell he was shaking slightly, though he hid it well.

"Where are my parents?" I demanded, standing up from my desk in my room. "I want to see them now."

Even at the age of twelve, I could tell my servants feared me. "Well?" I asked again.

"You can't see your parents, my prince," the general said. "The plan didn't go well, and..."

"And?" I prompted, holding on to the rim of my chair. I hoped they hadn't heard the quiver in my voice.

"Your parents died in the battle, Prince Shane. We're very sorry."

I stared at them. "That's not amusing."

"It's not a joke, Your Highness," he said, dismayed. "I saw it happen myself. The two kings and queens were fighting and magic was flying everywhere. One of the beams hit your mother and–"

"GET OUT!" I yelled at the top of my lungs. "Leave me alone, *right now!*"

The guards didn't hesitate before rushing from my room and closing the door behind them.

I sank down in my chair, staring at the map spread across my desk. Each of the kingdoms was sketched into the thick parchment. The Gale Mountains ran along the bottom of the map, but there was nothing below it. If there were any castles beyond the peaks, it was a mystery.

I stared at the map. My brain felt frozen. It couldn't be true, what the general had said. My parents weren't dead. There had been a mistake.

But deep down I knew that the general was right. My parents had been murdered by Rivallen's royal family.

I jumped up and grabbed my emergency satchel, which held everything I needed.

I was going to run away.

Without giving the idea another thought, I rushed down the stairs, past the groups of people clustered in the dim candle light. With all the turmoil, no one noticed me slip through the tunnels.

I entered the stable and found my horse, Triballi. He stomped his foot, clearly upset by the ruckus outside his stall.

He nudged me with his nose, smelling for treats.

"We're leaving," I told him. "We will travel past the Gale Mountains. I don't care that no soul has ever done it, *we're* going to do it."

I let him out of the stall, placed his bridle around his head, and his saddle on his back. I pulled the strap tight and pulled myself up.

No one else was in the royal stable, so I left unnoticed, riding into the dark night. The moon didn't shine, and neither did the stars. Gray clouds blanketed the sky.

We rode for hours – or what felt like hours. I hadn't brought a jacket and the air nipped at my exposed skin. The meadows had filled with rainwater, and although the storm had stopped before I left, it had turned the night into a frozen wasteland.

Lying against Triballi's warm body, I let his warmth pass on to me as I tried to find comfort.

I didn't know when I began to cry, but before I knew it, tears rolled down my face and dripped onto Triballi's skin.

He knew something was wrong. He kept flicking his ears back to listen to me. Smart horse.

I cried myself to sleep. Triballi carried me across the field to a rhythmic flow, which I found calming.

When I awoke the next day, I was back in my bed in Rapora.

"What?" I said groggily. "What's going on? Why am I here?"

The servants watched me. "Your horse carried you home last night. We found you in the stable and took you to bed."

I frowned. I must have slept hard if I hadn't woken up.

Tad, the man who planned my school every week, stood next to my bed. I looked at him.

"Are my parents really dead?" I asked.

He nodded, his shoulders slacking. "I'm sorry, Prince Shane, but they are gone. Rivallen's king and queen are dead as well, so the war is over. We don't have to worry about more death."

"So I will be king," I said slowly, knowing what this meant. "And I can do anything I need to?"

"You will have advisors to help you make decisions," Tad said cautiously.

"But I am the one with magic, with power. In the end, I will get what I want, when I want it. Anyone who opposes me can go straight to the executioner."

Tad's eyes widened. "Prince Shane, your advisors are there to help you gain wisdom, not hinder you. If they don't want you to do something, it's probably for the best."

"I want to avenge my parents. They didn't do anything wrong." I raised my chin, trying to look strong. "Rivallen's twins will pay for what their parents did."

"Remember, Your Highness," Tad said, wearily, "those girls didn't do anything wrong either. You cannot blame them for the war. This is a great chance to start over."

"It *is* Arely's fault the whole war happened in the first place," I pointed out, growing more annoyed with the old man. "Can you deny that?"

"Princess Arely could not help it. What was she supposed to do?" Tad watched me quietly. "Give the twins a chance. Maybe you can become friends."

I sank back into my pillows. "I highly doubt that."

"You have much to do and learn in the coming weeks," he said. "It would be best to give them a second chance. It will make things easier for you, and for them. There will be a peace meeting in a couple days—"

"I'm not going."

"Shane. Please," Tad said, wrinkling his forehead. "It's for the good of the kingdom."

"If my parents are dead, then I am already king by law, even if I haven't had a coronation yet," I said, stubbornly. "It's my decision if I go or not. Not an old teacher's decision."

Tad winced. I turned my head to stare out the window. It was still dark outside, and out in that darkness, thousands of bodies lay, motionless, slain.

"I'll never forgive them," I whispered, bitterly. "Never."

I had inherited my stubbornness from my father, to be certain. I hated what I couldn't control, because I wanted my plans to work every time. I wanted to plan far into the future, without needing to alter even one detail.

But I couldn't control whether my parents lived or died. And I'd had to watch all my plans crumbled to ashes, helpless.

Now I was facing another battle, another turn of events that I could not fully control. I couldn't focus.

My thoughts drifted back to Arely... she wanted the war to be over. And she was as desperate to end it as I was.

I gritted my teeth. I couldn't help it, but I missed her.

I stood, knowing I wouldn't be able to go to bed. I needed to read a book, to calm my mind enough to get a decent amount of sleep before morning.

I walked to my bookshelf and started scanning each of the titles. I had read these so many times, I'd memorized all the important information they held. But in the corner, several books sat gathering dust. These were my father's favorite books, but I hadn't touched them in a long time.

I started to pull one out when I noticed a piece of pink fabric poking out from behind an olive-colored book.

I paused and tugged at the fabric. A doll appeared, and I realized it was the same doll Arely had picked up after the carriage ride.

I nearly dropped it back onto the shelf, but something stopped me.

Arely had hidden it away. I didn't know why.

Perhaps she had kept it so that she could later give it back to the little girl. It seemed like something she would do.

Perhaps that was why she had snuck into the village in the first place.

I blinked, staring at the doll's button eyes and braided hair. It started to make sense.

I had made a terrible mistake.

I opened a drawer and laid the doll inside, where I would be able to find it later, and walked toward the door. As soon as I stepped out, I waved a guard over.

"Go to the head jail guard and tell him to let Arely out of the dungeon. Let her wash up and then bring her to my room immediately."

Only the sound of rain pattering against the windows echoed throughout the room.

It was a strange sound for me to hear, considering the circumstances. I had spent many nights listening to the pouring rain, all alone.

I was alone now, too, but I wouldn't be for long, and that's what made the sound so strange.

I had to make a decision. A difficult one. Over the last five years, I had made many decisions, most of which alienated me from my people. But there was a possibility of changing that. Of fixing my mistakes.

I had made mistakes, it was true. But it wasn't easy to admit.

A flash of lighting lit my room and a moment later, I heard a knock on my door. It had to be Arely.

I walked over and opened it.

Arely stood there, biting her lip uncertainly. She wore a light blue dress with white lace on the ends.

We met each other's gaze for a second, then I ushered her in.

I let go of the door and, without saying a word, walked back to the window. Arely hovered a few yards away, near the extinguished fire.

I hadn't gathered my words yet, and I had to wait a moment before I found them. Arely waited for me to speak first.

I chose my wording carefully, keeping my eyes on the view outside, with the black sky and raindrops sliding down the windowpane.

"I know you have your own kingdom to protect," I said, pausing. Arely didn't respond, so I continued on before I could back down.

"It's a tough job, isn't it? We have to work hard to rule our kingdoms... and that's the problem. Neither of us rules our kingdom the same way, because we were raised in different life styles. And so we're at odds with each other."

I glanced back at Arely, who nodded shyly but didn't say a word. I wished I could tell what she was thinking.

Taking a deep breath, I said, "I don't want us to be enemies, Arely. Not anymore."

Arely took a tiny step forward. "I know," she said, her voice quiet but steady. "And I'm sorry for sneaking out—"

"No. I don't care about that," I said. "I would've snuck out too, if I had been stuck here."

Arely nodded, her eyes wide.

"Come over here," I said, softening my voice.

She listened, coming to my spot next to the window, where the storm had grown ever more violent. Trees thrashed in the wind and water flowed down the walls of the castle. For a moment, we both watched the thunderstorm in silence, but then I turned.

"Arely," I said, and she looked up at me.

I took a deep breath to gather my courage, and say my next words.

"I'm sorry, Arely, for the selfish things I did. I can't excuse them. But you gave me a chance that no one else did. So I want to thank you. And... will you forgive me?"

She smiled this time. A real smile, bright and cheerful. "Yes," she said. "Of course."

Before I could fully grasp her answer, Arely stepped forward and hugged me.

I nearly stepped back from instinct, but stopped myself in time. No one had hugged me since my parents' deaths. I had forgotten what it felt like.

I recovered and, without saying a word, wrapped my arms around her.

"Thank you," I whispered.

It was a strange feeling, being close to another human being. I'd kept people at a distance for so long.

We both stood still for a moment, listening to the howling wind behind the window. The rain couldn't touch inside the castle. I smiled a bit. I had always enjoyed watching storms.

There was something nice about knowing it was cold and wet outside, but that we were sheltered from all that, and instead warm and dry. A castle was protection from a storm.

A knock disturbed the peace of the room. Arely let go of me.

"Who is it?" I called to whoever had knocked. I must've sounded irritated.

A deep voice answered, "It's General Collins, sir. I have urgent news!"

The tone of his voice sent a cold wave through me. My plan was about to unravel.

"Come in, then. Quickly!"

The general walked into the room, breathless. He must've ran up all the stairs as fast as he could.

"Your Majesty, Octavia is attacking, and she's almost here! I'm sure she captured Fort Maple. Our guards in the lookout tower spotted her army coming toward the castle, but the rain prevented them from seeing her sooner."

I glanced through the window. "Of course she had to attack during the muddiest time."

"I sent the army out," the general continued. "They're about to meet her own."

I reached down to tighten the buckles on my boots. "I'm going out there. Get my horse ready."

He nodded and left. I didn't have time to change into my battle armor. I was wearing my regular outfit, with chainmail underneath and a thick, black cloth covering it. It would have to do.

I threw off my robe and grabbed a woolen one, which would help keep the rain off my back and keep me warm.

I turned to walk out of the room, but stopped.

Arely was still standing in her spot, looking distraught. She met my gaze. "I'm going with you," she said, determined, even though her voice shook.

"What? You can't go!" I said, incredulous. "You proved last time that you don't do well in battle. You're staying here." I started to walk to the door again, but Arely stepped in front of me.

"But you don't understand! I know my sister. Maybe we can stop this whole war tonight."

I shook my head. "I highly doubt that's going to happen." I tried sidestepping her.

"It won't happen if we don't try," she argued, backing toward the door. "I can go and talk to Tavia."

"You're not going!" I yelled, throwing my hands into the air.

A look of disappointment crossed her face, but it wasn't about not letting her go.

I felt bad for yelling, but I had to get to my horse. She moved out of the way as I exited the room and ran down the hallway to the stables.

Chapter 30
Arely

Maybe I should have listened to Shane. Maybe I should have stayed in the room, warm and dry, under the blankets. I could have lit a fire and ordered the servants to bring me hot cocoa. That certainly sounded good. It was the perfect night for it, with the wind howling and the rain pounding.

But that's not what I did. I followed Shane down the hallway, stumbling and nearly falling. He was going so fast I almost lost him. Maybe he was right. I didn't do well in battle. I could stay in the castle and wait. I had done it before, but I didn't like it, either.

Maybe, just maybe, I hadn't learned my lesson.

That didn't stop me. I followed him all the way to the stables. When I reached them, I almost thought I had taken a wrong turn, because most of the stalls were empty. Only a few horses stood, munching on hay or flicking away flies.

I spotted Shane mounting his black steed only a few yards away.

I ran to him, almost spooking his horse. "Shane! This battle is going to be awful. I want to try to stop it before people die."

He gave me an exasperated look. "Honestly, it's like you've never been around horses before, Arely. You're going to get kicked!"

"I'm going," I said, stepping in front of the horse.

"No, you're not. Now get out of my way before Triballi tramples you!"

I sighed, retreating. There was no way I could convince him to let me go. I watched as his horse took off into the darkness.

It was all up to me now. I had to stop the battle myself.

An auburn mare stood in the corner. I didn't know who she was waiting for, but I didn't care. She already had a bridle and saddle on. I was sure I needed her more than the owner did.

I ran and jumped onto her saddle before anyone could stop me. Several guards yelled and started to run toward me, but stopped immediately when my horse reared up.

She started bucking. I held on for dear life until she calmed down, then I rubbed her neck and whispered, "I know I'm not your owner, but you have to trust me. Give me a chance."

The guards yelled and chased after me as my horse trotted out of the entryway. I kicked her and she broke into a gallop.

A giant wall of rain hit me as I exited the castle. It instantly drenched me and I could barely see. I had to blink and hold a hand in front of my face to make out the things around me.

Up ahead, I could see the blurry outline of Shane riding his horse. I headed straight after him. I didn't care what he would think, he couldn't send me back to the castle now.

After about a minute, I caught up with him. He must've heard my horse coming, because he turned to see me only a few yards away.

I expected the angry expression he threw me. "What are you *doing?* I told you not to come! Are you completely insane?"

"I know you're the king, but I'm the queen, and I am coming whether you like it or not!" I raised my chin, showing him my determination.

For a few moments, he didn't say anything. I didn't know what that meant.

At last he spoke, and his voice was softer. "All right. But stay close to me."

I nodded, turning to look ahead.

Out of the dark, a field of soldiers appeared. But the battle hadn't begun. Lords on horses stood silently, along with all the knights. I didn't understand what was going on, and I guessed Shane didn't either.

He stopped his horse, close to General Collins. "What are you doing?" he asked.

The general turned, but I couldn't see his face in the storm.

"Octavia wants to talk with you before the battle begins, without any guards. She's waiting at the lookout tower ruins."

Shane didn't move for a few seconds, but looked over the whole army. "Fine."

General Collins raised his voice. "Soldiers! Make a path for His Majesty."

The knights nearest heard, and slowly, the men moved aside to create a path through the army. I followed Shane as his horse trotted forward, leaving tiny craters in the ground due to all the mud and water.

After a couple minutes, I could see the old lookout tower. It had been abandoned years ago during the first war.

My heart started to race faster as we neared it. The dilapidated walls had moss and vines growing around it and the stones looked like they could crumble and fall any second. Inside, my sister was waiting.

That thought made me joyful and terrified at the same time.

We slowed our horses and dismounted them. Shane entered the ruins first, stepping carefully through the rubble. He looked around, as if expecting a trap. "Stay behind me," he ordered.

I wanted to burst past him and run to Tavia and throw my arms around her so we could laugh and cry together. It sounded wonderful in my head, but I doubted it would have gone that way.

One of her bodyguards would probably shoot me with an arrow before they realized who I was. The darkness and rain were not on my side.

I took a deep breath and stayed behind Shane.

We found our way to the middle of the lookout tower. A circle of cracked marble sat in the clearing, no longer a floor, but a home for weeds.

Standing in the middle of that circle was Tavia.

Tavia had her dark hair in a ponytail and it twisted in the wind. She stood as still as a statue, waiting boldly for Shane to come face her.

The silhouettes of her bodyguards were perched on the walls, overlooking the scene. One of them had to be Nico. Each one held a bow with an arrow nocked, ready to fire in an instant.

I knew exactly when Tavia spotted me, because she gasped. She took one step forward, but then stopped herself and motioned for the guards to lower their weapons.

Shane walked onto the marble circle, silently, until he was only a couple yards from her.

Tavia turned to give him a nasty look. "Well, King Shane," she said. "You actually made it."

I glanced at the knights on the walls and Shane followed my gaze.

"Why do you have bodyguards?" he asked, narrowing his eyes. "I thought you said none were allowed."

Tavia crossed her arms. "I had to make sure you wouldn't bring any, first." She hesitated, and then waved the guards away. "I'll deal with this myself."

The silhouettes disappeared down the opposite side of the wall, and then the three of us were left alone. I held my breath, not sure what to say and waiting for something to happen.

"Is this your secret plan to win the battle and kill me?" Shane asked, indicating the thunderstorm around us. "I must say, the rain *is* killing me. You really are stupendous at choosing battle times."

"No, and it doesn't matter because you will see in time. But I should kill you now," Tavia said, sparking her blue magic.

I ran up to them. "Hold on! Wait, we need to talk."

My sister frowned at me. "Arely. Stay out of this."

By now Shane had summoned a large swirl of his own red magic. I didn't have any magic to stop either of them.

"Tavia, listen to me, we need to stop the fighting. We've been at war basically our whole lives! Haven't you had enough?"

Her magic cast a blue glow on her face. "It doesn't work that way," she said stubbornly. "You don't understand war."

"I don't understand war?" I yelled. "What don't I understand? I know people die and people suffer and it's all for what? Getting revenge?"

"Good heavens, Arely. What did he do to you?" Tavia studied me, but she never put her magic out. "You never yell like this."

Shane stepped closer. "I treated her well. Do you think I starved her? I didn't do anything like that."

"You threw her in the dungeon!" Tavia yelled. "You made her marry you!"

I got in between the two. "That's all said and done. We need to think about what's happening right now."

Tavia threw an angry look at me. "Get out of my way! I'm trying to help you."

"What about the future?" I continued. "Don't we want to protect our future kingdoms? Killing each other is the worst way to do that!"

It seemed the storm was getting worse. Rain pounded against my hair and face, and my body was shivering from the cold, but I didn't dare move.

Tavia pushed me out of the way. "Okay, I'll think about the future. Shane is a horrible king and I bet his kingdom would prosper if I killed him."

"No!" I yelled, but both of them shot magic at each other at the same time. I dove out of the way to avoid getting hit by their blasts.

Mud splashed all across my face and dress as I landed in a puddle. Lightning flashed near us and the *boom!* that came after it shook the ground.

Horns blew in the distance, and the battle began. Now that the generals had seen the lights of the magic, they knew they could fight.

I stumbled to my feet. The light from both Tavia's and Shane's magic nearly blinded me.

I couldn't do anything to stop them, not without using my own magic, which of course I couldn't use because of the spell on me.

"Stop it!" I screamed.

Fear paralyzed me. I wanted to move, to do something, but my tense muscles kept me in place.

A blast hit Shane's arm and knocked him over. A gash on his arm spilled blood onto his robe and armor, and his eyes grew wide.

Tavia stepped forward, summoning a giant flame of magic and aiming it at Shane.

"Don't!" I yelled, running in front of her. She released it at the same second.

The magic hit me in the chest, sending me flying. I screamed as a wave of pain ran through my body, and a second later I hit a wall.

Everything around me disappeared in a heartbeat.

darkness falls
as I do
still waiting
for the Spark
inside.
hoping it will
remain
where I left it
last.
but I know
oh
I know
I never should
have
let
it
go.

Falling ~ by Arely

Chapter 31
Shane

Everything happened in a blur.

I remembered the pain that shot through my arm and how I hit the ground hard. I hadn't been able to focus. Suddenly Octavia shot a blast of magic at me that would have killed me instantly, but it never hit me.

A scream brought me back to my senses and I turned to see Arely hit a wall and crumple to the ground. She lay there, motionless.

Octavia ran past me and dropped down beside her sister. "No, no, no," she said, her voice shaking. Her expression was horrified.

The pain in my arm disappeared as I stumbled over to Arely and knelt down.

Her face was ashy and a trickle of dark red blood ran from her hair down her cheek. But I didn't see where the magic had struck her.

"I don't understand," I mumbled. "If your magic hit her, why doesn't she have any major wounds?"

Tears were running down Octavia's face. "B-because of Tvibura Magic. Twin magic. It's connected, so I can't injure her. But the force of my magic sent her flying into the wall. I have no idea how many bones she could have broken. It's enough to kill her." Octavia's face fell. "It's all my fault. I hit her!"

I held my breath as she reached down to move Arely's hair. There was a wound from where her head had smacked into the wall and blood was running down her neck and cheek.

"She has a skull fracture," Octavia whispered. She bent over to listen to Arely's heartbeat, and after a moment turned to me. "She's still alive. If we both use our magic, maybe we can save her. Can you help me?"

I couldn't help but pause. Octavia was asking me for help? But I nodded. "Of course."

I summoned as much magic as I could and set it to work, hoping and wishing Arely would sit up and smile.

She didn't.

Both of us worked, healing the wounds and broken bones she had gotten from hitting the wall. It didn't occur to me until halfway through what Arely had done.

She had jumped in front of me so that I wouldn't die.

Octavia and I continued to use our magic to try to heal Arely. After a couple minutes, Octavia sat back. "That's it. I think we healed everything."

I stopped my magic and studied Arely. Her skin had returned to its normal color and the blood on her neck had dried, stopping any more blood flow.

But she still lay motionless on the ground.

I realized the rain had calmed down. Only light sprinkles pecked at our backs. I could hear the sounds of our armies fighting outside the broken tower.

"I think she'll be okay..." Octavia said, pushing a strand of hair off her sister's face. She paused and I could tell her mind was at work. She turned to frown at me.

"Wait, why did you care what happened to Arely? You could've just killed me."

I stared at her, unsure of what to say. I opened my mouth, but before I could say anything, a rumble started to shake the ground. It was small at first, but grew so large, I couldn't have stood if I tried.

Chunks of stone fell from the wall above us. I grabbed Arely and pulled her out of the way right before half the wall collapsed into a giant pile of rubble.

Octavia whirled around to look at the battlefield. "What in the world? ...Oh no."

A roar filled the air, swirling around the three of us, in the middle of the shattered marble floor. Octavia's magic extinguished.

Golden wind broke through the darkness, like a tranquil breeze tickling the blades of grass beneath me. But it quickly turned into a harsh gust that threatened to bring the whole tower down upon us.

I covered my head as light exploded everywhere, illuminating the night as if it were day.

I blinked hard, trying to avoid the brightness that had filled my vision. I didn't remember Octavia's magic being golden. How much blood had I lost from my arm? Was I going mad?

Even after the light faded, I couldn't see. Blotches of colors floated in the air, but I had to be alive because I heard Octavia speak.

"You're late," she said.

I rubbed my eyes furiously until I could see the outline of Quay standing a few feet in front of me.

I leapt to my feet, trying not to lose my balance as the ground finally stopped shaking. Blond tufts of hair stuck out of the king's crown. He was much more prepared than I was, for he wore a full set of armor and carried a thick broadsword.

He looked me up and down, a smirk on his lips.

"What are you doing here, Quay?" I yelled, fury racing through me. He had taken Octavia's side in the war?

Quay raised his eyebrows. "The same as you, Shane. I'm here to fight."

Another blast of horns blowing across the field met my ears. I paid close attention to the pattern of the sounds, and after a second, I frowned. That wasn't right—

"Hold on," Octavia said, worry flickering across her face. "There must have been a mistake—"

"There was no mistake," Quay said, eerily calm, and as he spoke, the rain started to pick up again. "I ordered my army to attack both of you."

Behind him, I could barely make out his army as it raced toward my army and Octavia's. In a matter of moments, chaos broke throughout the meadow, with both armies fleeing from the wall of soldiers flooding into the field.

He continued. "I promised you one thing, Octavia. And I'm going to keep that promise. I'm going to kill Shane."

Quay turned and aimed a blast of golden magic at me right as I made a shield. The impact of his magic knocked me over, but I quickly stood back up.

Before I could fully comprehend what I was doing, I jumped to the right and shot a blast at Quay.

He quickly dodged it. I attempted to make a shield again, but my magic crackled and disappeared. I had used almost all of my magic to heal Arely.

Octavia sent a wave that hit Quay in the back and knocked him to his knees, but he stumbled up and aimed another blast at her.

She didn't move fast enough to dodge it and the magic hit her, binding her hands behind her back.

I had enough time to pull my sword out and stand. Quay turned back to me and laughed. "What, did you run out of magic, Shane?" he mocked, sending an orb of magic at me.

I raised my sword and the magic bounced off. It was all I could do, but I wouldn't last long like this.

I stepped back as the blasts nearly pushed me over again, until I hit one of the tower's walls.

Another surge of magic swirled throughout the enclosure, but this time it was blue, not gold. At first it seemed Octavia had made it, but it wasn't the right shade.

But I could see Quay controlling it with his hands. How was that possible? He couldn't have two colors of magic.

When the magic faded, Quay was standing next to Arely. She still lay, limp and bloody. I wished she would stand. I could release the spell on her so she could use her magic against him.

But that wasn't going to happen.

Quay lowered his hand. "You know what, I'll be kind and let you go. You don't deserve it, but I've always been the better king."

I glared at him, not fooled by his words. "I don't believe you. You said you didn't want war, Quay. But you lied."

"Oh, I didn't lie," he replied. "I hate war. That's why I'm going to make sure this is the last war that ever rages in the land."

"That's completely—" I started, but stopped when Quay reached down to Arely. "Wait, don't you dare touch her!" I ran forward but he raised his hand as if he was about to send another bolt of magic at me.

He picked Arely up and threw her over his shoulder.

"What are you doing with her?" I demanded, holding up my blade, which was slick from the rain.

He grinned. "This girl is going to help me take over both of your kingdoms. When I do that, I can rule and make sure no war ever breaks out between the three ever again."

"Let my sister go!" Octavia yelled. "You said you wouldn't let her get hurt."

Quay glanced at her. "I'm not going to hurt her. I'm just going to borrow her magic. After all," he said, looking me in the eyes, "according to Shane, it's okay to use other people for your own plans."

His magic swirled around him and he disappeared before I could stop him.

I wanted to throw my sword into the sky as soon as Quay disappeared with Arely. I wanted to blast the whole lookout tower to ashes with my magic.

How could he come here and try to kill me? How could he do that after all the years we had been friends when we were younger? How could he have changed so much in the past years? But the answers to these questions didn't matter as much as my realization.

I had a new enemy.

"You'll pay for that, Quay!" I yelled into the sky. "You can't do that to me without suffering!"

"Shane!" Octavia shouted at me.

The queen's voice broke me away from my anger. I glanced at her and realized Quay hadn't released her from the magic bond around her wrists.

"Can you help me out here?"

I paused and then walked to her. Using the enchantment on my sword, I sliced the bond and she stood up, breathless.

I walked out of the tower ruins and looked around the meadow. My army was nowhere in sight and neither was Octavia's. Across the field, Quay's soldiers marched home.

I whirled on Octavia, my anger at her renewed. "Why did you tell him to come here?"

She gritted her teeth. "I did it because you wouldn't let my sister go. If he helped me, I would win."

"Well, it looks like we *both* lost instead! And now he has Arely, too." I slid my sword back into its sheath. "To make matters worse, our armies have abandoned us."

"How could I have known he would do that?" Octavia said, defensively. "He's always been against fighting between kingdoms."

Her eyes held years of anger and regret, and I could only imagine what she wanted to do to me. But something held her back, because she crossed her arms and turned away.

I watched the army marching in the distance, dozens of questions racing through my mind. Quay's army was larger than both mine and Octavia's combined. Had he been training soldiers secretly day and night?

His magic was much more powerful than mine. I didn't understand. I had all three Blessings, so no one could have any more power than I did. But *Quay* did.

No one who had magic could disappear and travel from one area to another in a matter of seconds, either.

How was he going to use Arely's magic? Was he going to force her to do what he wanted, or something even worse?

I felt a pang of guilt as I glanced back at Octavia.

She was leaning against the wall, staring at the ground. I realized that must have been what Octavia had asked herself when I had captured Arely. Now she was going through it all again.

"I'm sorry," I said.

She tensed, and then turned toward the west and whistled. A moment later, a chestnut warhorse ran toward us, stopping a few strides away.

"I don't want your apology," Octavia hissed. "You're a selfish, careless halfwit, and if you keep ruining my plans—"

"Oh, right," I said bitterly, "I'm the one who convinced Quay to try and kill us."

She snatched the horn of the saddle and pulled herself onto the horse, prepared to leave.

"Wait," I said. "Quay is our enemy now."

Octavia looked at me, her expression hardened. "Oh, have you only now figured that out?"

"Of course not," I said, resisting the temptation to raise my sword. "But we stand no chance of defeating him because he's somehow broken the rules of magic."

She laid the reins down, her mind at work. "What are you suggesting?"

"That we work together. Until Arely's safe."

Octavia threw me a suspicious glance. "I am not forming an alliance with you."

"I never said an alliance," I said. "But we have a common enemy, and we need him out of the way to properly deal with our own kingdoms' problems."

She gazed at the meadow, silent for a few minutes.

"I agree," she finally admitted. "We'll form a truce until we deal with Quay. After that, our war will resume. Do you agree?"

"Yes," I said, holding my hand out. "For a truce?"

She hesitantly took my hand and shook it. "For a truce."

"We need to gather our armies," I said, starting to walk toward my horse, who was munching on a patch of grass.

Octavia shook her head. "No. First we need to figure out a plan. If we get the basic idea for a plan, we can go from there."

I put my foot into the stirrup and jumped into the saddle. A stab of pain raced through my arm, and I realized it was soaked in blood. I had completely forgotten about my wound.

I looked back at Octavia, trying not to show any pain. "We'll gather our armies and then devise a plan."

"You can't have control of everything, Shane," she said, putting her hands on her hips. "That isn't very thought-out anyway."

"I can give it more detail once I'm out of this horrid rain," I said, coming up with an excuse other than my throbbing arm. "I don't enjoy being drenching wet." I picked up the reins and made Triballi back up.

"Neither do I. But we have more pressing issues."

"If we wait to create a plan, we can do it better," I said, annoyed. Perhaps this truce wasn't going to work out. "We don't even know what Quay is up to," I continued. "We should send spies to check out his kingdom before we do anything else."

She looked in the direction of his castle and sighed. "You might be right about that, but we can't take long. Quay could to anything to Arely, and I don't want her to get hurt anymore."

"How about a week? Two days to travel, five days to spy? In the meantime, we can come up with several plans at Fort Oak. When the spies tell us everything they know, we can choose the best one for an attack."

Octavia nodded. "All right. That's a good plan for now."

She turned her horse around to face Rivallen. "We've got a deal. But one more thing..." she said.

"What?" I asked.

"Please quit calling me Octavia. It's giving me a migraine. If we're going to pretend to get along for the next few weeks, you need to call me by my nickname."

"Great..." I said, sarcastically.

She took off without another word. I touched my arm, the dark blood dripping from my fingertips. The wound needed to be bandaged immediately, but I didn't have any medics near. I had to get back to the castle.

And this time, Arely wouldn't be with me.

Chapter 32
Arely

At first, all I could feel was pain.

Everything around me was black. I couldn't see.

My memory blurred and faded, then came back like a lightning bolt.

I was a lifeless rock, sinking to the bottom of a lake or stream, but something was holding me, keeping me from going any farther.

I coughed, blinking. Light started to enter my vision.

There were gray walls to my left and right. Figures stood in the corners and by the one entrance in front of me. I tried to focus on them to see who they were, but exhaustion kept me from doing so.

A warm cloth was pressed against my head, and a medic spoke softly, but I couldn't tell what she was saying.

I realized a person was sitting a few steps in front of me.

I blinked hard and finally everything in my vision started to clear.

A man sat staring at me. He had blond hair, only a little darker than mine. His expression made me uncomfortable. It was almost like he was reading my mind.

"W-who are you?" I asked, wrinkling my nose. Was I supposed to know this person? Was he a friend or an enemy?

"I am King Quay, but you shall refer to me as Your Majesty."

"King Quay?" I scrunched my forehead. That name sounded so familiar, but I couldn't think of where I'd heard it before.

"I bet you want to know what happened to Tavia and Shane," he said. His voice was kinder now. He even smiled. "Right?"

"I'm not sure who you are talking about," I said, slowly.

The guards around us started chuckling. My skin grew warm as my gaze flitted around the room. Why was that so hilarious?

"Shush, all of you," Quay said, turning to his guards. He looked back at me. "I'm sorry about that. They aren't nice, are they? Tavia is your sister and Shane is... well, he's an enemy."

"Oh." I took a deep breath. "Why can't I remember anything?"

"That might be because of a little accident a couple hours ago," he replied, glancing at the medic. She stood and left the room, finished with her work.

"I found you wounded in a lookout tower ruin," Quay continued. "It seems you were knocked unconscious by getting hit in the head. I'm not exactly sure how it all happened, but we brought you here and now you're healing."

I nodded, realizing how much my head hurt as the numbness faded away. He was right. "So... where is my sister? ...Tavia?"

"Oh, she is in another kingdom. I'm afraid she can't come visit right now, but she knows you are here. You are safe in Greyston, Arely."

I hesitated. "Thank you."

I looked around the room again. My mind was still a little foggy, but as time passed, I became more aware of my senses. I was exhausted and hungry, and my body felt heavy. I wanted to sink to the floor and lie down, but I couldn't.

I looked to my left and right and realized my problem. Both my wrists were chained to two metal poles on each side of me. The cuffs were made of thick iron.

"What are you doing to me?" I said, starting to panic. This place didn't feel right. "Why am I chained up?"

He put his hand up. "Arely! Calm down," he said, soothingly. "Don't panic. Look, I'm not going to hurt you." He looked into my eyes, but I couldn't relax. "Do you want the kingdoms to stop fighting? Do you want the war to end and everyone to be happy again? Aren't you sick of all the arguing and killing?"

I paused, beginning to remember the war going on in the land. There were three kingdoms, I thought. Yes. And two of them couldn't stop fighting. Mine... and Shane's.

"Yes," I whispered. "And I want my parents back."

A look of sorrow passed through his eyes. "I'm sorry about your parents, Arely. I know you loved them. But now we need to focus on saving the people who are in danger. Your kingdom needs you. I have a plan to end this war – and prevent *all* future wars – but I need your help to do that."

I frowned. "Is that even possible?"

"It is possible, with a team and hard work." He gave me a smile. "What do you say?"

"What's your plan?" I asked, first.

He nodded. "That's fair. Okay, I'll tell you. Because you are my ally, our kingdoms won't fight. But we have one enemy, and that's Shane. He loves war and he'll start a new one even if we end the current one. If we can get rid of his threat, then we can manage the three kingdoms and make sure no war ever starts again! So our goal is simple: assassinate Shane and take over his kingdom."

I thought about his offer. "Are you sure Shane only wants war?"

"Yes," Quay said. "I've known him since he was little and he did the most horrible things you'd ever imagine to people. You and your kingdom have been at war with him for years."

"Then I'll help you," I said, "if it means my people are safe."

"Can you let me out of these chains?" I asked Quay. "We're allies now."

He paused. "There is a problem with that idea. I can't let you out because you need to heal more. You are still injured."

I stared at him, my eyebrows scrunched. "I don't understand. How is being chained up going to heal me?" I glanced at the thick poles. On the front side, a pink glow came from it, creating a fuzzy haze. "Is that my magic?" I asked.

"Yes," Quay answered. "It's, uh, hard to explain. You see, a couple of my inventors came up with the design recently, and I'm not an inventor, so whenever they try to explain it to me, I don't understand a word they speak. But it takes your magic and heals you. I'm afraid it's quite slow, though, so you might be here for awhile."

I stared at the poles, trying to wrap my head around it. "Okay, but why can't you heal me by letting me rest in a comfortable bed? This is the opposite of comfortable, if you haven't noticed."

"Arely, listen. You weren't injured in a normal way, so you can't heal the normal way. I have a suspicion you were struck by another royal's magic, which means it must have been Shane who hurt you. However, I wasn't there, so I don't know for a fact what happened. But you were close to dead. This mechanism will monitor how you are doing."

I nodded. "All right."

"I'm sorry it's not comfortable. Maybe I'll have a servant get a pillow. And I'll have to tell the inventors to change its design, for sure. But for now, I have a question for you: Are you hungry?"

A ghost of a smile crossed my lips. He had a weird seriousness to him, and he could say something and sound so deadpan. "Yes," I said. "Very."

"Okay." He turned to the guards behind him. "Go fetch a bowl of hot tomato soup and bring a glass of cold water too." They obeyed and he turned away. "There, Arely. Hopefully that will make you feel better. You can start getting your memory back as well."

"I hope," I said.

Quay stood up. "I have work to do now. I will come and check on you later. If you need anything, you can ask the guards. I'll have one of them bring a pillow too and you can get a little rest."

He walked out the door and disappeared. I wondered if I had known him before this accident a few hours ago. His name sounded familiar, so I suppose I had. Either way, he seemed all right and if he wanted to stop the war in the land, he had to be good.

Chapter 33
Shane

My arm and side were soaked in blood by the time I collapsed on the floor of the royal stable. The medics who had been waiting by the door ran to me.

My head was spinning, and I realized I had underestimated the urgency to care for my wound. I had pressed a cloth against it while riding toward the castle, but the blood had soaked through in only a couple minutes.

I groaned as a medic grabbed my arm to examine it, and soon, several others had surrounded me. I glanced at the wound as one of them pulled away the cloth, revealing slightly burnt, inflamed skin covered in dark blood that continued to dribble down my arm.

A medic pulled out a small knife and cut away at the fabric. The chainmail was high enough that it didn't get in her way.

I rested my head against the stone wall, closed my eyes, and let the medics work. After a little while, the medics had cleansed the wound as best as they could and wrapped clean bandages around it.

A hand rested on my shoulder and I opened my eyes to see that General Collins had sat on the floor next to me. His forehead was wrinkled, as if he had aged several years in the past hours.

"What happened to your arm?" he asked. "And where's Arely? Didn't she go with you?"

I didn't meet his eyes. "Quay took her."

Collins frowned, and I glanced at him as he said, "But what about Octavia?"

"We made a temporary alliance," I replied, forcing myself to sit up. My arm ached, but I stood anyway and Collins did the same. "Tomorrow we're going to visit Fort Oak and devise a plan."

"Are you sure, Your Majesty? You don't look well enough to make that trip again," Collins said, following me as I slowly made my way toward the doorway. I could feel the medics' eyes on me.

"I'll make it. Don't worry about me."

The next morning, it was agreed that General Collins and several of the lords would accompany me to Fort Oak to talk to Tavia. I needed everyone's help to plan.

We were halfway to the fort. The day was clear and blue. The grass was drying from the thunderstorm the night before, so the knights and I kept the horses at a trot so they wouldn't slip.

We reached the tower an hour later.

Tavia was already there, sitting inside the kitchen area drinking something brown that smelled like tea. She stood up when I entered.

"I've sent spies down to Greyston," she said. Her body was rigid, as if it took all her strength to stand still and speak evenly.

"So have I." I sat across the table from her seat. "I told them to return before a week was over."

Tavia walked to a desk with a large piece of parchment on it. She picked it up and brought it for me to see.

It was labeled Greyston and had the layouts of a castle. Each detailed level showed a description of how it was used. I could see the kitchen area, the gardens, the ballroom, as well as the king's quarters. It was exactly how I remembered it.

"Whoa, where did you get this?" I asked.

Tavia smirked. "My father had a giant collection of maps. I guess the space they took up will be worth it now." She pointed to a list in the corner. "I wrote all the possible obstacles we could run into if we tried to enter. He has a force field, I'm sure, plus a moat, and several walls between the castle and the outside towns."

"That's correct," I said.

She sat down. "The only way we'll be able to get Arely back is if we attack the castle. If he didn't have her, I'd say we should lure him from the castle and attack him... but this map will be crucial to our planning if we want to go with the first plan."

"This map lacks one thing," I said, sitting back in my chair and crossing my arms. "It doesn't have the secret tunnels and hideouts. That's going to be a problem for you."

Tavia frowned. "Well, of course it doesn't. What do you expect me to do about that?"

"I know all the secret tunnels because Quay showed them to me years ago. So I'll lead the way when we reach the castle."

She rolled her eyes. "Fine. As long as you don't get us caught and killed."

"His army was huge, too," I said, changing the subject. "I have around five thousand men, and you have around three thousand, right?"

Tavia narrowed her eyes at me as if wondering whether she should give me that information. "...Yes."

"Well, it looked like he had more knights than both of our armies combined. Although his kingdom is bigger, I don't understand how he has such a large army."

She nodded grimly.

"If we must go inside his castle, we will have to do it alone. We can send our armies to attack at a certain time and distract the kingdom's army," I said.

Tavia ran her finger over the map. "I suppose so. I also thought we could disguise ourselves and come in from the town. It could be easier, depending on what his rules for villagers entering and leaving the castle are. Then we wouldn't have to deal with the moat, and probably won't run into as much trouble with guards until we're farther inside."

I rested my arm on the table, my gaze falling on the throne room. "I... I feel he wanted to lure us to the castle by taking Arely, and he wants to weaken us by fighting in his territory. He doesn't have much experience in war, so he'll want to disorient us and use tactics no one else has."

I glanced at her.

"Then we'll keep our guard," she said, uneasily. "I agree with you, but we can't worry too much about it."

The generals from both kingdoms joined us at the table as I pondered her idea to sneak through the village. If we did worry about it, we risked not moving fast enough.

Within a couple minutes, papers and ink jars covered every inch of the wood as we brainstormed a plan for distracting Quay and entering the castle.

We discussed different strategies, listing the pros and cons. This resulted in arguments multiple times. The generals and lords didn't want to reveal any secret tactics to each other and I wasn't used to planning with Tavia.

We eventually had to take a break, to eat or stretch or get a breath of fresh air. But we didn't rest for long, and came straight back to the table to continue planning.

The sun was setting in the sky once I called it a night. Tavia agreed. It would be a long ride home and I needed to rest.

We had created a dozen different plans, many of which would probably never work and were therefore useless, but a couple we had devised were promising.

Tavia and I decided not to meet the next two days. Instead, we would begin to prepare our armies for whatever plan we chose.

On the third day, we would meet at Fort Maple. We would go over the plans and see if we could improve them at all. It was all we could do until the spies arrived to our kingdoms with all the information we needed.

Once they arrived, we would be well set on our way to winning this new war.

My horse trudged through the thick field of grass toward my castle. Night had fallen and hundreds of stars shown in the sky. Behind me, all my bodyguards followed after, not making a sound.

I rubbed my jaw, feeling the ache from clenching my teeth all day. How I had managed to be around Tavia for a whole day, I had no idea.

The lights shining from within my castle dwindled as people headed to bed. I could feel myself growing tired and I longed to be in my own room, reading.

Time hadn't slowed in the past few weeks and now I could feel the effects of it all hitting me. However, I did my best to ignore it.

I studied my castle as we drew nearer. The catapults sat on the top of the walls and guard towers dotted the area. No doubt one of the knights had spotted us in the distance and reported to a leader.

I wondered how well protected Quay's castle was. Had he done as much work as I had to create a secure place for the royal family and servants to live? He had a force field, but did he have anything else?

I bet he would tell me he hadn't done a single thing to the castle because he didn't fear attack, but he could easily lie.

I couldn't think of that now. It was stressful and I already had enough to worry about.

I tried to relax my jaw by taking a deep breath. I looked back at my castle.

With the moon's glow reflecting off the opposite walls, the brick towers created a massive silhouette hovering in front of us.

I had a strange feeling of smallness. The castle radiated power – as I had always hoped it would – and its creeping shadows swamped us in pitch black.

But it had never made me feel insignificant, as it did now.

"Why are you so different?" I whispered quietly, so no one else heard but me. "I've seen you a million times."

The castle only grew larger as we rode our horses closer.

I pulled on the reins and Triballi came to a standstill. My bodyguards stopped a few yards behind.

"Is something wrong, my King?" one of them asked.

"No," I said. "Go to the castle. I'll be there shortly."

They didn't argue, but headed into the darkness that shrouded the edges of the castle walls.

Triballi stomped his foot impatiently.

"Stop," I said, patting his neck. "Give me a moment, boy."

I watched the castle as the wind whistled past me, sending shivers through my body. Even with candles lighting the windows, it looked like a lonely, foreboding place to live. What used to be home was in question.

I could only imagine what Arely had thought when she learned she was stuck in Rapora Castle. Probably not the happiest thought.

The castle kept all unwanted people out, using armies, weapons, and magic. A person couldn't get in easily if they weren't allowed, and many weren't.

And to top that, the inside wasn't welcoming either if the person was a stranger. What would they do without knowing the customs and rules of the palace? He or she would get out before anything bad happened to them, if they were smart.

It was no wonder to me why I'd never had allies before. I had created a castle that shut people out, preventing anybody from hurting me.

This thought wandered through my mind the rest of the ride home. Triballi knew the way to the castle perfectly and I didn't have to pay much attention to guide him in the right direction.

When I finally entered the castle grounds and walked into the stable, I took care of Triballi's needs for the night and put him in his stall.

I was exhausted by the time I stumbled through the hallways. All I wanted was my warm, comfortable bed.

Halfway through my walk, however, a guard strode over to me. "Your Majesty," he said. "I found something in Arely's cell that you will probably want."

I scrunched my forehead, not sure what on earth he could be talking about.

He held out a circle of silver embedded with a blue gem, and I realized it was the queen's ring.

Her ring.

I lifted it up, letting the light catch the heart-shape. The edges weren't scratched or chipped, but I hadn't expected them to be.

"I guess she must have thrown it," the guard said. "It was lying on the floor."

I couldn't suppress the disappointment that filled me. Of course she had thrown it. Why wouldn't she?

"Thanks," I mumbled to the guard.

I sighed and slid the ring onto my own finger. Maybe once I found Arely and we left Greyston, she would take it and wear it again. Until then, I needed to keep it safe.

Chapter 34
Arely

I had no idea how long I had been chained to the peculiar glowing mechanism. I still felt exhausted, though it was supposed to help me.

Quay must've been wrong about the device. It couldn't possibly heal me if I felt worse and worse the longer I was attached to it.

I needed to tell him to let me off it. Perhaps this one was broken. Or maybe the whole invention was a fail. Whatever it was, I needed to lie down in a soft bed and sleep.

My head ached. It pounded as if someone was hitting me in the back of the head.

I looked up at the guards. "Let me off this thing," I mumbled. "Please, it's making me worse."

"We need Quay's permission to let you go," one of the guards replied calmly.

"No, you don't understand," I pleaded, my headache growing more painful. "I feel completely ill."

"I'm sorry, Arely, but that's not possible."

"Then go get King Quay! I'll tell him how I feel and he will see that I shouldn't be attached to these poles."

The guard slowly nodded. "All right. That's fair." He turned and walked out of the room, but all the other guards stayed with me.

I closed my eyes and tried to breathe deeply. The headache didn't want to go away, it seemed. I had no idea what happened when I'd gotten injured, but it had been serious.

After a while, the guard came back with Quay following him. The king looked unconcerned and walked without urgency. His white cloak swished across the floor.

A whole new wave of nausea crashed over me and everything swam in my vision.

"Quay!" I whispered. "I can't be on this thing anymore. It's hurting me."

He stopped in his steps. "What do you mean?"

"I am sick. I'm worse than before and I feel like I might throw up," I admitted. "This device isn't working. I need to lie down in a bed. Please!"

He frowned and stared at one of the glowing poles. Its pinkish light faded away, and I shook my head.

"What's going on?" I asked in bewilderment.

Quay waved my question away. "All right. I'll let you off it, since it doesn't appear to be working for you."

I breathed a sigh of relief as he unhooked the cuffs and dropped them to the floor. As he stood, he offered me his hand, and I took it.

He helped me up, and although I was a bit wobbly, I stood and rubbed my wrists, looking over at Quay.

"There is something incredibly wrong with that mechanism of yours," I said, straightening myself. "It didn't help my injuries at all."

"I'm sorry about that, Arely," Quay said. "Perhaps you would like to come meet my family so they can take care of you."

"But... what about helping you? With the war?"

He shook his head. "We'll wait till you feel better."

"That sounds good," I said, taking a deep breath.

King Quay's castle was spectacular. I wondered if all castles were this amazing, or if his was the most magnificent. As hard as I tried to remember my own castle, I couldn't think of a single detail, which puzzled me.

The windows fluttered with colorful drapes, the sun glowed against the polished-white tile of the floors, and the halls bustled with maids and knights.

I wanted to stick around and wander the palace, but Quay ushered me quickly through the hallways and into a large room with a half dozen people inside. There was a row of beds by one wall, a fireplace, a desk with several bookshelves near it, and a dining table. Another door on the far side must have led to a washroom.

"Whoa," I said, taking it all in.

A little girl sat next to a roaring fire, poking at the kindling. A man cleared the table of used plates and cups. A young lady sat on the side of a bed, next to a little boy who appeared to be sleeping.

As soon as Quay and I walked in, most of them turned to look at us. I counted seven people in all.

"Arely, this is my family," Quay said. "My mother, my three sisters, and my three brothers."

I brushed my hair behind my ear, a slight memory flickering through my mind. "But... don't you have a wife and son?" I asked.

He nodded. "Yes, but they are in another kingdom right now, doing visits with other royals and such."

When I didn't say anything else, Quay nudged me forward. "You should go meet them. I have to go, but you can stay here with my family for as long as you need."

Without another word, he left and shut the door behind him. A second later, it clicked.

As long as you need, I thought. I wasn't sure I wanted to stay here that long.

I bit my lip, unsure of what to do. In the corner, sitting at a desk and writing on a piece of parchment, was a woman in a green gown. She looked like the mother.

I hurried over to her.

"Queen Osanna!" I said, beaming because I had remembered her name. I dropped into a curtsy. "It is an honor to meet you, Your Majesty."

She looked up at me, dully, as if she was exhausted and nothing could surprise her anymore. "Oh, aren't you one of Allister's twins? The younger one?"

"Y-yes. I'm Queen Arely."

She bobbed her head, then tilted it, concerned. "Are you all right, darling?"

I tried to smile, but I couldn't. "I feel a little ill," I admitted, touching my forehead.

Osanna stood and led me to one of the beds in the room. "How do you feel?" she asked as I sat on a mattress draped with a red quilt.

"Like I have a fever. But it's on and off. I also have a horrible headache from hitting my head a few days ago..."

"I see." Queen Osanna pulled out a corner of the blanket and I climbed under the cool covers. As I laid down, I closed my eyes.

"There." Osanna's voice was quiet as she pulled the quilt around me. "You're not the only one who's sick. Lily and Rafi have been sick for several weeks now."

I opened my eyelids enough to see her, my curiosity piqued. "Do you know what they have?"

She pursed her lips, silent for a moment. "Maybe. But I don't know for sure." She glanced at me. "Do you still have your magic?"

I blinked, surprised I hadn't thought about it since arriving at the castle. I pulled my hand out from underneath the blanket, and tried to create a spark of magic. Nothing happened. I didn't feel the usual tingle of magic underneath my skin. It was as if I'd never had magic at all.

I sat up, confused. "Did I... lose my magic when I hurt my head?"

Osanna watched me, but didn't offer an answer.

I knew that royals had lost their magic from getting injured before, but I'd never imagined it happening to *me*.

"You need sleep. I'll get you clean clothes to change into," she said, glancing at the muddy fabric of my dress.

Too tired to wait, I closed my eyes. It only took a few moments to drift into sleep, and I must have slept for a good while because when I opened my eyes again, the room was dark and a couple candles flickered on the table. Two people were awake.

I turned in the bed and spotted the rest of Quay's family sleeping on the other beds in the room. I wondered which beds Lily and Rafi were sleeping in.

Osanna had laid out a dress at the end of my bed. It was a plain yellow nightgown, nothing fancy, but I was happy to see a clean dress to change into.

Osanna apparently heard me wake up, because she stood from the table and walked over to me. "Do you feel better?" she asked.

I shook my head. "I'm still dizzy and tired. I may need help putting the gown on..."

She picked up the dress and helped me change from my muddy, blue dress into the new one. It was strange, because although I hadn't recovered my memory, I felt completely comfortable around Quay's mother, like she was my own mother.

I wiped the sleep from my eyes, and as I did, my stomach growled.

"We have fruits at the table," she said, pointing at a large bowl filled to the brim.

I happily stood, though slowly, and walked to the table. The man I had seen clearing the table was bent over a book, reading.

I sat down and picked an apple from the woven basket. Now that I held it, I realized how hungry I was. Without taking the time to slice it up, I took a bite.

Quay's brother looked at me. "You might be stuck here for a while," he said, rather ominously.

"Why will I be stuck here?" I asked.

He closed his book. "My brother's been different. Ever since Father died. I'm not sure I trust him anymore." He squinted. "Did you notice?"

I frowned. "No. I'm afraid I can't remember much."

"Oh." He tilted his head. "Well, everything's been strange lately. And then my two younger siblings started getting sick, and I haven't felt well myself..."

Osanna took her seat next to me, her expression stiff as she looked at her son.

I took a breath and leaned forward. "Please, Your Majesty. If you will, can you tell me more about the illness they have?"

She gripped the fabric of her dress, and began to shake her head, but I spoke.

"I've been studying illnesses for years. There's not enough information in our kingdoms and the people need to understand what they're up against."

Osanna regarded me carefully. "It's no ordinary illness, Queen Arely."

"So it's rare?"

"More than that. Only royals can get it, if my observations are correct." She untangled her hands from the dress and reached for a tattered book. "It's called the *Vorlenmagie* Illness, or the Lost Magic Illness. I only found this book about it in the library, and as you can see, it's falling apart."

I pulled out my leather notebook, wanting to write this down for later reference.

Osanna continued, looking through the window. "I noticed Rafi and Lily's fevers weren't normal. We knew they had lost their magic, of course, but I had never heard about this disease. I began studying it and realized that they only showed signs of it."

I glanced up. "What do you mean?"

"They don't actually have the illness," she answered. "Yet. It's as if some invisible force is keeping them right on the edge of life and death."

"But how could they *not* have it?"

"That's the part I don't understand."

I sat in silence, thinking it over. I didn't have any experience with magic-related illnesses, although my other experiences with diseases could help.

I placed my notebook back in my pocket, having only one question left.

"How did they lose their magic?" I asked.

Osanna pursed her lips, unwilling to speak. She met her son's gaze, but I couldn't read whatever passed between them. They either didn't know or weren't ready to answer.

Deciding not to press the matter anymore, I stood. "I'm heading back to bed, if you don't mind."

"Wait!" Quay's brother said. He glanced at the row of beds, then back at me. "Just don't take anything for granted."

I frowned, paying attention to his warning. I knew he was talking about his brother again, so I said, "What's Quay doing now? Do you know?"

"Yes, actually," he replied, cautiously, folding his arms. "He said he's going to attack our enemy. Doubtless he's leaving to attack King Shane as we speak."

Chapter 35
Shane

Time flew by as my castle and army prepared for the upcoming battles. I found myself lost in the process. It was easy to go from knight to knight, making sure all the people in charge were ready and prepared for whatever might happen next.

I was so lost in the rhythm, in fact, that the cooks had to stop me and ask if I'd eaten at all, which I hadn't. This wasn't terribly uncommon for me when a new battle was coming up, however.

By the time night arrived and I had finished all my tasks, I took one more long walk around the castle, seeing that everything was well for the night. I was pleased to see the castle in top order.

That finally soothed my energy. I had done enough that day, and I'd have a new set of tasks the next day... but for now I had more than earned myself a good night's rest.

I headed to my room, ready to sleep. Within a couple minutes, I lit a fire and crawled under the blankets of my bed. It took only seconds to fall asleep, but I didn't sleep for long.

Slivers of dreams drifted through my mind, and the ones that did come to me left me restless and uncomfortable. There was something wrong – something I didn't know.

I slept only a couple hours before that *something* disturbed my sleep.

It was dark when I awoke. The stars were out and the sun wouldn't rise for many hours. I had a feeling it wasn't past midnight. Maybe the pressure of the upcoming battles had awakened me.

I sat up in my bed. The strange feeling that something wasn't right crept over me again. And then my magic began sending me a warning. There was an unwanted presence in the kingdom...

It was Quay.

I raced to the balcony, where the shockingly cold wind sent a chill down my spine. He was there. At the bottom of the castle, Quay's golden magic disappeared and I spotted the tiny figure that replaced it.

I couldn't really see him, but I knew it was him thanks to the magic.

His massive army stood behind him, unmoving at first, and then charged toward the castle walls.

I threw open the doors and raced from my room.

"Quay is attacking!" I yelled to the guards. "Go, wake everyone as fast as you can!"

I ran down the stairs, nearly tripping and falling multiple times. The lookout towers must have missed his army. It hid perfectly in the dark and I would never have seen the mass of soldiers if I hadn't known they were there. Quay, of course, hadn't appeared until now.

We couldn't protect the castle with our knights. The walls were our best protection at this point, and with all of Quay's magic, I didn't know if they stood a chance.

I reached the knights' section in the dungeons and found many of them were already rushing about. One of the lookout guards must have seen Quay appear and alerted the knights.

I found the chief knight giving orders to his men.

"Get everyone into their positions along the walls," I told him. "We will use the catapults against the army. It's our best option."

The chief followed my orders and started gathering the knights.

I had to use my magic to defend the castle. I ran up a flight of stairs to the innermost wall and burst into the cold air once again. I stood on a platform overlooking the approaching army.

It wouldn't be long before they reached the castle.

I started to summon my magic. A flaming orb slowly formed in front of me like a small star, casting a red glow across my skin. I had to focus on the magic and nothing else.

The castle walls needed extra protection, in the place where Quay's army was headed. I spread the magic out and sent it flying toward the castle walls standing before the large army. "Make the walls stronger," I whispered.

For a second, the walls appeared to burn with my touch, but the magic disappeared inside as if I hadn't done a thing. I needed to reserve my remaining magic.

Knights filed into the wall's tunnel, where the catapults were located. A snap filled the silent air and a boulder flew into the sky and plummeted onto the soldiers, though they continued forward.

The force field rippled as the army plunged through it.

Either my castle was about to survive a brutal attack or I was going to learn about escaping through the tunnels built underneath it.

Boulders rained down as smoke billowed from the stone walls, making it even harder to see in the dark.

A voice rang out behind me. "My lord! You need to get into the bunker!"

I turned to see Tad standing in the entrance of the stairway.

"I've never gone in there for an attack," I said. "I need to see what's happening so I can use my magic against Quay and his army. I can't leave my knights to fight alone."

Tad fidgeted, eyeing the battle below. "King Shane, you have to come inside. He's going to get in no matter what. The last thing we need is for him to enter while you're still here. We'll take the escape tunnels into the meadow. The castle is already being evacuated."

I looked back at the massive army. Thousands of knights attempted to move around or climb the wall. The years spent fortifying the castle were being tested. I hoped my work had been enough.

"Give me a few minutes," I said to Tad. "He might not get in."

I frowned at the scene. Is this why Quay hadn't killed me when he had the chance? Had he planned to attack my castle all along? I couldn't imagine what his other plans could be. He was unpredictable.

An explosion of gold magic crashed into the wall and stones flew into the air, leaving a gaping hole in the border wall.

I watched, in dread, as the army flooded into my kingdom.

Tad grabbed my arm and pulled me toward the stairs. "You must come. I swore to your parents I'd protect you and I'm keeping my promise."

I followed him down the stairs into the chaotic castle. People swarmed everywhere, trying to escape.

We pushed through the crowd, heading to the dungeon stairs. With all the panic, I wasn't sure if we'd be able to navigate our way to the bunker.

Battles had never made me nervous, but the fact that I was escaping from an enemy with magic much more powerful than mine made a difference. My heart raced as we squeezed past dozens of people. Would we make it to the stairs? Would Quay find us first?

I barely recognized the door that led to the dungeon. Tad had to pull it open and usher me in before I could accidentally pass it.

The dim torchlight made it difficult to see, but I ran down the stairs nonetheless.

More explosions rang overhead and I winced.

We reached the end of the stairs and had to find another set of stairs to reach the bunker. I darted to the door and fumbled to find the keys in one of the stone crevices.

Once I found it, I unlocked the door and let Tad in, then rushed down the rest of the steps.

I ran into dozens of spider webs and realized how long it had been since my family had used the bunker. It'd been abandoned for eight years.

Igniting my magic, I let light bounce across the tunnel and clear the webs.

After several minutes, I came to another door and had to unlock it as well. When I opened it, I came into a minuscule chamber.

Four old mattresses sat in the corners of the room, and by the smell, water had soaked into the fabric and mold had grown inside.

With Tad's help, I pulled one of the mattresses out of the way to reveal the tiny entrance to the second escape tunnel. This one led to the meadow, while the first one led to the village.

I tugged at the rusty, metal door until it flew open. I stared at the hole, my claustrophobia threatening to change my mind. Water dripped from the top, leaving a small stream underneath. I wasn't sure if I would fit, because the tunnel was jagged and dark, with a tight entrance.

"How long is this tunnel?" I asked Tad, my stomach tightening.

"Uh, maybe two thousand feet long?" he answered.

"Oh no," I groaned. "Why didn't my father make it wider? Maybe a little less... wet?"

"He never thought he'd need it." Tad stepped in front of me. "Shane, I won't be able to fit inside the tunnel. You know the tunnel leads to a horse stable outside of the castle grounds. The people there will give you a horse to ride. You must go to Rivallen."

I nodded. "All right."

"The army and castle will be destroyed. But you and Octavia must go and fight Quay. We need you to stop him."

"I will do my best." I handed Tad the keys to the bunker. "Thanks. And Tad, take care of yourself."

The old man smiled. "I will."

I unhooked my cape and crouched next to the tunnel, taking a deep breath.

I pulled myself through the hole and started crawling through the narrow space. I couldn't see anything in front of me, but I didn't want to use more magic in case I needed it later.

As I crawled, slimy objects rubbed against my skin, hanging from the tunnel. Spider webs stuck in my hair and on my face, convincing me that a spider was skittering down my back. I tried to keep from gagging, but that was impossible. I had to get out of here.

At one point, I heard squeaks and knew I would run into a rat soon, and I did. I bumped into its fuzzy body and pulled back.

With one spark of my magic, it fell over, dead.

"Yuck," I hissed.

I climbed over it hurriedly and continued up the narrow tunnel.

I scraped my arms and elbows against the ragged rocks so many times, I had to be bleeding, but the adrenaline kept me from feeling any pain.

I felt like I'd been in the tunnel forever by the time I reached the trap door. I pushed it open and climbed into another dark area, like a space under a porch.

A slit of light shone under a small door, which led into a house, and apparently the kitchen.

"Good heavens!" a voice exclaimed as I stood up, gasping. A woman rushed to me, wrinkles forming on her forehead. "King Shane! Is the castle under attack?"

"Yes," I panted. I shook myself, making sure there weren't any spider webs left on me. "And I need a horse."

"Of course!" she said. "Billy! Go fetch the best horse, fast!" She grabbed a towel from the table and gave it to me.

I wiped the slime and water off my skin. "That is the worst escape tunnel," I muttered. "Ever."

A boy and man appeared at the door.

The man stepped forward. "The best horse is already saddled. You were lucky, because we were about to use him. I'm sure you will find he is a great horse, my King."

He bowed.

"Thank you," I said. The man took me outside, showing me a dark brown steed in the pasture.

I mounted the horse without a word.

"May I ask what your plan is, Your Majesty?" he asked.

"I'm going to Rivallen," I answered. "Tavia and I will attack Greyston tomorrow. There's no reason to wait."

"Then I won't keep you." He stepped back and I nudged the horse into a gallop.

The castle burned behind me. Even at my distance, I could see the bright flames that climbed the towers.

My kingdom wouldn't last long.

I pulled myself closer to the horse as it ran faster.

Rivallen slowly grew larger in my vision. Tavia was my only hope now.

Chapter 36
Arely

The night was bitter cold. The raging wind beat upon the stonework of the castle. Windows were locked up tight, doors closed and barricaded. Everyone wanted to keep the cold out and light a fire to warm themselves up.

It was the first night I felt the true effects of fall. It was here.

I wrapped myself in a blanket and turned to glance at the sleeping figures in the room. I had spent much time with Quay's family and gotten to know them better. They had made me a little spot to stay with them while I continued to recover.

My sickness had been coming and going throughout the night. It didn't make sense, but at least I felt well for the moment.

It seemed everyone else was asleep, and I would have been too, if the young man's words hadn't bothered me so much.

"He's going to attack Shane."

I don't know why this bothered me so. It was as if I had forgotten something important – something just beyond my memory.

I picked up the ends of my blanket and bent down beside the wooden door, peeking through the keyhole.

Guards were stationed outside. My heart flipped in my chest. They weren't there to protect us, but to keep us inside. Did Quay distrust his family so much as to keep them prisoners?

But after a moment, it appeared they were all fast asleep. However long they'd been guarding this door, they must've decided the royal family had given up escape.

I couldn't disturb their slumber, not if I wanted to find any answers to my questions.

I quietly pushed the door, slipping out. The corridor was empty, at least at the moment. I tiptoed through the deserted hallways, not sure where I was or if I'd run into people.

If I did, what would they do? Would they know I'd left the royal quarters without permission?

I hugged the quilt closer to me as the chill in the air nipped at my skin.

"Arely?" a voice said, the sound echoing throughout the hall.

I whipped around. Quay stepped up a long flight of steps. His bodyguards, who watched me warily, surrounded him.

Quay's armor had blood running down it and the sight made me freeze.

"Where have you been all day, Y-your Majesty?" I asked. "I didn't know whether I should see you again."

He glanced at his guards as he walked. "I've been... fighting in a battle."

"Really?" I said, taking a step back. "What happened?"

The King frowned as he made it to the top. "I attacked Shane's castle and destroyed it."

"Is Shane... dead?"

"Unfortunately, he escaped."

"Oh." I tightened my blanket around me, wondering what this meant for my kingdom.

"You should get to bed," Quay said, ushering me back the way I had come. "I have a feeling tomorrow will bring lots of work. For you and for me. There are more battles on their way, after all."

He walked me all the way to his family's room again and said good night. I hesitantly entered the room. But as soon as I pressed my back against the cold oak door, I had the same feeling from before: the feeling that I had missed something.

I peeked into the hallway, watching as Quay left for his own bedroom. His bodyguards weren't looking back.

Abandoning my blanket on the floor, I squeezed through the door and followed silently. Quay was murmuring to a man who appeared to be an adviser. I assumed that he was telling him how the battle had gone.

Quay didn't go straight to his bedroom. First, he stopped at the kitchen for a late night meal. I waited, out of sight, in a small sitting room until I heard him and his guards leaving, now filled with food and ready to crash on their beds.

They looked tired just by the way they dragged their feet down the hallways.

I followed a safe distance behind, but made sure I didn't lose sight of them because I didn't know where Quay's room was.

After a dozen or so minutes, they stopped at a door. I slipped behind a curtain and watched by peering around it.

Quay waved his bodyguards away and then waited for them to leave. I narrowed my eyes as he looked around before entering his room. It seemed odd to me that he would stay in his own large room when the rest of his family stayed in a room the same size. Why did he avoid them like the plague?

I sat on the edge of the window, safely covered by the fabric. I didn't know how long I sat there, only that by the time I stood up, my legs were cramped.

I still was unable to use my magic, even though Quay had said I should have gotten it back sooner or later. I had my suspicions.

Perhaps I could uncover a bit of information that would help me understand what was going on. After all, I couldn't rely on my memory for anything.

I walked to the guard-less door and slowly pushed it open. My heart started to hammer, knowing what the consequences would be if I was caught. But I *had* to figure out why Quay was acting so strange.

There had to be answers in his room.

I glanced around the dark chamber. Quay was fast asleep, or if he wasn't, he did a fine job at faking it. Luckily, he snored pretty loudly.

Not knowing what to look for, I wandered to the desk, brushing my fingers over a pile of papers. An inkbottle had been spilled over the desk, staining the wood. Several quill pens had drifted to the floor, forgotten.

I couldn't read any of the words in the dark, but I didn't dare light a candle.

I walked to his wardrobe, but he only had a stack of books sitting on top. The bookshelf held several trinkets, but they proved to be nothing of importance, at least to me.

I stepped silently to his nightstand, where Quay had left his gleaming dagger. I had no interest in this either.

Then I saw it.

Quay wore a necklace – a *glowing* necklace – and his fist was tightly clenched around the chain, even in his sleep. The way he held on to it made me think of the villagers who clung to food like their life depended on it. This was no different.

I wanted to study it, to hold it, but I could never pry it out of his hand without waking him up.

I could see eight crystal tubes hanging from the silver chain. Each one held a different color of swirling mist. They pulsed with life, and in the darkness, the combined glow was brilliant.

I glanced down the line. One of the tiny bottles was pink.

I bit back a gasp as I realized where they had all come from. One was from his mother: the purple one. And the other six belonged to his siblings, both younger and older.

The pink one... that was mine.

I stumbled back and nearly ran into Quay's desk. My fingers brushed the corner of a piece of paper, and it slipped off the desk and drifted to the ground.

In the pale moonlight, I could make out a few words.

Three united kingdoms... Octavia... Shane... kill...

I picked the parchment up and carried it to the window, allowing me to read the words better.

It appeared to be something Quay had written, his perfect cursive in straight, even lines.

My eyes scanned the page, looking for the most important information.

I want the three kingdoms to become one, to be united under my rule, so that no war can ever happen again. This, of course, means I will have to kill the current rulers. Octavia will be difficult, but she is surely still in shock from recent events. Arely will be easy, because I've already captured her and she has amnesia from a head injury. Shane will be the most difficult. He has always trained hard and taken safety seriously. But he will fall with the other two, and I will make my kingdom.

I stared at the paper, almost unable to take in the words. It was a letter, and it was addressed to an earl in one of Greyston's villages.

Behind me, there was a sound of rustling and I turned to see that Quay was waking up. Something must have disturbed his sleep.

I stuffed the parchment into the pocket of my dress and ran. I pushed through the door and took off down the hallway, not knowing if the door would slam or not. I didn't care. All I wanted was to get far, far away from Quay.

I didn't stop running until I reached the royal family's room and shut the door behind me. I clicked it into place, then sighed in relief.

My heart started to slow down, but my mind spun, telling me I needed to escape, to find my sister. Greyston was dangerous. The spinning didn't stop, and within seconds, I felt myself slam into the stone floor. The illness was returning, faster than I thought possible.

I'd never escape in this condition.

Osanna rushed to me, holding out her hand to help me into bed. She didn't say a word.

As I climbed under the cold blankets, I closed my eyes.

Quay had asked me to help him in the war, to become his ally. But he'd only done it to create the illusion I was safe in his kingdom. He'd wanted me to sit back comfortably and not worry about a thing, when the reason he'd brought me here in the first place was to steal my magic and gain more power.

Quay was a liar. A thief. And he was also a killer in disguise.

Chapter 37
Shane

My horse raced into the borders of Rivallen, passing small farming villages and homes. I slowed the horse as we came closer to the wall and stopped at the drawbridge.

I took gulps of the cold air, then calmed my horse and waited. I needed guards to let me in.

The sun had risen in the sky hours ago. I hadn't eaten, and after the long trip, I was fatigued.

A group of four knights approached me cautiously from the castle walls.

"King Shane?" one said, his eyes wide.

I dismounted my horse and grabbed his lead rope. "I need to talk to Queen Octavia," I told the four men. "It's urgent."

"Why are you alone?" another asked.

"I had to escape my castle by myself. That's why I need to talk to Octavia."

Before they could reply, the drawbridge began to lower. I steered the horse toward it. The guards followed as I walked toward the bridge, and once it reached the ground, we headed inside.

Tavia stood inside the castle walls. Her magic must have alerted her as soon as I came into the vicinity of the castle. She walked up to me, her eyebrows knit together in suspicion. Clearly she still didn't trust me.

"Queen Octavia," I greeted her, deciding that it wouldn't hurt to call her by her title. "Quay attacked my castle last night. He broke the wall with his magic and his army came inside. I had to escape through the tunnel under my castle."

Worry filled Tavia's eyes. "He blasted the wall apart?"

"Yes," I answered. "And if he destroyed my castle, what if he comes for Rivallen next? We have to attack him, even without my army."

Alarm flickered through the knights' expressions as they looked from me to their queen. Tavia's expression was dark, but not surprised.

One of the guards behind her stepped forward. "Would he do that?"

Tavia shook her head. "I-I don't know, Nico. We shouldn't underestimate him though." She looked back at me. "Are you sure we can defeat him without your army?"

I paused. "We planned to fight him ourselves. The army was only for a distraction."

"True..." Tavia ushered me farther into the tunnel, away from the slicing wind. "Then we'll have to leave in the morning."

I nodded.

"I'll take you to a guest bedroom. We will need good rest if we want to win."

She motioned for the knights to raise the drawbridge, but a shout in the distance made us pause.

A horse barreled forward, trying to catch the bridge before it went up. The knights paused, and a couple moments later, a rider clambered toward us. He skidded to a stop a few yards away.

Tavia's bodyguards shielded her, but as soon as they realized the man riding on the horse wasn't a threat, they lowered their swords.

The man gasped for breath and slid off his horse.

"Your Majesty," he said, bowing to Tavia. "You told me to return from Greyston in a week, but I have important news."

She stepped toward the man, who I assumed was one of her spies. "Did you figure out Quay's plan?" she asked.

"No," he said. "But I saw strange things in his castle."

"What did you see?" I asked, my exhaustion gone.

Tavia shot a look to silence me. "Tell us," she ordered the man.

"Yes, milady. Yesterday morning, I met with two of the spies in Greyston. We told each other what we had seen, and realized we had to come back to tell you, Your Majesty. But while we were traveling, knights captured both of them. I couldn't save them, even though I tried. I'm afraid King Quay ordered all suspected spies to be executed without trial."

The man twiddled his thumbs, his expression distraught. Why would Quay order such a thing? He was supposed to be the fair king.

"I looked around the palace," the spy continued, "although it was difficult with all the guards. I couldn't get anywhere restricted for you, but I did come across the royal family's quarters. I told Quay's family that a maid had told me to check on them."

The man pulled at the sleeve of his coat. "I made small talk and they enjoyed it greatly. I asked if they had practiced using their magic lately, and Osanna said that Quay had asked to borrow their magic to end the war and they had given it to him. Isn't that crazy? How did they do that?"

I paused, bewildered. "You mean all the magic that belongs to his family... that all belongs to him now?"

"That's the way I understood it, sir. I did my best to listen carefully."

"Thank you," Tavia said. "And the other two stories?"

"The second spy said he saw Queen Arely, Your Majesty."

"He did?" Tavia asked, and I couldn't ignore the hope in her eyes. "Is she all right?"

"She was in a gray room with guards, two days ago. He only got a glance, but it was definitely her. She was chained to two metal poles and her magic seemed to be stored inside them. He didn't know if she was awake or not."

Tavia frowned, clearly disappointed, but she said, "At least we know that much. What about the third spy?"

"When we talked, she said she walked into the royal gardens surrounding the castle. In the middle, she found a memorial for the past kings of Greyston. When she reached the last one, she realized it was Quay's father."

I crossed my arms. "Wait, his father's not dead."

"It said he died a couple months ago," the spy said. "I thought you might want to know."

I paused. How would news like that not spread to my kingdom, or Tavia's? Why hadn't Quay said anything about it to me? And how had his father even died? He was in perfect health and he hadn't died in battle because he'd never been in a war in the first place.

Perhaps there had been an accident. But that still didn't explain why the news hadn't reached me.

"I already knew that," Tavia said.

I stared at her. "You did?"

"He told me a couple weeks ago. He said his father died from illness."

"I didn't even know he was sick!"

Tavia glanced at me. "I suppose Quay didn't want you to know."

I bit back a frown, and said, "Perhaps that is why he's been acting so strange. He always looked up to his father."

"It doesn't matter now," Tavia said. "We have to find Arely."

I nodded silently.

She rubbed her forehead, looking more tired than ever. "It sounds like he's stealing magic. I bet that's why he wanted Arely as well."

I stopped to ponder this and remembered that Arely couldn't use her magic.

"Maybe Quay won't be able to use her magic," I said. "I placed a spell on her so she'd never use it."

Tavia glared at me, but sighed. "Okay, but you placed the spell on her, not the magic. So it's very possible he could still use it."

I frowned. She was right. I held onto the rope of my horse, thinking of Quay's large family. No wonder he had been able to teleport to us. He had more magic than anyone could ever need.

That put us in constant danger of attack.

Tavia must have had a similar thought, because she was pale, and I had never seen her that way.

"How is he even taking their magic?" she exclaimed. "I thought that was impossible!"

I watched the drawbridge reach into the midday sky as the knights pulled on the chains and secured it in place. I turned back to Tavia.

"The only way we will be able to defeat him is by taking him off guard. If we can sneak up on him, he'll never get a chance to use his magic on us. But that's harder than it sounds, because he will have force fields and other magical things protecting the castle."

Tavia nodded. "And we need to attack before he can get a chance to attack Rivallen."

"Right. So you want to leave tomorrow morning?"

She raised her eyebrows at me. "Shane, I want to leave right now, but it doesn't look like you're fit to head into battle at the moment. So tomorrow morning will have to work."

The morning came faster than I would have liked. Although I headed to bed hours before the sun set, I found that I couldn't sleep, and instead tossed and turned. I eventually sat next to the window, where I fell asleep.

 262

Tavia had to send guards to wake me. It was still dark outside, and the last thing I wanted was to get up and ride across the endless meadows. The trip would take all day.

But I thought of Arely. Who knew what situation she was in? We had to get to Greyston to find her.

I had left everything I needed on the coffee table, so I was prepared to leave in a couple minutes.

I followed the guards outside, and once I met with Tavia, we started on our way.

The army followed us. This made the trip long, and it was twilight before the castle and city came into view.

At this point, Tavia halted on her horse and motioned everyone else to do the same. Here, the army would wait until the proper time to create a distraction for us.

She began issuing orders, and I waited and listened.

"All right," she said, riding next to me when she had finished. "Are you ready, Shane?"

"I was born ready," I replied.

"Well, good." She dug through the bag her horse was carrying and pulled out a cloak. "Take this."

She threw it to me and I caught it. By the smell and appearance, Tavia had bought the cloak from actual villagers. I hesitantly put it on, and once I had, I saw that Tavia and her bodyguards were putting on their own.

When everyone was ready, Tavia took the lead, weaving her way down a dusty road.

She'd done a good job of disguising us, I had to admit. She had packed real merchants' items into the bags we carried so if anyone stopped to ask us our business, we could show them the goods we were "selling."

The walk to the village took a half hour and I was ready to dismount my horse as soon as we entered it.

Tavia and her guards did the same.

As much as I didn't want to work with Tavia, we had to get along or else we'd draw unwanted attention.

I walked next to Tavia and spoke quietly. "We need to search for the force field, but there's too many people who would see us doing it."

"You're right," Tavia whispered, looking around. "And we could run into it any moment."

I held onto my hood, afraid the wind would blow it off. I didn't know how easily the people would recognize me.

"I can find a secluded area if you'll watch my horse," I told her.

She paused, and then nodded. "Hurry."

I handed her the lead rope and walked down an alleyway. People milled about, but not just any people. These villagers were the creepiest humans I'd ever seen.

One was hovering over a crystal orb, muttering to himself. Another was staring at me with one eye, the other covered by a patch. A woman shrieked with laughter at everyone who passed her.

I did my best to avoid those people. This was the last place I'd choose to be, but I was doing it for Arely.

I finally found a place that was empty. Someone could possibly see me from a window, but the chances of being spotted were much slimmer.

I cast a small spell toward the distant castle, counting the seconds. Only a couple blocks down the street, a green ripple coursed through the air, showing me its location.

As soon as I saw it, I waved to Tavia and her guards.

When they reached me, I showed them the spot where the force field had rippled.

I walked slowly as I neared it and listened for the hum of magic fizzing through the air. If I touched the force field, Quay would instantly know we were here and he'd come and kill all of us.

Tavia stopped next to me and listened.

"The magic was green," she whispered, "so it's part of the stolen magic." She stared at the air where the invisible force field waited. "It'll take almost all our magic to disable it."

Tavia's bodyguards stopped a few feet behind us.

"What do you want us to do?" the one named Nico asked.

"Follow us inside," she answered. "You can secure an escape route for us while we fight Quay." Tavia lifted her hand. "We have to disable a small section long enough so that we can all get through. Quay shouldn't feel any disturbance if we do it quickly."

I summoned my magic and pushed it forward. "Get ready," I said to the guards.

Tavia did the same with her magic. Together, we fought against the force field. At first, the magic struggled, and I had to use more against it.

A line of red, blue, and green appeared in the air, creating sparks and fizzles.

Tavia climbed through the circle first. "Come on," she said. "And don't touch the magic!"

The seven guards stepped through the void and I went last. As soon as I made it through, I cut off my magic and so did Tavia.

The hole closed up in a millisecond.

Tavia gave me a small smile. "Good job."

"Wait, did you actually just say that?"

"Don't get used to it," she said, walking back onto the crowded road.

I paid close attention to the village as we walked. It had changed quite a bit from the last time I had seen it.

Quay had always bragged that his people had the best lives and that he took great care of them, but as I walked down the streets, it seemed his villagers didn't have it much better than mine, and I had long neglected my people.

The people were dressed in rags, shivering in the night air, without a place to go to stay warm. A woman called out to those who past her, saying, "Does anyone need clothing patched or knitted? I can do it for a low price."

Tavia walked with her hands curled into fists. She looked as uncomfortable as I felt. "Has this place always been like this?" she asked me in a hushed voice.

"No," I said. "It used to be a beautiful town."

In truth, the beauty was still apparent. The buildings' brightly painted colors had faded over the years, and the stores hand-painted signs hung over the streets. But many of the buildings appeared to be in disrepair. The people that crowded around them looked unable to take care of themselves.

As we neared the castle, I grew wary. I had a bad feeling that we weren't done with the force fields yet.

A hum reached my ears and I instinctively stopped and put my hand out.

I nearly whacked Tavia in the face.

"Hey!" she hissed. "Watch it!"

"There's a second force field," I warned.

She stopped and listened. "Darn it, you're right. He must have several. He certainly has enough magic for it."

"I've used half of my magic," I said, frowning. "If we disable this one, we won't have any left to attack Quay."

Tavia bit her lip. "Then we're trapped!"

"Not really. We can go through without disabling it. Quay will know we are here, but we will still have magic."

"What if he has trackers on it?" Tavia asked. "What if it takes our magic away?"

"Well, then it'll make for a very interesting battle." Before she could respond, I marched straight through the force field.

A hundred alarms shrieked through the air, loud enough for the whole kingdom to know what I had done.

"Hurry up!" I yelled to Tavia and the guards. People were starting to stare and I didn't want them to recognize us.

Tavia hesitated, her eyes wide, and then plowed through the force field, along with her guards. The villagers looked into the sky, where the magic pulsed, many covering their ears.

"I'll take you to the nearest secret entrance," I said, running through the grass to the outer wall.

"Won't Quay guess you'll use the secret passage?" Tavia yelled over the alarms.

"Yes, but there are so many, he won't know which one I'll take!"

I reached the outer wall of the castle and started looking around for a specific crevice in the wall. This passage wasn't far from the castle gate, and I could see knights guarding it. They had their spears crossed, not letting anyone inside the grounds. I didn't know how much time we had before they noticed us.

I fumbled with a little rock inside of the stones, and pulled it out. This enchanted rock would open a passage inside the castle.

I placed it on one of the stones, when a knight shouted at us. "Hey! Stop in the name of the King!"

"Hurry up!" Tavia said, her eyes wide.

A dark tunnel appeared in the side of the wall, and I climbed in. I let everyone pass me and then used the rock to close the stone door. I heard a cry of outrage right before it banged shut. Thankfully the knights had no way of getting inside, because I had the only magic key.

Now in the blissful silence, I turned to the others, who were all panting. Tavia stood in the back, next to a ladder that would lead us to Quay.

I stepped forward, and gave her a weary grin. "And that isn't even the worst of it."

"Great," she said sarcastically.

I waved her to the ladder. "Time to get your sister back."

Chapter 38
Arely

I jolted out of bed as alarms shrieked through the night air. I had never heard such a horrid sound in my life, and it made my blood run cold.

The other beds rustled as Quay's family sat up, confused.

I ran to the window, feeling a burst of energy, and looked outside. A red light pulsed through the air, and when I blinked the sleep from my eyes, I realized it was the force field.

Without waiting for the others to see what was happening, I changed into a yellow dress and raced out the door. I had a strange feeling that whatever was about to happen was important, and I needed to be there.

Unlike the day before, I didn't feel ill. My memory and magic had betrayed me, but I knew there was a way I could help.

People came out of their rooms, bewildered and even panicked. I dashed past them, trying to get to Quay.

I turned a corner and saw him at the opposite side of the hall, walking toward me.

He halted, his expression cross. Narrowing his eyes, he ushered for me to follow him. "I came to find you," he said. "Shane is in the castle. He must have fallen for my second force field and tripped it. Lucky for us, because he got past the first one."

I pressed my lips together, trying to keep in what I wanted to say. The chain necklace hung around Quay's neck as he walked, and I remembered the eight crystal containers filled to the brim with magic. He was the one keeping my magic from me.

Shush, I told myself. *Follow him and see what happens.*

Quay continued to talk. "I'm heading to my throne room. I'm expecting Shane to meet us there."

I nodded, to keep myself from speaking. When we reached the throne room, I glanced around.

Giant statues of scholars lined the aisle, surrounded by marble carvings on the walls. Red tapestries depicted old fables that had existed for hundreds of years.

Quay stalked up to his throne and sat, as if this were merely another day at work.

I hesitated near the door, and Quay motioned for me to sit. "I don't know how long we'll be waiting," he said.

I walked down the aisle, feeling small, and sat on the edge of the queen's throne. Quay didn't speak, so I watched the front doors, wondering what to expect. If Shane and Quay started fighting, whose side was I to choose?

Quay had stolen my magic and lied to me, but I didn't remember anything about Shane... Was he untrustworthy like Quay or worse?

I must have been lost in thought, because the next thing I knew, Quay was tapping me on the shoulder and pointing at the ceiling.

"W-what?" I said, looking to him and then looking up.

Far above me, I could see the area where the large banisters hung. The servants used this area to remove the cloth if it needed cleaning, but I didn't see anyone up there.

Quay summoned his gold magic and shot it toward the rafters. I stood, bewildered, and a moment later, he brought down a struggling person, dropping him on the ground.

It was Shane.

"That was unnecessary!" he panted, pulling himself to his feet. He glanced at me, his eyes questioning. But I had no idea what he could be thinking. His eyes didn't hold any anger or annoyance, like Quay's did, only a familiar look that I should have recognized.

My memory started to return to me, slowly at first, and then it hit me, like a shadow spinning backwards on a sundial and revealing events buried in the past. I remembered when I had gotten injured, when I had jumped in front of Shane and Tavia's magic had struck me. And I remembered how Shane had apologized to me while the thunderstorm raged outside.

Shane wasn't my enemy.

I took a step forward, but Quay jumped and blocked my way, as if reading my thoughts. "Welcome, Shane. I see you decided to use our old eavesdropping route. Adorable."

Shane narrowed his eyes. "Yes, I did," he hissed. "Thanks for showing it to me."

Quay turned to the rafters again and called, "Come on, Tavia! Don't be shy. We cannot complete my task without you."

I could only imagine the malevolent glare my sister was giving Quay right now.

"Fine, I'll bring you here myself," he said. He shot another blast of magic and in seconds, he brought Tavia down next to Shane.

Her usually tidy hair had fallen into a tangled mess of curls and a cut on her cheek dripped blood.

"Hey!" I said, attempting to push past Quay, but he blocked me. "Don't treat my sister like that!"

He looked at me, and I could see the silver chain on his neck again. The magic containers were safely out of sight, tucked underneath his robes.

"I'm sorry," he said. "I'll try not to."

 270

But I knew perfectly well he was mocking me.

Tavia stood, wincing, and glared at Quay. "You've made a foolish mistake," she said.

"Foolish," Quay repeated. "That's interesting. It looks like I'm the one winning this battle and we haven't even begun fighting."

In the corner of my vision, I saw Shane roll his eyes. "Keep telling yourself that," he muttered.

Quay stepped forward. "Oh, you've never lost your competitive personality," he mused. "But it doesn't mean you will stop me."

He formed an orb of liquid-y maroon magic, preparing to strike. Shane gathered his own magic, forming what looked like a shield.

A beam of Quay's magic ricocheted off the shield and shot toward me. I dove behind the throne, and it missed me by inches.

Coming from the opposite side, Tavia crouched beside me. "Arely, we must go. Now."

"Wait," I whispered as she tugged my arm, "we can't leave Shane!"

"Forget about him," she said, gritting her teeth. "Quay will kill us all if we don't run."

I let her pull me from behind the throne, uncertainly, and we took off toward the doorway. But before we reached it, a dark orange magic swirled around it, barricading us in.

"You can't leave yet!" Quay said. "I haven't dismissed you."

I turned to look at Shane. He had his blade out, blocking Quay's magic. It didn't look easy, and with how little magic he possessed, Shane didn't stand a chance.

Quay smirked. "How does it feel to be the underdog, Shane? Bet you don't like war so much anymore, do you?"

Shane clenched his fists, his face red from exhaustion. "What makes you think I like war, Quay? *What?* I've never liked war, despite what you might believe."

"You're lying," Quay said, waving his hand to dismiss what Shane had said. "And it'll cost you."

I turned to Tavia as they spoke, and pulled her closer to whisper in her ear. "We have to find a way to make Quay stop using his magic, and *fast*."

She nodded right as I heard Shane say, "You can kill me. I deserve it after all I've done. But you can't kill Arely or Tavia. They've done nothing wrong."

Quay shouted, "You *all* have caused problems! This war has been creating trouble in my kingdom."

"You have an obsession with gaining control of the kingdoms around you, weather by forming alliances or manipulating people," Shane said. "You've interfered with our war by attacking *both* of us and made it twice as hard to bring peace to the land."

Quay looked like he was ready to blast Shane to pieces. I stepped as calmly as I could to stand by Shane, with Tavia a few steps behind.

"Wait, Your Majesty," I said, looking up at Quay. "I have something I need to tell you."

He stopped his magic, and turned his eyes toward me. He didn't know that I had regained my memory. "What is it, Arely?"

I pushed down the fear climbing my throat and squared my shoulders. "You want peace, Quay. We are all willing to compromise, I believe. If we agree on a peace treaty, we can stop the current wars."

Quay snorted. "Like that would work."

"Maybe it would if you tried," I said. "There are times when war is necessary, but diplomacy should be our first option."

"I won't let Shane and Tavia try to trick me," he said, tightening his grip on his dagger.

"They aren't going to try to trick you—" I argued, but he cut me off, his eyes glinting.

"Forget it Arely! Out of the four of us, I am the oldest, the most qualified to rule the kingdoms. You are still children, and trying to form a compromise will not work."

"We've had just as much experience ruling our kingdoms as you have!" I said. "And we will work together with or without you."

Quay stared at me. "Shane is not your ally. Perhaps that memory hasn't—"

"My memory is perfectly fine, thank you!" I said, flustered. "And I know that Shane is on my side."

"You do?" Quay raised his eyebrows. "Then why are you still in a war with him?"

Shane held up his blade. "We wouldn't be if you hadn't intervened. If you hadn't taken Arely, we could have ended it days ago."

"Oh, so it's my fault now," he said. "Amazing."

"Quay," I said, trying to get back to my point. "You destroyed Shane's castle. You told me so yourself. When I was injured, you didn't send me a medic because you didn't want me to gain my memory back. And the worst thing of all is that you stole your family's magic. You left them defenseless, and then you began meddling in our war and deceiving people."

Quay shook his head in disbelief. "You have no idea how false that is. I only want to get rid of Shane, because he is the cause of this war. I want to help you."

"You haven't helped me at all," I said, crossing my arms. "You've stolen my magic as well."

The king started to laugh, as if I had told him a joke.

"I see you are confused, Arely, probably due to your head injury. I never—"

Before Quay could end his sentence, I pulled the crumpled piece of paper from inside my dress pocket. I smoothed it in my hands and lifted it for Quay to see.

"What about this? Am I confused about this?"

His face turned dark red as he scowled at the page. "How dare you—" he said, trying to snatch the parchment from my hands, but I pulled away. "Did you sneak into my room?"

"Y-yes," I said, freezing in place. "I thought this wasn't like you. What changed your mind?"

Quay stopped, his eyes widening in surprise for a second.

In his moment of hesitation, Shane tackled him from the side and pressed the jeweled sword against his neck.

Tavia stepped beside me, holding a flame of blue magic.

"Wait, Shane," I said. "Let him answer."

Shane wavered, and then lessened the pressure, leaving a small cut on Quay's skin. But he didn't let him go.

I crouched and Quay regarded me carefully before speaking.

"I've learned since my father's death that I need to accomplish more than he did," he said slowly. "And he passed many opportunities. Perhaps he was a coward. There was a reason he chose me to lead the kingdom instead of my older brother. I had more ideas and plans for the kingdom."

"So why won't you return the magic to your family?"

"Because," he hissed. "They disagree with my plan for the three kingdoms to unite under my rule. They'd only oppose it."

Shane met my eyes, his lips parted in confusion. He glanced down at Quay. "My people will hate you. You attacked my castle and everyone inside evacuated. How would you gain their trust?"

A muscle in Quay's jaw twitched. "You ran away like a coward and abandoned your people during the attack. So you're not in a great situation either, I see."

"I had no other choice," Shane argued.

I stood, my head whirling. Though a month ago I had struggled with my responsibility as queen, now I had realized its importance.

No one could take that knowledge away from me, and I wasn't about to let Quay rule over my people. I knew them better than he did.

I needed to return to my kingdom, without the worry that Quay would try to take everything from me.

"No," I said, shaking my head. Quay turned his gaze to me, frowning. "I won't let you rule Rivallen. And neither will Tavia."

My sister held onto her dagger, a few steps away, and nodded.

Silence fell over the room, beside the sound of the howling wind from outside. I took a deep breath to try to calm my nerves.

Shane relaxed his grip. In a second, Quay pushed off the ground and leapt up, sending Shane tumbling.

A burst of magic shot from his palm, but Shane dodged, and it hit a towering pillar several rows away.

The room shook as the structure cracked and crumbled. I jumped as a chunk slid across the floor, nearly tripping me.

Tavia raised her dagger to throw it, but the magic knocked it from her hand and it skittered across the marble.

I dove forward and snatched it, the cold handle fitting my hand perfectly.

"Try to disable the barricade!" I yelled to Tavia. "Now!"

Quay blocked Shane, gathering more magic, as if it was limitless. This time it was pink. He was using *my* magic.

While he was distracted by Shane, I stepped behind him and wrapped my fingers around the silver chain on his neck. I pulled. It snapped in two, the crystal bottles clinking into my palm.

Quay whirled on me, his eyes blazing with anger.

"Arely," Quay said, his voice tense. "Hand those over. *Right. Now.*"

My heart raced but I refused to let the necklace go. "I will not," I said, stepping back.

He lunged forward and collided into me, knocking us both to the ground. I held tight to the chain as he attempted to yank it away.

Navy magic shot over my head and left a gash on Quay's arm. He yelled in pain and I jumped up, as cracks appeared in the containers.

Before I could run, he summoned magic and it wrapped around the necklace, pulling it from my grasp.

Though the chain cut into my fingers, I didn't dare let go. I braced myself, fighting the strength of Quay's golden magic.

As Shane ran over to help, the necklace snapped and several of the containers flew into the air.

The bottles fell at Quay's feet, shattering into miniscule shards of glass. A cascade of colors ignited the air, wild and uncontrolled as the magic exploded, and it wrapped around Quay and the pillar beside him.

He tried to escape it by running, but a shockwave soared throughout the room, sending him crashing onto the floor.

The force knocked Shane and me to the ground. With the magic left in the container, I raised my hand and formed a force field around us. It took all my strength to hold it in place as Quay's stolen magic bombarded it.

The ground shook as the pillar beside us crumbled and marble rained onto my magic.

Panting, I held onto the force field for several seconds, even after everything had fallen still.

Shane sat up, wiping the sweat off his face. "I think we're safe."

I released the magic. In my hand were two bottles, one with purple mist and the other with pink. All the other magic had been released into the sky.

I peeked at where Quay had stood moments before. But as soon as I did, I regretted it.

He lay on the floor, motionless as he bled from multiple wounds. He had taken the majority of the impact from the magic explosion.

I rubbed my head. Shane stood, shakily, and held out his hand to help me up. After I had regained my balance, I whirled around and scanned the area for my sister.

"Where's Tavia?" I asked, my voice rising.

"Here."

I turned to my right. Tavia crawled from under a pillar hanging precariously against the wall, in one piece. She paused, looking past me to where Quay lay.

"He's dead?"

We didn't answer. It was enough to see his wounds.

None of us had known the power of the magic Quay possessed. Not even him. And the ignorance had proven deadly.

Chapter 39
Shane

My old friend lay on the floor, dead.

This realization hit me harder than I would have liked.

A chunk of the pillar had fallen on him after the magic exploded. That alone would've been enough to kill him. Although he had tried to kill me, I didn't want it to be true.

The castle rumbled and I heard a large crash. Then another. "What's going on now?" I asked, wishing I didn't have to be in this castle any longer.

"Quay's storm," Tavia said, frowning. "His magic dispersed and now it's going to cause a storm."

"Wait a second," I said, turning to Arely. "What did Quay try to grab from you?"

"The magic containers," she said, oddly quiet. "All of them."

So Quay had kept the stolen magic in containers. That explained how he had used it, but I still had no idea how he had taken it in the first place.

"If all of that magic causes a storm, that means this will be one of the worst royal storms in history," I said. "Like the Massacre of Khristyna."

Tavia stood up. "We have to get out of here. I don't know how much time we have."

"Wait!" Arely said before either of us could move. "We can't leave Quay's family. They are on our side. He tricked them into giving him their magic. And besides," she added, "who will rule the kingdom if we leave them to die?"

"How quickly can you get to them?" I asked, but she was already heading up a flight of stairs.

"Follow me!" she called. "It's only a couple minutes away."

Tavia and I glanced at each other, not entirely sure this was a good plan, but we couldn't let Arely go alone.

"You should gather your guards," I told her, "and I'll go with Arely."

With a nod, she disappeared down the hall and I raced to catch up with Arely. She wasn't too far down the hall.

After a couple minutes, she slid to a stop at a door and threw it open. Inside, several scared faces looked over at us, the rest aggressive.

Even though most of the people looked quite different from the last time I had seen them, they were most certainly Quay's family.

"Arely?" the youngest boy called.

"We need to evacuate the castle immediately," she said. "I'll explain things later, but we have to hurry."

A couple of them started to shuffle toward the door, but the others stood, incredulous.

"Come on!" Arely said, desperation taking over her voice. "If you won't come now, we'll have to leave you behind."

This got the family's attention, and soon they filed out of the room. Right when the last girl left, Arely said, "Let's get out of here."

She began to sprint down the hall and I follow right behind her.

We ran through the halls as fast as we could, and soon reached Tavia and her guards. They joined the group without us having to stop, and we continued down the hall.

With everyone, a total of seventeen people, we couldn't move through the narrow halls quickly.

The hall ahead went on forever. The twists and turns never seemed to end, and I wondered if we would get out in time before the castle was blown to ashes.

Lightning lit the whole castle as if it was daytime and the thunder sent us crashing into walls. I struggled to keep my balance.

Ahead of me, Arely started to slow down. She was panting dreadfully and I didn't know if she'd be able to make it.

With the next clap of thunder, she fell to the floor. I hurried to her and crouched down.

"Are you all right?" I said, giving her my hand. She clutched her side, and she looked dizzy and disoriented.

"Shane," she said. "I can't—"

Another flash of lightning lit the hall, and I wrapped my arms around her and lifted her up. If I didn't carry her, we'd never make it out alive.

Her dress had so much fabric, I could barely see, but she clung to my neck and I had to keep going.

"We are almost there!" Queen Osanna said. "Keep running!"

I could see cracks zigzagging through the ceiling and tiny rocks started raining on us.

Ahead, I spotted a large chunk rumbling and slid to a stop before it fell and created a crater in the marble floor. One of Tavia's guards crashed into me and I nearly fell over.

"Come on!" Tavia said, waving at us.

I could see the stable entrance not too far away. Queen Osanna stood at the door, counting us as we raced inside.

The horses were bucking and whinnying. Castle guards attempted to calm and saddle each one. I scanned the row and carried Arely to one of the bigger horses. A guard had placed a saddle on its back.

Queen Osanna yelled over the booming thunder. "Give us the saddled horses! We need the fastest escape."

The guards instantly handed over the horses and began preparing others.

"Can you get on the horse?" I asked Arely.

"I-I think so," she said, her face pale.

I put her back on the ground and she wavered. I held the horse still as she slowly climbed into the saddle. Her hands were shaking and I suspected she'd fall off if she rode alone. The horse was big enough to carry both of us though.

I climbed behind her and took the reins. Arely held onto the horn of the saddle for dear life. She fell into a fit of coughing.

"Are you all right?" I asked again. "What's wrong?"

"I feel sick," she said, rubbing her forehead. "When I broke Quay's necklace—"

Her next words were drowned by another clap of thunder. Tavia, Quay's mother, and everyone else had found a horse and climbed on.

"Let's go!" Tavia yelled. "Shane, you go first!"

I lifted the reins and steered the horse from the stable. He gladly bolted out of the collapsing building and dashed through the tall grasses of the meadow.

As soon as we took off into the woods, I dared to peek at the sky. Above the castle, a swirling mass of magic hovered, emitting blasts of lightning and rumbles of thunder. The turrets were crumbling like a sand castle, colliding with the lower walls. Stones cascaded down into piles of rubble below.

A couple guards dashed from the stables before it caved in, but the rest weren't as lucky.

We'd barely made it out. Just barely.

Arely was leaning precariously to one side, as if she was losing consciousness. With one hand holding onto the reins, I wrapped my other arm around her to prevent her from tumbling down.

"Arely!" I said, but she didn't respond. Her eyes fluttered and she held her head. "Hold on a little longer, okay? We will get you to the castle as soon as we can."

She mumbled a reply that I didn't catch. Her skin was cold. Unnaturally cold, as if she were a piece of stone ice, carved to look like a queen. She closed her eyes.

Tavia rode next to me, looking dazed. "What happened to her?" she asked, eyeing Arely.

"I... I don't know," I said. "She fell unconscious."

"We should take her to Rivallen," Tavia said.

I squinted at her. "But we can get to my kingdom faster."

"She needs to be home again," Tavia argued. "Besides, you have no idea what condition your castle is in."

I winced, remembering my narrow escape from Quay's attack two nights before. In the rush, I had nearly forgotten.

"What is that?" she asked.

I looked down to where she was pointing. In Arely's hand were two glowing tubes of magic, the only two that hadn't been destroyed.

Afraid they would fall, I reached out to take them. With the explosion of magic, it hadn't crossed my mind that Arely was using her magic to create a force field over us. But now I understood what had happened.

"These are powerful," I whispered.

"He stored the magic in containers?" Tavia said, frowning. "Arely must've figured it out. I didn't know what was happening when he turned on her."

"Imagine what we could do with them," I said. "I wonder how much it took to travel wherever he wanted. Maybe we could travel to Rivallen right now!"

"They're almost out for tonight," she said. "Besides, there are too many of us."

"True…"

"Let me have them," Tavia said, reaching to take them. "I'll keep them safe until we reach the kingdom."

"Wait, no." I pulled back, frowning. "I'm perfectly capable of doing it myself, thank you."

She crossed her arms. "One is my twin's magic. I should carry it, at least."

"Fine," I said, handing her the pink bottle. I slid the second into my pocket.

"We'll figure out what to do with the magic when we reach the castle," she said, kicking her horse to take the lead.

Rivallen was hours away. The magic storm had faded in the distance, so we were safe from it, but I didn't know if Arely would be all right.

The night was cold. The harsh winds from the field whistled around us. I held on tightly to the reins, preparing for the long trip ahead.

Chapter 40
Shane

We rode through the field until we felt like we might fall off the horses from exhaustion. By the time we reached the castle, the sky was lightening and the sun was due to appear any minute.

I followed Tavia through the gates and we stopped near the stairs. I made sure Arely wouldn't fall, and then dismounted the horse. I carefully pulled her down from the horse's back.

Tavia hurried toward me. "We need to get her to my bedroom," she said.

I watched as her chest rose and fell with her breath. She was still breathing. "She's burning up," I said. "I don't understand. When we left the castle, she was freezing cold."

Tavia shook her head. "I'll have to get the medics to check on her."

She led me through the castle, waving away the people who tried to talk to her, though she asked one of the servants to get a medic.

We walked up several flights of stairs until she entered a hallway and stopped at one of the doors. She pushed it open and walked into her room.

It was larger than my room, with two pairs of doors that both led to balconies, one king sized bed, two dressers, and everything else one could need in a bedroom.

I laid Arely on the bed and pulled the covers around her.

Not long after, a pair of medics rushed into the room and stopped beside her. They felt Arely's skin and took her pulse first, and then began to ask Tavia questions.

"Where did you find her?"

"Was she conscious?"

"Has she lost all her magic?"

Tavia recounted everything we knew for them. She told them about finding her, taking her out of the castle, and riding home with her.

The medics left the room for a couple minutes as we waited in silence.

I hoped Arely would be all right. She had become my friend and I didn't want to lose her now. I hoped whatever condition she was in wasn't serious, but as I looked at her pale face, I didn't think that would be the case.

The medics returned with a cart of herbs and medicines.

"We believe we know what Queen Arely has, Your Majesty," the woman said, looking at Tavia. "And it's not good."

"What does she have?" she asked, leaning forward from her perch on the bed.

"We think she has the *Vorlenmagie* Illness," the man answered, "where royals get very sick if they lose their magic, whether from an accident or birth flaw. It's deadly."

I buried my head in my palm. Of course that's what she had. I should have figured it out myself, because I had read about it in books before.

In the past, many royals had died after getting a sickness caused by the lack of magic. Many powerful rulers had died due to the illness.

Tavia had clearly heard of it as well, because she said, "I knew it, but I'd hoped it wasn't true. Will she make it? How much time does she have?"

"We don't know," the woman said. "It's not easy to know if a royal will survive. We barely know anything about the illness because it's so rare. And the effects it has on each and every individual differs widely. I can't tell you much else, but it's a short illness. By tonight she'll either be awake... or gone."

"Can we do anything?" I asked.

"The best thing you can do is watch her temperature and give her medicine. I can make a special mixture for her and I'll give it to you. All you need to do is cover her with a warm blanket when her body temperature drops, and take it off when it spikes again. And besides Arely, you two could do with some soup, I bet."

"Yes, go get bowls of soup, please," Tavia said. "For both of us."

The medics nodded. "We will see to the cooks to do so." They both left the room.

"Oh!" Tavia said, digging in the pocket of her cloak and lifting the pink bottle. "I have Arely's magic."

During the trip, the magic had replenished itself and it was ready to be used.

"But how do we return it to her?" I asked. "If we open the lid, it will disperse through the air."

"Maybe if she wakes up..."

"Even then, she used it herself when Quay's throne room was collapsing. It didn't return to her. What if it's stuck in this container forever?"

"Perhaps she will be fine if she wears it as a necklace like Quay did."

"I highly doubt it."

She narrowed her eyes. "Quit being so pessimistic!"

"I'm being realistic," I argued. I glanced down at Arely as her eyelids fluttered.

"Arely?" I whispered, and she looked up, her face ashen.

"Shane..." she said, then spotted her sister sitting on the bed next to her. "Tavia!"

"Hey, wise girl," Tavia said, brushing a strand of blonde hair out of Arely's face. "How do you feel?"

"Not well," she said, quietly. "I don't think I—"

Arely started coughing and buried her face into the blankets. After a couple seconds, she mumbled, "It's my magic... Now that I don't have it, I don't think I'm going to survive."

"Don't be ridiculous." Tavia lifted the pink container. "We have it right here."

Arely took the vial carefully, studying the inky magic inside. She was silent for several minutes, before she sighed.

"This is useless to me."

"It will save your life," Tavia argued, her hands clenched. "You must try something."

"Quay's castle was destroyed... along with the machines that took my magic. If anything could return it to me, it was them. This – this will not heal me."

"How can you be so sure?"

"I can't. There is always something to learn about illnesses. But Queen Osanna said she tried to take back the stolen magic several times and it never worked."

As I studied Arely's pained expression, I knew she believed it. Her face was an ashy gray and she could barely keep her eyes open to talk to us.

"If I die, you must destroy it," she finally said. "Perhaps it was supposed to happen this way."

"Don't say things like that!" Tavia snapped, fear in her eyes. We both knew that Arely wasn't lying.

Arely turned from her sister to look at me. "You know I'm telling the truth, right?"

I didn't reply, just swallowed and looked away.

She coughed again. "It'll all turn out for the best. As long as all of the kingdoms have a good ruler and the three rulers work to preserve peace. But it can't be one person ruling the kingdoms, like Quay wanted it to be. We need everyone to work together."

Tavia and I both nodded.

Silence filled the room. Uncomfortable, painful silence.

I looked back at Arely to see that she was watching me. She managed to smile, though it wasn't as bright as usual.

"I owe you," I said, before I could stop myself. "I owe you more than I can repay."

"There's one thing I'd like you to do for me," she said, squeezing my hand. "Can you find the doll that I picked up after the carriage ride, and return it to the little girl who dropped it?"

"Yes," I said, "yes, I will."

"Thank you, Shane."

Her eyes drifted over to her sister, who was wiping tears from her eyes, and then to the window, where the sun was rising in the east.

"I love you," she whispered. "I love you both."

I watched as she closed her eyes, and then, she was still.

I don't know how long we stayed by Arely's side, but I didn't care. I didn't want to do anything else.

Eventually, a maid came with two bowls of hot tomato soup. She saw us, and must have decided she shouldn't bother us, because she left the bowls on the coffee table without saying a word.

Neither of us stood up to get the soup. The steam curled in the air, until finally, it grew cold and mushy in the bowls.

Tears stained my cheeks, but I didn't bother to wipe them away.

Tavia had buried her head in a pillow, but she slowly sat up, her eyes puffy and her hair a tangled mess.

"We... we need to release the magic. No one will be able to use it for wrong again, which is what she wanted."

"What about the second one?" I asked, pulling it from my pocket. "It belongs to Quay's younger sister."

"Oh," Tavia whispered. "We should let her decide, if she hasn't gotten the illness, too."

I nodded, slowly. "Without it, Greyston's royal family has no protection. It's the only stolen magic left. And they won't repeat Quay's mistake, so it will be safely kept."

"I agree," Tavia said, without looking at me. "But we can deal with that later."

She handed Arely's vial over. "I'd rather you release it, if you don't mind."

I hesitated, and then tugged the cork from the top. The magic curled into the air, reminiscent of smoke from a fire.

Within a few minutes, lightning crackled outside the window and thunder gently rumbled the castle. But it wasn't violent, as Quay's had been. Instead, it lit the night with soft pink zigzags and covered the stars with rare clouds.

It was a couple minutes before Tavia spoke.

"I found Arely's poetry notebook the other day," she said, breaking the endless silence that had fallen over the room once again. "There was a piece inside that I think you'd like to read."

"Okay..." I said.

Tavia ushered me to follow her to a desk in the corner of the room. On it lay a leather bound notebook. Its sides were worn from years of being carried around.

She opened it gently and showed me one of the pages. The date was only a couple weeks prior, and the page next to it was blank. It must have been the last thing Arely had written inside.

On the top, scrawled in cursive, Arely had written "Peace Treaty."

She had written below it, in a smaller size:

"On this day, when the summer is turning to fall, we three rulers, of Rivallen and Rapora, agree to settle the war that has raged between our kingdoms for far too long. We realize our differences and will work to accept them, providing the fact we will change if need be. We have all learned and we know we were not always right in our assumptions of each other.

"We will now form an alliance between our two kingdoms to promote peace and friendship for our people from both lands. We will protect each other if other kingdoms threaten, but also do our best to form new alliances with other nations.

"Our people will be allowed to travel freely from kingdom to kingdom, to explore and to interact, to trade and to learn. We will make a clear path from Rivallen to Rapora, so everyone can travel easily across the meadows. Our people will be as one, so that the wounds of war may fade and be healed.

"On this day, when the summer is turning to fall, our kingdoms will be united. We will not forget the past, but we will learn from it. We will make a bond that will last for ages, will work to solve problems through peaceful means, will grow our knowledge through meeting new people, and will learn to forgive and forget so we may live happily together.

"This I write in the name of love, for my kingdom and my people. Signed: Queen Arely of Rivallen."

I looked at Tavia, who had pressed her lips into a thin line.

"Did she always want to end the war by forming an alliance?"

"Yes," Tavia said. "She wanted to have a meeting with you, to try to talk it out, but I never listened. I didn't believe it would work."

I looked down at Arely's peace treaty. She had written it only a couple days before the attack at Fort Oak, when I had captured her. It was the day after Tavia had taken over the fort.

"I want nothing more to do with this war," I said. "I guess revenge for my parents has been paid for, though I didn't want it anymore."

I twisted the cork off the nearest ink jar. "I've made a huge mess. But I do plan to repay for what I've done. I suppose the first thing we should do is settle this war once and for all."

Tavia smiled, only for a moment, and then took the notebook in her hand and carefully tore the peace treaty out. She laid it on the desk.

"You can go first."

I took a feather, and, below Arely's signature, I added my own. After I was done, I gave it to Tavia and she signed her name.

For a moment, neither of us spoke. The parchment lay there, suddenly the most important parchment in all the kingdom. But although it should have felt completely different now that the war was officially over, I felt exactly the same.

"Well..." Tavia said, slowly, "Arely would be proud of this paper."

I lifted it to the light. "Now we need to tell the people."

Epilogue
(One Month Later)
Shane

The morning glistened with dew and fresh rain. The streets were full of mud puddles, but the sun peeked out behind the clouds and a rainbow arched across the pale blue sky.

A cool breeze slipped through the alleys and chilled the air. Smoke puffed out of chimneys and the smell of baking bread drifted from homes. I stepped along the road, my bodyguards at my side. People watched me curiously from the side of the road or from their homes.

I followed the directions I had been given, looking for the butcheries and coffee shops that were on the way. After a couple minutes, I arrived at a small cottage with weeds growing around the walls and windows.

"This is it, right?" I asked.

My top bodyguard nodded. "Yes, sir."

I took a deep breath before knocking on the door. I was half convinced it would fall off if someone tried to open it.

The door creaked open and a woman appeared. Her eyes widened at the sight of me and she froze in place.

"Hello," I said, giving her my best smile. Or, at least, what I hoped was my best smile. "I believe that you are the one with a daughter named... Nolwenn?"

"Y-yes," the woman said, and her voice suddenly raised. "If she has done anything wrong, Your Royal Majesty, you must forgive her. Please, she is only three years old—"

"You misunderstand," I told her. "I have something for her. May I see her?"

The woman's eyes squinted with confusion. "Uh, yes, Your Majesty." With a shaky voice, she called her daughter's name, and a couple moments later, I heard her say, "Honey, the King is here. He wants to see you, okay? Be respectful."

A little girl with long, dark hair appeared, half hiding behind the doorway.

"Hello," I said, kneeling so that I was eye level with her.

"H-hello," she said in her high-pitched toddler voice. She slowly edged out of the house and toward me.

"I think you lost something a couple months ago, am I right?" I asked her.

She nodded.

I reached into my satchel and pulled out the ragged doll that Arely had hidden in my room. It had taken me days and days to find, searching through the ruins of what used to be my bedroom. I had almost given up hope of being able to find the doll and finish Arely's request.

But after almost a week, I had been digging in a corner full of rubble and books when I'd come across the doll.

It had been so filthy from the attack on the castle, I had asked the maids to wash it twice. Arely's assigned maid, Lori, had taken the task and cleaned it as best as she could, but it still wasn't perfect. Either way, Nolwenn's face lit up as soon as her eyes landed on the doll.

"My doll!" she squealed.

I couldn't help but smile. "Yes. Here," I said, handing it to her. She beamed and hugged it to her chest.

"Thank you, Mr. King."

"You're very welcome."

Her mother watched from the door, a surprised smile on her face. She ruffled Nolwenn's hair. "That was beyond kind. How were you able to find us?"

I stood up. "Let's just say I had help from two children who came to the castle with information. They said Queen Arely had sent them to find you."

The woman hugged Nolwenn close to her. "Well, Your Majesty, it is most appreciated. She missed the doll greatly."

I tipped my hat and turned to leave. Out of the corner of my eye, I saw Nolwenn wave at me.

The walk home didn't feel quite the same. I supposed Arely had known that, and that's exactly why she had asked me to do it.

My castle was a mess, and as I looked up at it from the village, I knew it could never be built just like the old one. But I was okay with that. I didn't want it to be the same. In fact, I had plans for a better castle (with a few ideas from Rivallen).

Things would never be the same as they had been, and for once, I was glad.

In the darkness
There is a spark;
In the silence
A singing lark;
Within the enemy
Find a tentative friend
To seek a new beginning out of
The End.

Farewell ~ by Arely

Acknowledgements

First of all, I'd like to thank Millie Florence for writing the poetry in this book. It added a special touch to the story, and I am super grateful! Millie has written two books, Honey Butter and Lydia Green of Mulberry Glen. I've read both and highly recommend!

Second, I've had several amazing teachers who encouraged me in my writing adventures. My second grade teacher, Mrs. Clark, gave me a beautiful rainbow notebook and told me to write my future stories in it. My IEW teachers, Mrs. Bundscho and Mrs. Phillips, taught me much about the craft of writing and using my skills to make better stories.

Also, I had several beta readers who helped me improve my novel and encouraged me while writing it! So thank you Adeline, Megan, Elise, Lynn, and Taylor for helping this idea become a reality.

My writing buddy, Vada, helped me brainstorm and edit my manuscript. She listened to all my crazy ideas and how I came up with the novel (which is a long story!).

Finally, I can't forget my family because they helped a ton as well! My brother helped me when I had writer's block and didn't know what to write, my mom listened to my rants about whatever writing problems I was dealing with, and my dad proofread the novel and helped me improve the writing.

Thank you to everyone who helped me with this book, whether in a small way or a big one. I appreciate it!

~ Zoe

About the Author

Zoe Anastasia is a dreamer by day and writer by night. She loves puppies and dragons, and is waiting for the day when she finally spots a sasquatch in the woods. Her debut novel, The Love of Her Kingdom, was written while she traveled through many different states and explored new landscapes and cities. One day, she plans to travel throughout Europe and learn even more about the history there. Her favorite word is idiosyncratic (in case you were wondering).

Follow her blog to find more stories and writing tips: zoeanastasiastories.wordpress.com

Follow her on social media for more adventures:
Instagram: @zoe.anastasia.author
Facbook: